The Persian Pickle Club

Also by Sandra Dallas

Buster Midnight's Cafe

The Persian Pickle Club

Sandra Dallas

ARROW

Published by Arrow Books in 1996

1 3 5 7 9 10 8 6 4 2

Copyright © 1995 by Sandra Dallas

The right of Sandra Dallas to be identified as the author
of this work has been asserted by her in accordance
with the Copyright, Designs and Patents Act, 1988.

Arrow Books Limited
20 Vauxhall Bridge Road, London SW1V 2SA

Random House Australia (Pty) Limited
16 Dalmore Drive, Scoresby,
Victoria 3179, Australia

Random House New Zealand Limited
18 Poland Road, Glenfield
Auckland 10, New Zealand

Random House South Africa (Pty) Limited
PO Box 2263, Rosebank 2121, South Africa

Random House UK Limited Reg. No. 954009

A CIP catalogue record for this book
is available from the British Library

Papers used by Random House UK Limited
are natural, recyclable products made from wood grown in
sustainable forests. The manufacturing processes conform to
the environmental regulations of the country of origin

ISBN 0 09 972701 3

Printed and bound in Great Britain by
Cox & Wyman Ltd, Reading; Berkshire

*This is for
Mary Dallas Cole
with love.
Sisters, like friends, are forever*

Acknowledgments

In 1933, shortly after my parents were married, my father lost his job, and he and Mom moved to my grandparents' farm in Harveyville, Kansas. A neighbor offered Dad a dollar for a day's labor. Dad worked so hard, he finished by noon and was paid just four bits, the only money my parents saw all season. In our family, that was known as the "Fifty-cent Summer." The rest of *The Persian Pickle Club* is fiction.

Like the scraps of a quilt, the elements of this book came from friends. Thanks to Mom and Dad for the stories that are its pieces; to my extraordinary agent, Jane Jordan Browne, and her assistant, Danielle Egan-Miller, who supplied the design; to Marjorie Baxter and the Harveyville United Methodist Quilting Ladies for assembling the parts; to Bob, Dana, and Kendal for warmth and substance; and to my editor, Jenny Notz, who stitched it all together.

The Persian
Pickle Club

chapter
1

The first time she saw the members of the Persian Pickle Club, Rita told me after I got to know her, she thought we looked just like a bunch of setting hens. She'd learned all about setting hens that very morning after she'd gone out to the henhouse to gather eggs. Rita's luck must have been under a bucket, because Agnes T. Ritter saw her checking the roosters, and in that nasty way Agnes T. Ritter has, she told Rita just why she wasn't going to find eggs under a rooster. Then she told Rita to leave the broody hens alone unless she wanted scrambled chicks for breakfast.

How would anybody expect Rita to know about hens and roosters when she'd never lived in the country before? Like most town folks, Rita never cared where eggs came from, and after she found out, why, then she didn't care if she ever ate one again. Rita was a big city girl from Denver who had more important things to study in college than chickens, like learning how to become a famous writer. I'd never known a woman who wanted to be anything more than a farmwife.

Rita was right about us looking like a coop full of biddies. We sat there at Ada June's dining room table, clucking as Rita walked in. Then our eyes bugged out, making us look dumb enough to knit with wet spaghetti. I stopped sewing, with my hand in the air, and held it there so long that Mrs. Judd told me, "Put down your needle, Queenie Bean, and don't stare."

Well, I can tell you, I wasn't the only one staring! Even Mrs.

1

Judd was peering with watery eyes through her little gold-rimmed glasses. How could she help it? How could any of us help it? We'd all heard Tom's wife was a looker. After he met Rita at the Ritter place, Grover came right home and told me she was the nicest thing he'd seen since rain—not that he remembered much about rain, or that Grover was a good judge of what was pretty, for that matter. He thinks Lottie, the two-year-old pie-eyed heifer we just got, is a looker, too.

Grover was right about Tom's wife, however. Rita was as pretty as pie. She had curls like fresh-churned butter, not at all like my straight brown bob, and eyes as big and round as biscuits. Rita was little. I am, too, but next to me, Rita was a regular Teenie Weenie, not much over five feet or a hundred pounds. Her hands were as plump as a baby's, smooth and soft, and the nails were polished. She smelled good, too, not just a little vanilla behind the ears the way I do it, but real perfume, the nice kind that they sell in the drugstores in Topeka. We were chickens, all right, and Rita was a hummingbird. It gave us all pleasure just to look at her.

All of us except for Agnes T. Ritter. She stood behind Rita looking sour as always, like the wind was blowing past a manure pile right in her direction. President Roosevelt could get out of his wheelchair and ask her to dance, and she'd act like she was two-stepping with the hired man. Agnes T. Ritter had turned up her little sliver of a lip at Rita's dress, which was as dainty as a hanky, made of strips of lace and red silk. I could see the strap of a red slip that she wore under it, and I meant to ask Ada June where anybody bought a red slip. Grover'd think I'd gone to town for sure if I put on red underwear. We always dressed up for Persian Pickle Club, but none of us wore anything as fancy as that, certainly not Agnes T. Ritter, who wore $1.49 housedresses from the Spiegel catalog and made her own slips. It didn't matter how she dressed, of course, because she was as knobby as a washboard. Agnes T. Ritter, you sure are jealous, I thought.

That's when I decided I would be a good friend to Rita. She could use one, with Agnes T. Ritter for a sister-in-law. And with

Ruby gone to California and never coming back, I myself needed a best friend my own age.

"This is Rita, Tom's wife," said Mrs. Ritter, who was Agnes T. Ritter's mother and Rita's new mother-in-law. Naturally, we knew Rita was Rita, but I guess Mrs. Ritter felt it might be a good idea to say something, since not one of us had given her a word of welcome. Our manners must have been under that same bucket with Rita's luck.

I was the first one to speak, as I usually am. I smoothed the rickrack around the neck of my dress and said, "I'm Queenie Rebecca Bean, Grover's wife. We're glad Tom came back and brought you with him, because Tom is Grover's best friend, even though Grover went to farming instead of to the university. We live out in the country, three farms down from you, in the yellow house that looks like dried egg yolks. The place is even brighter in the fall when the willows turn. Grover says it's like living inside a lemon." I stopped long enough to take a breath, then added before anyone else could speak, "Welcome to Pickle. I'm the youngest member." Grover always says I'm the talkingest woman he knows when I get nervous. Grover doesn't say a word when he's rattled, so together, we're about normal.

Rita ran the tip of her tongue over her upper lip and looked at me out of the corner of her eye.

"I like a stand of willows," muttered Opalina Dux, who said something queer most times she opened her mouth. So no one paid attention to her.

Ada June Zinn, who was the hostess that day, said, "I guess Queenie spoke for all of us. Welcome to the Persian Pickle Club."

Rita put out her hand, and Ada June stared at it until Mrs. Judd said, "Shake it, Ada June. That's what it's there for." In Harveyville, women didn't shake hands with one another. Ada June wasn't quite sure what to do, so she put the tips of her fingers into Rita's palm. Rita went around the circle, offering her hand to everybody, and when she came to me, I shook it hard, and she winked at me.

When Rita was finished with the handshakes, she and Mrs. Ritter sat down in the two empty chairs at the end of the table. It was a minute before Ada June realized she hadn't counted Rita when she'd set out the chairs. She was one short, and there was no place for Agnes T. Ritter to sit. Ada June jumped up and got an old straight-back from the kitchen, and we all moved around to make room. Left standing is the story of Agnes T. Ritter's life.

"Did you bring sewing?" Mrs. Judd asked Rita. Mrs. Judd knew she hadn't, of course. Rita couldn't have gotten a pin into that tiny purse of hers.

"Oh," Rita said. "I don't sew."

I'd never met a woman who didn't sew. None of us had, and we stared at her again, until Ceres Root said with a nice smile, "You modern women have so many interesting things to do. In this day and age, there's no good reason to make thirteen quilt tops before you marry, like I had to when I was a girl." We all nodded, except for Mrs. Judd, who wasn't one to make excuses for other people. Agnes T. Ritter didn't nod, either. A hundred quilt tops wouldn't help her find a husband.

"Sewing's a snap," I told Rita. "You'll pick it up fast."

Agnes T. Ritter snorted. She opened her work basket and pulled out a sock and put it over a darning egg. "You could try mending. I hope to say I'm not going to darn your husband's socks for the rest of my life."

Agnes T. Ritter was the only one who took mending or plain sewing to the Persian Pickle Club on what we called Quilter's Choice Day. That meant the hostess didn't have a quilt ready for us to work on, so we brought our own piecing or fancywork. We all liked Quilter's Choice because we saw the designs the other club members were working on and swapped scraps of material. There wasn't a quilt top turned out by a member of the Persian Pickle Club that didn't have fabrics from all of us in it. That made us all a part of one another's quilts, just like we were part of one another's lives.

Agnes T. Ritter was as good a quilter as any of us—except for Ella, of course. Nobody quilted as well as she did. But Agnes

4

T. Ritter wasn't any good at piecing. Her quilts were just comforts made of big wool squares cut out from old trousers and blankets and tacked instead of quilted. You put one of those on the bed, and you thought you were sleeping under a flatiron. She said she'd just as soon stitch the pieces together with her sewing machine as sew it by hand. Agnes T. Ritter was not born to quilt like the rest of us. We'd rather quilt than eat, even in times like these, when some didn't have much choice. I hoped Rita would learn to like quilting as much as I did.

"If Rita doesn't sew, she can read to us," said Mrs. Judd.

"Oh, Septima," Nettie Burgett said as she bit off the thread on a tea towel she was embroidering. "Can't we skip the reading just this one time? We want to get to know Rita."

Mrs. Judd didn't answer, just squinted at Nettie through her thick lenses until Nettie blushed and looked down at her sewing. Mrs. Judd liked to remind us that the Persian Pickle Club had been formed to improve the mind, not just to make bedcovers.

"I don't care if I do," Rita said. I guessed she was tired of people staring at her and asking her questions. Maybe she was afraid we were all like Agnes T. Ritter and would start picking at her.

"Choose something from *One Hundred and One Famous Poems,*" I said. It was the only book in Ada June's house except for the Bible and the dictionary and a set of *A* through *C* and *P* through *R* of the encyclopedia. We'd heard every poem in that book, but it was better than Scripture. I did wish, however, that one day Mrs. Judd would open the *P* through *R* volume and suggest that we read about the pygmies who didn't wear clothes. I'd seen the picture. So had Ella, who'd been looking over my shoulder. She'd giggled, then put her hand over her mouth like we were naughty girls. She had a child's sweet disposition, and things tickled Ella so these days.

Ada June handed the poetry book to Rita, who leafed through it, then stopped and read something to herself.

"Out loud," Mrs. Judd said, and Rita turned red, while Agnes T. Ritter snickered.

5

"It's Carl Sandburg," Rita said.

"Oh, that's not poetry. Give us something that rhymes," Mrs. Judd told her.

"How about 'Trees?' " I asked.

"You know that by heart, Queenie," Mrs. Judd told me. "Read Mr. Longfellow's *Paul Revere.*"

The rest of us sighed. *Paul Revere's Ride* was Mrs. Judd's favorite, and it lasted an hour. It made a nice rhythm for quilting, but, my, I was tired of it.

Rita read until she was hoarse, while the rest of us stitched and drowsed and made little sewing noises. Nettie's big shears sounded like tin snips when she cut a thread. Opalina's damp needle squeaked every now and then as she pushed it through her fabric. Her hands sweat a lot. Forest Ann's quilt pieces rustled and crackled. She was making a Grandmother's Flower Garden, and had backed each little five-sided piece with same-size patterns cut from a letter. Mrs. Judd kept time to the rhythm of the poem with her needle, flashing it back and forth before taking tiny stitches in her quilt square. I never knew how a woman with hands as big as chicken hawks could make such neat stitches.

It seemed that there never was a poem as long as *Paul Revere's Ride,* and when Rita finally read the last line, Ada June snatched the book out of her hands and said, "The teakettle's on. Rita, would you help me put out the refreshments?"

"I'll help, too," I said, and put my sewing down before Mrs. Judd could fuss at me. You didn't need three people to serve refreshments, but I wanted to tell Rita not to let Mrs. Judd bother her, because she had a nice side when you got to know her. She was loyal, too. There never was a woman as loyal as Septima Judd, but that was true of all the Pickles.

Ada June had the same thought, because when I reached the kitchen, I heard her whisper to Rita, "Don't mind Mrs. Judd. Her bark's worse than her bite. She's as good a woman as you'll find in the state of Kansas."

"If you can put up with living in the same house with Agnes

6

T. Ritter, Mrs. Judd's no trouble at all," I added, picking a thread off my dress.

Ada June laughed behind her hand at that, then put on her apron and went to the icebox for the bread pudding, which was her specialty. She wasn't much of a housekeeper, her quilt stitches were big enough to catch a toenail, and with six kids, she'd grown as lumpy as a Kansas sand hill, but Ada June Zinn sure could make bread pudding. Buck Zinn said he was a goner the minute he tasted it. Buck rode into Harveyville on a sorrel named Roxie one day on his way to Wyoming, where he was going to be a cowboy. Then he caught sight of Ada June sitting on her folks' veranda and stopped to pass the time of day. He stayed for supper and ate a dish of Ada June's bread pudding, then a second helping, and asked if anybody in Harveyville was looking for a hired hand.

"Wait till you taste Ada June's bread pudding. She's famous for it," I said. When I saw Ada June blush, I knew she'd made it in honor of Rita, so I laid it on as thick as cream. "Bread pudding's like quilting. Ada June and I can take the same pattern and the same material, but our quilts are as different as the sun and moon. I use stale bread and milk and eggs, but my bread pudding's as dull as Jell-O, while Ada June's is fine enough to take first prize at the state fair. It would if the fair had a category for bread pudding, that is. You know what I mean?"

"Oh, I've never made bread pudding. I don't like it much," Rita said.

Of course, Rita couldn't know that she'd hurt Ada June's feelings, because she didn't know how special that bread pudding was. I patted Ada June's arm and called into the other room, "Guess what we've got for refreshments?"

Everybody else carried on over Ada June's dessert just as I had. Ella clapped her hands and said, "My favorite!" The others put aside their sewing so they'd have room in their laps for refreshments. Ada June, Rita, and I carried the dishes into the room, and nobody said another word, except for compliments, until the pudding was gone and Ada June began clearing the bowls. Ceres Root, who is the only living founding member of the Persian Pickle Club, picked the last raisin out of her dish with her fingers and asked Rita if she'd met Tom in college.

Rita glanced at Agnes T. Ritter, then said, "He was a customer at the Koffee Kup Kafe, where I was a waitress. Tom came in for coffee and left me a twenty-five-cent tip. He did that every day for a week. Then he invited me to the picture show. It was *Son of Kong*."

"How romantic," Ella Crook whispered. She was small and wispy and blushed when she talked, as if she ought not to have spoken. We had to listen hard to understand her, but we always strained our ears, because she didn't speak up often. Besides, we loved her so.

"There wasn't anything romantic about *Son of Kong*. Don't you remember? We saw it over to Topeka," Mrs. Judd said. She was the blusteriest member of the club and the hardest to please, but in all the years I'd known her, I never heard Mrs. Judd say a cross word to Ella.

"I like that monkey," Ella said, then blushed and picked up her sewing.

"Rita's cafe was one of those places that never heard of nutrition and spells Koffee Kup Kafe with *K*'s," Agnes T. Ritter said. She meant for us to frown, but I thought using *K* instead of *C* was classy. Make that *klassy*. I thought Rita would appreciate the little joke, and I hoped I'd remember to tell it to her. I also decided that as soon as I finished the Double Wedding Ring quilt I was piecing, I would make a Koffee Kup Kwilt. Just you wait, Agnes T. Ritter!

"I thought you went to the university," Forest Ann Finding said. Forest Ann was a widow lady and Nettie's sister-in-law, because Nettie was married to Forest Ann's brother, Tyrone. Forest Ann was still pretty and slender, with hair the rusty color of ripe maize and freckles like a sprinkling of cinnamon across her nose, while Nettie, even though she was younger, had gray hair and skin. Being Tyrone Burgett's wife was harder than being his sister.

"Oh, I did, but I worked, too. After Tom and I got married, I worked full-time, since there wasn't enough money for both of us to go to school. I want to get a degree, too, like Agnes, only in English. Agnes has a degree in home economics."

"They know that," Agnes T. Ritter said. She'd always thought she was better than the rest of us, even though home economics wasn't something important like teaching. I thought it was stupid to spend all that money going to college to learn the very thing you learned growing up on a farm.

"Tom and I had a small wedding. Just the two of us. We were married by a judge, but I had a new pink dress."

"Married in pink, your fortune will sink," Forest Ann said.

"No such a thing," Nettie told her. "It's 'your husband will stink.' "

Rita didn't pay any attention to them. "Then I lost my job . . ." she said, and she didn't have to finish. We understood. She wasn't the only one going through hard times.

"We needed Tom on the farm," Mrs. Ritter added quickly. "We'd been trying to talk him into coming home."

"Well, I for one am glad Tom went to farming," I said.

"We all are," Nettie added. But we all weren't. We were glad Tom had come back to Harveyville and brought Rita, but going to farming that summer meant you had reached the end of your row. With the crops burning up and the dust blowing in, farming was the last thing anybody wanted to do. I looked out the window, the way we all did from time to time, hoping I could be the one to say, "Why, lookit there. It's raining off to the west." It wasn't raining, however. It never was. The air was hot and dry and dusty. I picked up my needle and felt the grit on it. The quilt piece I worked on was smudged from the dust, and so were my hands, which were as wet as Opalina's.

"You're a city girl, are you?" Mrs. Judd asked.

Rita nodded. "Tom wasn't sure I'd like it here. Once, he wrote me a letter asking if I thought I'd like this part of Kansas or whether I thought it would be too much like heaven for me." Rita blushed and ducked her head. Ella sucked in her breath, and I thought I'd never read anything that pretty in all of the one hundred and one poems in Ada June's book. No wonder Rita fell in love with Tom.

"Well, is it?" Ella asked, and we all laughed, even Mrs. Judd. Ella looked confused.

We returned to our sewing and were quiet for a time. Then Mrs. Judd cleared her throat, and I wondered what we were in for. "The Reverend Foster Olive called me," she said, and I let out a little groan. I wasn't alone. Reverend Olive was the pastor of the Harveyville Community Church, which even the Catholics attended, because it was the only house of worship in town. Grover said he'd rather listen to a dog bark than Reverend Olive preach. But that wasn't the only reason I didn't care for him. He was always asking the Persian Pickle Club to make a quilt so he could raffle it off to our husbands to buy hymnals or a fancy new altar to replace the one Grover's grandfather had carved.

"He's like a hard woman. He always comes back," muttered Forest Ann.

"What is it this time?" Mrs. Ritter asked. "I wouldn't mind it so much if we were helping less fortunates, but Foster wants money to buy things the church doesn't need."

"You'd think he'd ask our opinion about what to spend the money on, since we're the ones who've got to raise it. Reverend Olive doesn't ask our husbands to plant corn for the Lord. What makes him think we want to be quilters for Jesus?" Nettie asked, looking at Forest Ann. Sometimes Nettie blasphemed just to make Forest Ann blush. The two of them always tried to get the better of each other, although I knew they were close, closer than either one of them was to Tyrone, in fact. But that figured. Who'd want to be close to Tyrone Burgett?

Forest Ann pretended she hadn't heard, and Nettie added, "That man's like a sore thumb, always on hand."

Mrs. Judd stuck out her chin with its little collection of warts that looked like the tips of screws and said, "He wants a steeple, like the one they just got for the Methodist church over to Auburn."

"Oh, it's ugly. It looks like it came from the ugly-steeple factory," I said, which made Rita laugh out loud. Everyone turned to stare at her, because it wasn't a joke.

"How are we going to tell him no?" Mrs. Judd asked.

"Why, it looks like Foster has put the fear of God into you, Septima," Mrs. Ritter joshed. I looked over at Ada June, who put her hand in front of her mouth to hide her smile. There weren't many people Mrs. Judd wouldn't stand up to, so you almost had to admire Reverend Olive for that. I was disappointed, however, because if Mrs. Judd didn't have the nerve to tell him we weren't going to make him a quilt, who would?

"I say we tell him we're busy with our own charity," Nettie said.

"What charity's that?" Mrs. Judd snorted.

We all thought it over for a minute. Then I piped up. "There's a home in Kansas City where girls who aren't married but are in the family way can go and live until their babies are born. We could make a quilt to raise money for them."

Nettie and Forest Ann looked at each other and frowned, but they didn't object until they heard what Mrs. Judd had to say. Mrs. Judd took off her glasses and pinched the bridge of her nose while she thought it over. I held my breath until she said, "That's an awful good idea, Queenie. I guess I'd rather help girls like that than buy a steeple." Nettie and Forest Ann stopped frowning and nodded.

"We can make a Rocky Road to Kansas," Opalina suggested.

"Not if I have anything to say about it," Mrs. Judd told her. "I've seen too many of those Kansas rocky roads to put them in a quilt, especially one that goes to help a less fortunate."

Before anyone else could suggest a pattern, I spoke up. "Let's make it a Celebrity Quilt. You send a square of fabric to famous people and ask them to sign their names to it." I'd read about Celebrity Quilts in the *Kansas City Star* and had wanted to make one ever since, but who'd autograph a quilt square for me?

Now that the quilt was for a good cause, famous people all over the country would want to send in their names. I said we should each make a list of the people we admired and bring it to the next meeting. Then we'd write letters to the celebrities, explaining what the quilt was for. The rest of the club agreed that was a fine idea.

"Here's something else. Famous people are pretty busy, and they won't answer by return mail. So it's going to take a long time to get that quilt put together, and by then, Reverend Olive will have given up on the steeple or found some other way to buy it," I said.

"Besides," Ada June added slyly, "us raising money for unmarried mothers will surely get under Reverend Olive's skin. Lizzy's, too."

That tickled us all.

"What do we do if Foster sends Lizzy over to help us?" Opalina asked. "Do we have to let her sew?"

"In a pig's eye! You leave Lizzy to me," Mrs. Judd said, being her tough old self again. She glanced at Ella, who never was nasty to anyone and once or twice had said it would be a kindness to invite Lizzy to join Persian Pickle. "Now, don't you say anything about it," Mrs. Judd told Ella. "You've got the problem of thinking people are nicer than they are. Pickle just wouldn't be the same if Lizzy was to join."

We all nodded. Lizzy Olive was thin as whey and just as tasteless. She wanted to be in the Persian Pickle more than anything. It was odd the way women were about our club. There were some, like Lizzy, who would have given six months' rain to belong, but we didn't invite them. Others, like Nettie's girl, Velma, who was automatically part of the club because her mother was a member, never came.

Velma Burgett worked at the Hollywood Cafe in Harveyville until Tyrone heard about how the men acted around her. He slapped her face, dragged her home, and said he'd take a strap to her if he ever heard of her going in there again. I guess he was afraid she'd turn out to be a drunk like him. Forest Ann told me that Velma sneaked out nights. She was wild as hemp, which worried Nettie and Forest Ann, but I knew sooner or later she'd settle down. She'd start coming to club after she found a husband. It was marrying that made women appreciate other women.

We had our differences in Persian Pickle. "My stars, we'd be as dull as checkers if we didn't," Mrs. Ritter told me once. But when any one of us was in need, she got the support and understanding that a man never provided. There wasn't anything we couldn't share or a secret we wouldn't keep.

Forest Ann must have been thinking the same thing, and she spoke up. "Lizzy's such a gossip. Why, if she had the least idea—"

"Be still!" Nettie interrupted her, glancing at Rita.

Ada June changed the subject. "I have just the thing for you, Rita," she said, standing up and going to the sideboard. She took an envelope out of the drawer and handed it to her. "Here's my templates for a Nine-Patch. It's a good quilt pattern for you to start on."

I wish I'd thought of that. "Nine-Patch is as easy as pie, and it goes fast," I told Rita. "It's made up of nine patches, three to a row. Three up and three across. That's why it's called Nine-Patch. You make a big patch out of nine little patches; then you put it next to a square of fabric that's the same size as your nine-patch."

"Oh, like geometry," Rita said. It pleased us all that she'd gotten the hang of it right away.

"I like to think of it like cornfields next to wheat fields," Ceres said, rubbing her hands. They were crippled with arthritis and Ceres couldn't quilt the way she used to, but she came to Persian Pickle Club, anyway. She said she'd die if she gave up quilting.

"When there isn't a drought and you can tell the difference between wheat and corn," Mrs. Judd threw in, and we all sighed.

"That's the truth," said Mrs. Ritter. "Maybe that Nine-Patch ought to be all black and brown."

"I could make it in yellow and white," Rita said after she

studied the scraps. "I'll buy the material next time Tom takes me to town."

None of us said anything for a minute. Rita had plenty to learn about quilting. You didn't just go out and buy all the fabric even if you had the money, which most of the members did not. You made quilts out of what was on hand, like flowered feed sacks or pieces remaining when you cut out a blouse, or from trading scraps with one another. You got pleasure knowing this piece was left over from your high school graduation dress or that one was passed down from your grandmother. Forest Ann said quilt scraps were just like "found money." Of course, sometimes you went out and spent a nickel at the Flint Hills Home & Feed for an eighth of a yard of material you just had to have, but you didn't buy yards and yards to make a quilt top.

We couldn't explain that to Rita when it was something you didn't say, you just knew. Who would be that rude?

Agnes T. Ritter would. That's who. "I guess Tom has a pot of money buried someplace," was the way she put it. Agnes T. Ritter was the only one of us who was mean-spirited.

Rita didn't get it. She looked at me—the way you look at somebody who is your friend when you need help. That pleased me.

"We're used to making do," I explained, looking around the table. "Rita's too polite to ask us for scraps, but I expect we have enough to get her started." Since I don't always say things right, I was pleased with the way that came out.

Ella was right behind me. While I was speaking, she took out her scissors and snip-snipped a little piece of yellow-flowered goods with green dots in it. The cut piece was exactly the size of Ada June's small template, even though Ella hadn't measured. Without a word, she pushed the patch across the table to Rita with her needle.

Before you knew it, we'd all reached into our work baskets for our best material, everybody but Agnes T. Ritter, that is. She didn't have any scraps, anyway. Ceres gave Rita a piece with cherries printed on it, saying it came from the Marshall Field's

14

store in Chicago. She wasn't bragging. She just wanted Rita know it was special. Forest Ann handed her a sliver printed with windmills in what we called "that green." It was the color of the enamel trim on my stove and Mrs. Judd's double boiler, and it was in all the new material nowadays.

Then Opalina handed Rita a small piece of gold velvet with a pansy that she'd embroidered that very afternoon for her crazy quilt. "You cut that into a little square and let it peek out of your Nine-Patch," she said. Of course, velvet didn't have any place in a plain old Nine-Patch made of wash goods, but it was the thought that mattered, and later, long after Rita was gone and Mrs. Ritter had brought out the top for us to quilt, I got to make the stitches around the pansy. After we quilted it, Mrs. Ritter kept the Nine-Patch in the kitchen, over the rocker, and whenever I looked at it, I searched first for the yellow zigzags I gave Rita that day, then for the pansy.

Time always went fast at the Persian Pickle Club, but that day it just flew. Even Mrs. Judd, who usually gave the high sign when it was time to go home, forgot to keep track of the hour. Not until we heard the parlor clock chime did we realize that we'd gone an hour past our time.

"Oh, dear, it's five!" Forest Ann said, as upset as if she'd looked out and seen a dust storm boiling up over the house. Ada June and I exchanged glances, and Nettie shot out an angry look, but whether it was to show her disapproval to Forest Ann or to warn the rest of us to keep our mouths shut, I couldn't tell. None of us would have breathed a word of criticism, anyway. If Forest Ann let that man stop by her house every night at five o'clock, it was her business, not ours, even if he was married.

"Sometimes I wish I didn't have a man to feed each and every evening. It'd be nice to go home to the radio and my sewing," Opalina said. She wanted to let Forest Ann know she thought being a widow wasn't always such a bad thing. I didn't look at Forest Ann, however. I looked at Ella, who didn't have a husband, either. She didn't have even a radio to keep her company. In fact, the old Crook place had no electricity, but Ella didn't

15

mind. She sewed in the evenings by kerosene lamp—or even candlelight sometimes, because it was like having stars inside her house, she said.

Mrs. Judd looked at Ella, too. "Come along, sweetheart. You can stay to supper with me. You're better company than Prosper. He can't talk about anything but the crops drying up." The rest of us sighed, because that's all any of our husbands talked about. Mrs. Judd tucked the sugar-sack square of cloth with the butterfly she'd been embroidering on it into her sewing basket and stood up. "What do you say we make us a big dish of popped corn for dessert, Ella, even if it is the middle of summer? I haven't had popped corn for the longest time."

"Oh, my favorite!" Ella said.

Outside, Rita passed her hand around again for us to shake, and Ella couldn't resist touching the hem of Rita's pretty dress. "It's just like milkweed silk," she murmured.

Mrs. Judd told Rita, "You have any sewing you want done, you come see Ella here. She sews better than anybody in a hundred miles." Then she added, "She's a worker." We all nodded, because that was the biggest compliment you could give a Kansas woman. You didn't say she was smart or pretty. You said she was a worker. And Ella was a worker. In her embroidered white dress, with the wisps of hair curling around her thin face, Ella resembled the girl on the Whitman's candy box, but she was a regular farmwife who chopped wood and slaughtered pigs. She was stronger than she looked—and older. She was as old as Mrs. Judd, which was more than sixty.

"Oh, I would, but I'm going learn to sew myself," Rita said, and blushed. What she meant was that she was broke like the rest of Kansas.

"You do that." Mrs. Judd opened the driver's door of the yellow Packard, and Ella scooted in across the leather seat. The old touring car sagged as Mrs. Judd stepped on the running board. I noticed she'd rolled her stockings down around her ankles when it got hot during quilting and had forgotten to roll them back up. Her legs above the rolls were angled from rickets and as white as birch sticks. Mrs. Judd sank into the seat beside

16

Ella and started the motor, and we watched as the Packard lumbered out onto the road. Sometimes it didn't make it, and then Mrs. Judd had to tinker with the motor.

"I always think of Mutt and Jeff when I see Ella and Mrs. Judd together," Ada June whispered.

"Or Laurel and Hardy," I said.

"Or Edgar Bergen and Charlie McCarthy?" Rita chimed in. The three of us laughed about that all the way over to my car. I drove a Studebaker Commander that Grover's father had bought back when farming paid enough to live on. As I opened the door, I knew Rita was going to be more fun than a shoe box of kittens, and I turned around and hugged her, saying how glad I was she had moved to Harveyville.

That's what this story is about—Rita coming to Harveyville and joining the Persian Pickle Club and learning the meaning of friendship. It's about me, too, of course, and about how I never can keep my mouth shut.

chapter 2

The minute Grover came in, I knew something was eating at him. I knew because he didn't tell me. In fact, he didn't say a word, which is Grover's way. When something's gnawing on him, he's silent as the dawn. Not me, however, and I got edgy knowing Grover was upset, so I talked a mile a minute.

"The cream doesn't last in all this heat. I put it in the Frigidaire and it should have stayed cool in there, but when I poured it into the churn to make butter, it'd already gone bad. I had to scald the dasher to get out the sour smell. Funny thing is, the buttermilk's fine. I don't know why the cream'd go bad and the buttermilk wouldn't. Maybe it was bad when I put it away."

Grover didn't reply, just took off his hat and tossed it over the knob on the back of a kitchen chair, so I kept on talking. "The bread's moldy, too. It's only two days old, and already I found mold. Tell me why there's mold when everything's so dry. Sometimes, I think I can hear the crops out there crying for water, calling, Grover, give me a drink." I stopped, hoping Grover would laugh, but he was washing his hands and still not paying any attention to me. He had a little scrub brush at the kitchen sink that he rubbed on the cake of Ivory, then on his knuckles to get out the dirt. His shirt was wet all down the middle of his back, and the hair on his great big head was damp and matted in a ring on top where his hat had perched.

"I've got to clean out the refrigerator again and sprinkle it

18

with baking soda to get rid of the moldy smell. I hate that smell as much as I do the stink in the hired man's cabin. That shack smells like rotted oilcloth no matter how many times I air it out. Oilcloth and molasses and old pancakes. I don't suppose hired men care about things like smells, though."

"Uh-huh," Grover said at last, still not listening. The water ran over his hands, but Grover didn't pay attention to how he was wasting it. He just stared out the window, stared at nothing.

"That's why I'm going to run away. I'm driving to Kansas City this afternoon to be a burlesque queen, or else maybe I'll join the Catholic church so I can be one of those sisters. That way, I'll never have to worry again about what to wear."

"You going to keep the car, or you want me to go along to Kansas City with you so's I can drive it back?" Grover asked. He shut off the water and turned around and grinned at me. "I sure would hate to lose that radio." He'd spent a whole day installing a radio in the Studebaker.

"I thought you weren't listening."

"I wasn't until you got to the interesting part about the burlesque queen." He pronounced it "bur-le-que." "I expect I'd buy a ticket to see that. Maybe I'd get a private show ahead of time." I pointed my toe and swung my leg up in front of me—not too high—while Grover reached for the towel and dried his hands. "You upset about something?"

"Just you. What's on your mind?"

"What makes you think something's on my mind?"

"Grover." I sighed. "We've been married five years, and it might as well be a hundred, because I know you that well. Either you tell me what it is or say you're not going to tell me, but don't say nothing's wrong, because I know different."

Grover used his fingers to comb through his hair. It was as thin as Depression wheat, but Grover was touchy about his hair, and I never mentioned he was going bald. "How come you're so smart?" he asked, and I told him not to change the subject.

"Got any cookies?" Grover asked. I knew then that he'd tell

19

me. Otherwise, he'd have turned around and gone out to the barn to brood.

"I've got jumbles and hermits, made with the black walnuts we gathered down on the creek last fall."

"Both kinds."

I took out my plate with the peach-and-plum decal on it and piled it with cookies. Then I put the pitcher of buttermilk on the table with a glass. The outside of the pitcher was damp, and little drops of water ran down the sides, forming a wet ring on the tablecloth. I took off my apron and sat down at the kitchen table across from Grover.

"You sure make cookies better than anybody, Queenie," he said, putting a whole hermit in his mouth, washing it down with buttermilk, then eating a jumble in two bites.

"Grover Bean, don't try to wiggle out of it with the compliments."

"You won't like it." Grover picked up a jumble, and I pulled the plate away. Grover knew he'd have to tell me what was wrong before he got any more cookies. "There's squatters down on the creek."

I set down the plate, and Grover put his hand over mine. I was sorry I'd made him tell me. There wasn't anything that scared me as much as drifters. We didn't get many this far off the main road. Still, every now and then, I saw a man tramping past the farm or driving an old car jammed with kids and belongings, driving slow, like he was looking for something to steal. Sometimes they even came to the door, asking for work. If Grover was there, he'd give them a handout, but I always locked the screen and called Old Bob up onto the porch.

I knew most of them meant no harm, but some were desperate and would kill you for a quarter. Down in Kiowa County, a drifter put a pitchfork through a farmer who'd caught him stealing off a clothesline. And I myself had had three dollars and a meat-loaf sandwich stolen off my kitchen table while I was in the chicken coop, and I knew it was a back-door knocker, because nobody in Harveyville except Grover would eat my meat loaf. I had good reason to be scared of drifters.

"They didn't break into the hired man's shack, did they?" I asked.

"No, they just pitched a tent by the creek. That's all."

"I hope you shooed them right off. You know how I hate tramps."

"They're not tramps, Queenie."

The way he said it made me look up at him. "Well, gypsies, then. It's almost the same thing."

"No, they're not gypsies, either. Not these folks. They're just people, hill people, down-and-out. They're pretty near as broke as anybody I ever saw."

"You told them to move on, didn't you?"

"No," he said, rubbing the little port-wine spot on his chin.

"We can't have people like that camping on our land."

"What do you mean, 'people like that'?" Grover asked. He moved his hand away from mine and picked up a hermit and bit it in half, spilling crumbs on the table. "They're people like Ruby and Floyd. People like you and me."

"Don't say that."

Grover ate the other half, then picked at the crumbs on the cloth, putting them into his mouth. "Whether you like it or not, they are. There but for the grace of God—"

"Don't you preach to me, Grover. Are you going to tell them to move on?" I interrupted. Grover looked at me so long without replying that he made me nervous. So I got up and took out another glass from the cupboard, then poured myself some buttermilk, but I don't know why, because I hate buttermilk. Grover took the glass out of my hand and set it on the table. "You hate buttermilk," he said. "Look at me."

Grover didn't tell me what to do very often, so I looked at him.

"Queenie, these people aren't moochers. They're just about our age, with a boy no more than six or seven years old and a baby. They're in need, and it's our Christian duty to help them."

"You sound like Lizzy Olive," I told him. And when I said it, I thought, No, he doesn't, but I do.

"That's not you talking, Queenie. I met these people. There's nothing wrong with them except they're broke. I'm sorry for them, and I want to tell them they can camp out there on the creek until they're ready to move on. Maybe we could offer them the hired man's cabin."

I just stared at Grover.

"We've got no use for it," he said. "There's no reason in the world some family in need can't live in it for a bit."

"Are you telling me or asking me? I guess it's your farm, so you can do what you want to with it."

Grover sighed, and I could tell he was disappointed. "I'm asking, Queenie. It's *our* farm. You know that. I'm not saying you have to invite them over to supper or to let them join your stitch-and-itch club." He'd started calling it that this summer because the chiggers were so bad. When I didn't laugh, Grover added, "I'll tell them to move along if you really want me to."

I don't like to go against Grover, but sometimes he can be a sap, believing every hard-luck story he hears. He could call those squatters anything he wanted, but they were tramps to me. "There was a man and wife in Missouri who got killed when a tramp set fire to their farmhouse. They'd chased him off, and he waited until dark, then burned them alive. When he got caught, he said he wasn't sorry. I read it in the newspaper last week."

"These folks won't hurt anybody, Queenie. I promise."

"You can't promise any such thing, because you don't know them," I told him.

"Well, I know you, don't I? You wouldn't turn your back on a less fortunate, and that's just what they are."

"If you want to help the less fortunates, what about Tom and Rita? We ought to extend a hand to our own kind first."

"Tom and Rita may not have money, but they aren't poor. Besides, they don't want to throw up a tent on the creek."

There was no use fussing with Grover when he had his mind made up, so I said, "I guess it wouldn't hurt to take a look at them."

Grover reached across the table and squeezed my hand. "I

misspoke about the shack. All I'm asking is that you let them camp here for a while. If you still think they're tramps after you meet them, I'll tell them straight off to hit the road," he said. "Oh, and why don't you put the rest of that buttermilk in a jar, since you're not going to drink it. They could use it."

He reached out for another jumble, but I swatted his hand. "They might like some cookies," I said.

❧

I packed up the cookies and the buttermilk and most of what else we had left in the refrigerator, telling Grover things were going bad so fast in this heat that giving them to the squatters would save me from having to throw them out later. I didn't want Grover to think I'd gone soft.

"You're not so tough, Queenie. That peppermint candy doesn't go bad."

"Now you watch out, Grover. Don't you pick on me. They won't be as likely to murder us if we fill up their stomachs. If they're hard cases, I'll tell them myself to move on."

But I didn't. Like Grover, I thought they were the saddest, sorriest people I'd ever seen, and my heart went out to them right off, especially the two kids.

When we drove up, the woman was kneeling down at that little trickle of water in the creek with a bar of harsh, home-made lye soap, washing out clothes. A pair of overalls and some shirts were already spread out on the rocks to dry. She was scrawny, but she was clean. They were all clean, and I knew they'd taken baths in the creek that day. The woman wore a dress that was more patches than dress, and the little boy had on a pair of homemade drawers made out of gunnysack. It made me itch to see that tough, old material next to his skin. I wondered why his mother hadn't used a flour sack or a sugar sack to make underwear for him, then realized it must have been a long time since they'd bought a sack of anything.

Their old rattletrap Ford with a ripped canvas top was parked under a black-walnut tree, next to their tent. They'd laid stones in a ring for a fire and rigged up a tripod over the fire pit to hold a kettle. I knew there couldn't be much in it. Jackrabbits were pretty poor pickings these days.

The man sat on the running board, with a stick in one hand and a pocketknife in the other. He stood when we drove up and threw the stick away, then carefully closed the knife and slid it into his overalls. He wasn't wearing a shirt, just the overalls.

The woman stopped washing and put on a felt hat, even though she was barefoot, and came to stand at attention beside her man. She jabbed him with her elbow and jerked her chin at his head, and he snatched off his hat, holding it in front of him with both hands. The little boy stopped playing and joined them, not looking at us because he was shy. I didn't see any baby.

"Afternoon," Grover said. They didn't say a word at first, just stared and maybe wondered if we were going to tell them to pack up. "This is my wife, Mrs. Bean," Grover said, and the woman nodded just the slightest bit. She glanced at the food basket I held, then looked away. Then she looked at it again.

After a minute, the man said, "Proud to meet ya." But it sounded like he wasn't sure.

Then the woman wriggled her toes and said softly, "How do."

"Hi," I said, and we stood there looking one another over. Then because silence is a burden to me, I said, "I've got buttermilk. It's cold. There's cookies, too. I hope they won't spoil your supper." Then I knew without anybody saying it that the cookies and buttermilk would be their supper. "In all this heat . . . things spoil so fast. . . . There's just Grover and me. . . ."

The woman nodded again without smiling, and the man said, "We sure do thank ya." They didn't move, and neither did I, so Grover took the basket out of my hand and handed it to the woman.

"You ought to drink the buttermilk soon, so it doesn't go bad," I said. The woman fetched two tin cups out of a wooden box on the ground while the man opened the basket and took out the jar.

"Would you have some?" she asked me, which made a lump come into my throat. As poor as they were, they had offered to share their charity basket with us.

"Why, thanks just the same. We already finished ours," I said, reaching into the basket for the sack of cookies and holding it out. "Your little boy might like one of these hermits. The nuts came from the very trees we're standing under. You go right ahead and help yourselves."

The woman nodded her thanks and passed a cookie to the man, then to the little boy. "You say ' 'Bliged,' " she told him, and he muttered something, his mouth full of cookie.

"Where do you folks come from?" I asked.

"Missouri," he replied. "We been on the road two months. We took a wrong turn and ended up in Oklahoma. There sure ain't nothing there. We're headed for California is what we are, but we ain't got the money for gas, so we figured we'd give Kansas a try. We'll move on toward California when we get a little money in our pocket. We're looking for work."

"Any luck?" Grover asked.

"Plenty of luck. Luck, jes' like a grasshopper in a chicken house's got luck," the woman said. "The car give out right here—two days ago. Blue says let 'er sit. I says we ain't got the choice. We cain't move till he gets a part."

The man nodded. "Blue's my name. Joe Blue Massie, but folks call me Blue. That's Zepha. This here's Sonny." Sonny scowled at the buttermilk in his mother's cup but took a drink, anyway. He didn't look up when his father introduced him. "Baby, she's in the tent."

"Blue says the part's going to cost us. We'd like to move along. We don't mean to camp out on private property. We got respect for what belongs to other folks. The fact is, we just cain't move till we get that part. You tell them what part, Blue."

"Water pump."

"That's a problem all right," Grover said. "Do you have the money for it?"

I wanted to kick Grover for being such a dope. Of course they didn't have the money.

25

Blue sized up Grover for a minute, maybe wondering if Grover was thinking of robbing him. "Bit. I'd be 'bliged to find work. I work hard."

"Most people'd like to find work, but there's none around here that I know of," Grover said. "You can see how the crops are burning up. That creek there, it ought to be up to the bank. If this was a good year, those rocks in the stream you're drying your clothes on would be underwater, but it's not a good year. We haven't had a good year in a long time. I'm not hiring, myself, and I don't know anybody who is. If they did, they'd give the work to local boys first."

Blue nodded, expecting that answer.

"I sew right smart," Zepha said, looking at me hopefully.

"I wish I had a need for it," I told her. "There's a widow lady here, a friend of mine, who does sewing. She needs all the work she can get."

None of us could think of anything else to say, so we all watched the boy cleaning out the cup with his tongue. "He sure does take to that buttermilk," Zepha said.

"You send him up to the house after milking tonight. We'll give him some fresh milk. Your baby might like it," I said.

Zepha was so grateful, she couldn't even reply, just looked down at her toes. So I glanced over at Grover and nodded. He knew what I meant and said, "You folks are welcome to stay here for a few days, until you get that part for your car. The fact is, I know a little about engines and could take a look at it for you. Maybe I've got something on hand that will do. I can't see any sense in paying good money for a part if you got it on hand."

Blue and Zepha looked tickled, and Blue wiped his hand on his overalls and shook Grover's hand. "By dogies, that's real nice. We won't be a bit of trouble, will we, Zeph? We'll be careful with the fire, too. We won't hurt your land none, Mr. Bean."

Zepha added, "No need for you'ns to trouble yourself about the car. Blue's real good at that."

"We've got a better place for you to stay," I said, looking to Grover for approval. Now it was his turn to nod, and when he did, he smiled at me. "There's a hired man's cabin between here and the house. It's not much, and it'll have to be cleaned up, but it'll keep you out of the rain."

The two of them looked startled, then realized I'd made a joke, and they laughed, the man slapping his leg. "That's a good 'n." Lack of rain was something we all shared, and we felt a little easier with one another.

Then the woman realized we'd offered them a place to live, and she asked, "You mean that? I never heard of nothing so nice. Last week, we got dogs sicced on us. Show them where you got bit, Blue." But Blue only scowled.

"We could drive you folks over there right now," Grover said. "You just load what you got in our car."

"We wouldn't want to trouble you none," Zepha said.

"No trouble at all," Grover told her. He helped Blue move things out of the tent while Zepha and I packed them in the cardboard boxes that were stacked on the ground. Then I heard a cry from the tent, and I handed my load to Zepha. "Let me see to her," I said. Zepha nodded.

The baby didn't put much effort into crying. She was a little bit of a thing, with the face of an old woman, but she was precious to me, and I felt a stab of pain as I picked her up, knowing that although I wanted a baby more than anything in the world, I'd never have one of my own. Grover and I had been married only a year when I miscarried, and the doctor took out most of my insides to save my life. I was lucky to have a man like Grover who didn't blame me for being childless and never once brought up that I was the reason we had an empty place in our lives. Still, every time I picked up a baby, I felt as if I'd let Grover down.

I hummed a little song to the baby to get the lump out of my throat, and after she quieted down, I asked Blue her name.

"Baby."

"I mean her Christian name."

He looked at me kind of funny and said, "Baby."

We couldn't get everything into the car at once, so Grover and Blue said they'd take a load over by themselves and come

27

back for us. Zepha went along to unpack. I volunteered to sit with Baby and Sonny.

Sonny looked me over until they disappeared, then asked, "You got a dog?"

"Old Bob's his name. He's a big dog, a hunting dog, but he's nice and gentle. You come see him sometime," I said.

"Our dog, Pup, is in the bushes. He don't take to strangers. Got more cookies?"

I nodded.

"I like cookies. Hate buttermilk. It makes me puke. Drink it only 'cause I'm real hungry. What else you got in that basket, lady? Got a bean sandwich?"

"I've got your supper. We'll wait till your mother gets back."

"Got possum?"

I made a face and shook my head. "No possum. Possum's as bad as buttermilk. I brought chicken." I wouldn't eat possum, which was as bad as eating squirrel. I'd starve to death before eating some things.

"No sir. Possum's the best eatin' they is," Sonny said. "We been eatin' fried dough. Ma made a fried doll cake yesterday. It was real pretty. Day before, we had taters." He stared at the basket for a minute. Then he went down to the trickle of water in the stream and squatted down to make a dam by piling rocks across the water. Circles of blackened rock along the bank showed that other drifters had camped there. I wondered if Grover had known about them, too.

As I watched Sonny play in the creek, I hummed a little song to Baby and was still singing when Grover came back with Blue. When Blue got out of the car, he wouldn't look at me or thank me for letting them stay in the cabin, and I was afraid his feelings were hurt by that dirty old place. We should have let the Massies stay where they were. Blue kicked the rocks out of the stream, then nudged Sonny up with his bare toe. When Grover walked by me, carrying a box of battered pots and pans to load into the car, I asked if the Massies were disappointed with the shack.

Grover shook his head and whispered, "I think he's afraid

he'll cry if he opens his mouth. The woman said that shack was nicer than any place they'd ever lived in, even at home. You'd have thought it was a palace, the way she acted."

The Massies were poor indeed, because the shack wasn't anything more than upright boards with battens to cover the cracks and keep the snow from sifting in during the winter. The stove was held up by wire, and the built-in bunk was narrow. I remembered when Nettie once made a cover for a daybed, and Mrs. Judd called it a "hired man's quilt" because it wasn't very wide. The only other things in that cabin were a table with a warped top and two nail kegs for chairs. I hoped Grover had thrown away the 1931 calendar with a picture of a naked woman on it that hung on the wall.

"This house is pretty dirty," I told Zepha after Grover drove us all over there with what was left of the Massies' things. "I'd have cleaned it myself if I'd known somebody was moving in."

"I like to clean, missus," Zepha said. "It'll be real nice when I'm done."

"The roof leaks," Grover said, "but I guess you don't have to worry about that. If we get rain, we'll all just stand outside and dance."

"It don't look like much to fix. You got any boards around? I'll fix it if you got boards," Blue said.

Grover told him he did, and when Blue went inside, I prodded him with my elbow. "You can fix it, Grover. We shouldn't let them move into a shack with a broken roof."

Grover shook his head and said, "That's his way of paying us back. It helps his pride."

"I guess pride's the only thing they've got."

"And not much of that, I'd bet."

Before we left, I stuck my head inside the cabin and said, "After supper, we'll come around with the things we stripped from here last fall and took up to the home place. With nobody living here, we didn't want to leave things lying around, for fear somebody would steal them."

When I got into the car, Grover asked what things were those. We'd never had anything else in that cabin.

That evening, Grover filled up the little cream can with milk and put some boards, a bedstead, and an old feather tick into the truck. He thought I should take along some quilts since I had so many, but I told him he wasn't the only one who was sensitive about the Massies' pride. Zepha had quilts of her own, folded up inside the tent, and she might be ticklish about accepting another woman's second best. The easiest way to insult a woman was through her quilts.

Instead, I took along a big basket to make a bed for Baby, a can of stove black, a decent broom, and some old feed sacks I'd bleached for dish towels. Grover said those rags were better than what the Massies had on.

"That's the idea. I'll give them to Zepha for cleaning cloths, but she'll use them to make clothes for the kids."

The Massies were lined up, waiting for us when we arrived after supper. Zepha wore shoes and had pinned a scrap of ribbon to her hair. Sonny stood straight and tall, with his feet together, as if he were a clothespin soldier, and I was especially glad for his sake that we'd brought along the surprise.

"I've got something special for you," I said, pointing to Sonny. "But you've got to help with it." Grover lifted the ice cream freezer out of the car and set it on the ground, and the three of them gathered around and stared at it. When they didn't respond, Grover and I realized at the same time they didn't know what it was.

"Ice cream," we told them together.

"Ice cream? I ate ice cream once. From a store," the boy said, his eyes wide.

"This is just as good, but it doesn't make itself. You have to turn the handle on top until it won't turn anymore." Grover put Sonny's hand on the crank. "You do that till your arm gets too tired. Then your dad will take over, and when his arm gives out, I'll take a turn. The harder it is to move, the closer we are to eating ice cream."

Sonny began turning the handle, and the Massies stood over him, their heads moving in a circle with the handle. "What do you bet when it's his turn, Blue won't cry uncle?" I whispered to Grover.

"I'm counting on that."

Zepha looked up at me, her eyes wide. "By golly, I never saw nothing like that. Does it make them little brown cones, too?"

"It's a mean trick to play on that boy of yours," Grover said. "Mrs. Bean and I get too tired to turn the crank. We figured we'd get Sonny to turn it for us so we could have a dish of ice cream without doing a lick of work." That was another of Grover's fibs, because he would sit on the porch all day turning that handle.

While Sonny and Blue cranked the ice cream freezer, Zepha showed me the shack. I told her I'd never seen it so clean. In fact, I'd never seen it clean at all.

"I hope you don't mind if I picked your flowers," she said, pointing to the brown-eyed Susans that were in a broken bottle on the table.

"I like them. I'd like to make a quilt like that some day."

"Oh, you'ns patch?" she asked, her eyes lighting up.

"There's not much else I'd rather do."

"I'm the same. I look across the land, and all I see are quilts. I carry my scrap bag in the car so's I can go to patching while Blue drives. If I didn't have my quilting, I'd have gone crazy with all this moving around. I quilt every chance I get, 'cept on Sundays, of course. Every stitch you take on the Sabbath, you got to take out with your nose in the next life, but I expect ev'-body knows that. You'ns want to see my quilts?" she asked, blushing and looking at her dusty shoes in embarrassment.

Blue, who was listening from the doorway, said, with a touch of pride in his voice, "That one's got a hot needle and a galloping thread."

"Go'n, Blue. You talk too much," she told him, but I could tell she was pleased. "I didn't bring all my quilts. If'n I did, they'd reach to the sky. I left my lumpy comfortables at home, and some I traded for gas and such on the road. These uns that I got with me are Blue's favorites." Three quilts were stacked on the rusty iron bed, and when Zepha unfolded them, I held my breath. They were made of old homespun, and the stitching was almost as fine as Ella's. "Why, that's Wandering Foot," I said, pointing at a quilt made of home-dyed blue and white.

"No sech a thing. I ain't fool enough to let my Blue sleep under a Wandering Foot. He's hard enough as it is to keep to home. I call that Turkey Tracks. He can sleep under Turkey Tracks and not run off," Zepha said. She spread out another quilt. "This has got the pieces sewed on instead of patched. It's a Piney."

"We call that a Peony," I told her.

"That's what I said, a Piney. Now, here's my pride. It ain't my work. Granny Grace, our neighbor lady, made this one." Zepha unfolded a quilt made up of tiny triangles no bigger than my thumbnail, and they all met perfectly at the corners. Even Ella had never made a quilt like that. "People was always asking Granny Grace to sell it. Why, some woman offered her twenty-five dollars, but Granny wouldn't take it. She wouldn't sell a quilt that was made out of the dress Aunt Bessie drowned in. That was her youngest girl. Granny give it to me the night before me and Blue left home. You could have knocked me over with a feather. I never was so tickled with a thing in my life." Zepha looked up at me. "I guess Granny Grace give it to me because it's called Road to Californy."

"Oh, isn't that the best name! Will you let me copy it? Someday when I'm good enough, I want to try it."

Zepha was pleased and promised to draw it out herself if I brought her some paper. Then I said if she did that, I'd trade her the pattern for fabric scraps. It's funny how quilting draws women together like nothing else.

After we'd eaten our ice cream and bid the Massies good night, we drove down the old road to the highway. "I've got an errand to run. You want me to take you home first?" Grover asked, fiddling with the radio dial in hopes of getting the weather.

"I guess I'll go along for the ride. Did you offer him work?"

Grover chuckled. "I told him a dollar a day wasn't much, but it was as good as anybody around here ever paid. Blue'll mend fences, spread manure, do other chores. It won't be for long."

"What about Tom? He'd be glad to work for a dollar a day."

Grover thought that over for a minute. "Tom's got a place to live, and he doesn't have a family to support. I'll offer him work at harvest, when I need men, but I can't ask my best friend to be my hired man." I understood. I wouldn't ask Rita to be the hired girl, either.

Grover and I rode out into the country. In the moonlight, it looked like the Kansas farmland Grover and I knew when we were growing up and there was plenty of water. I could almost smell lilacs and honeysuckle. We passed a fallow field that all of a sudden made me shiver, it was so dried up and ugly, and I slid over next to Grover to get warm. He put his arm around me, asking if I was cold, and I told him I was.

We drove toward Auburn and stopped at a house just this side of the river. Grover got out of the car and knocked at the back door, spoke with a man for a few minutes, then followed him into a shed. A few minutes later, Grover came back to the car and put a box into the back of the truck.

I waited until we were on the road again before I said, "Is it a good water pump?"

Grover put his arm around me and asked how come I was so smart. I turned the dial until I found Fred Waring's Pennsylvanians on the Topeka station, and we drove on through the dark without talking. I didn't know I'd fallen asleep until Old Bob jumped up on the car and Grover said softly, "Wake up, honeybunch. We're home."

chapter 3

I'd come to be Rita's friend. Of course, I couldn't say anything so silly to her. I told Rita I was there to get to know her better. It took me longer to come calling than I'd planned, what with the Massies moving in and, after that, me having to put up tomatoes and to dry peaches. Bottled tomatoes I like, but dried peaches are a waste of good time, since there's nothing that tastes worse than dried peach pie, unless it's a rail fence. Grover likes them, however, but then, Grover likes anything.

"That's nice of you, dearie," Mrs. Ritter said. "You girls go sit out where it's cool." Mrs. Ritter smelled like the blackberry jam that was cooking on the stove.

Rita smelled like a hired hand. Her bangs were plastered to her forehead, and sweat rings stained her dress under her arms. There were blackberry stains on her apron, which was really one of Mrs. Ritter's and was big enough to go around Rita three or four times.

Agnes T. Ritter started to take off her apron, too, but Mrs. Ritter spoke up. "Agnes, would you help me with these dishes while we wait for the berries to cook?" Agnes T. Ritter sighed and retied her apron. She filled the teakettle from the pump on the sink and put it on the cookstove.

"Don't spill the dishwater on the floor. Nettie says if you do that, you'll marry a drunk," I told her.

I guess it served me right for being mean, because Agnes T.

Ritter said right back, "I hear you set up a squatter village on your place."

"Agnes!" Mrs. Ritter said. "It's not our business."

"It is if we all get head lice," she muttered.

I itched my head for fun and turned to Rita. "Let's go sit under the trumpet vine and scratch chiggers." I could see the red welts on Rita's arms and knew she hadn't waited for my invitation. She'd probably gotten them in the blackberry patch.

We walked across the yard, where Mrs. Ritter's hollyhocks and morning glories were in full bloom despite the heat that wilted man, beast, and even Grover, and sat down on a wooden bench. It was as cool a place as you could find, being in the shade of the sod house that Tom's grandfather had built when he moved onto the land, way back in the 1870s.

Now, the old place was a toolshed, but it was still pretty, because somebody had planted trumpet vines to hide the sod, and those orange flowers covered the house and hung down over us, blocking out the sun.

Rita wiggled back on the bench, then stood up fast and said, "Oh, hell. If it's not the chiggers, it's splinters." She pulled a half-inch sliver out of the back of her leg and sat down again carefully and fanned her face with her hand. "I don't know what's worse, the cookstove or the heat out here."

"Were you helping with the jam?" I asked.

"No, I was just heating water to rinse the dinner dishes. Agnes says we have to pour boiling water over everything. I forgot to do that yesterday, and she washed the dishes all over again after I'd dried them and even put them away. Agnes sure knows her onions about dirt. All she does is criticize, criticize, criticize. I wish she'd stop telling people about how I didn't know the difference between salt and sugar. She's brought that up ten times, and even if it had happened to someone else, I wouldn't have thought it was funny. Why, a person who cooks every day could get them mixed up." Rita pulled a trumpet flower off the vine and put the end in her mouth and sucked out the sweetness.

"What happened?"

35

Rita threw away the blossom and picked another. "I made a cake, only I used a cup of salt and a pinch of sugar instead of the other way around."

"Anybody could do that," I said, even though it seemed pretty peculiar to me. "Shoot, I bet even Agnes T. Ritter could get them mixed up."

"Why do you call her that?" Rita asked me, pretending the flower was a little horn and blowing through it. "Why do you always call her Agnes T. Ritter instead of just Agnes?"

The question made me blink. She'd been Agnes T. Ritter all her life, and I'd forgotten why, so I had to stop a minute to remember. "We started calling her that when we were kids. You know that baby rhyme, 'Jack, be nimble, Jack, be quick?' Well, one day Floyd said, 'Agnes T. Ritter, Agnes T. Quick.' And Agnes T. Ritter got so mad that it just naturally stuck."

"I can tell she doesn't like it. She frowned every time you called her that at the club meeting. She frowns a lot." Rita seemed pleased about that. She peered through the end of the trumpet flower as if it were a spyglass. "How come you're called Queenie Bean?"

"Because that's my name."

"Oh." Rita scratched the back of her neck, and I could see a little red chigger bump. "Try not to scratch. It's better if you don't," I told her. "Sometimes a little butter and salt mixed together help."

Rita made a face.

"You don't eat it," I said quickly. "You rub it on the welt." I didn't tell her Grover used tobacco spit.

Rita stretched back, leaning her head against the dry wire grass of the soddy behind her, and that was when I realized she was pregnant. Seeing me look at her stomach, she said, "Six months. It seems like ages."

I started counting backward, and Rita knew right off what I was doing. "December. We were married the end of December. I got pregnant the first month," she said. "Oh, don't be embarrassed. Everybody counts. Agnes even counted out loud."

"Well, I'm sorry," I said.

36

"Me, too. I didn't want a baby right off."

"Oh, I don't mean that. I mean the counting. I think you're so lucky to have a baby."

"You can have it," Rita said. I must have looked shocked, because she added, "Queenie, it was a joke." She didn't sound like it was a joke, however.

Rita was quiet for a minute. A hummingbird stopped in midair and stuck its beak down the throat of an orange trumpet, then flew off.

"I like the green hummingbirds best. The red ones are mean," I said, changing the subject. It wasn't polite for me to talk about the baby if Rita didn't want to.

But she changed it right back. "I shouldn't have said that. I mean, it's nice to have a baby, only with things the way they are, it's not a very good time. Sometimes I get awfully down in the dumps. Agnes said getting pregnant is all my fault. Maybe she doesn't know it takes two to tango."

"Agnes T. Ritter is sour cherries," I said indignantly.

"Agnes is bad cheese." Rita giggled.

"Agnes T. Ritter is stepping into fresh cow pie—in your bare feet."

"Are cow pies what I think they are?" Rita asked. I nodded, and she laughed so hard, she bent over double and then sat up straight, as if she'd picked up another splinter.

"You all right?" I asked.

Rita put her hand into her pocket and pulled out a needle. "I forgot this was here," she said. She took out a wadded-up quilt square and held it up for me to see. "It's bum, isn't it?" It was.

"You'll learn. My first one was worse than that," I told her, although that wasn't true. I'd worked so hard on my first piece of patchwork that it had turned out to be almost perfect. But I wanted us to have more in common than being short and not liking Agnes T. Ritter, which was nothing special. Everybody didn't like Agnes T. Ritter. Then I reminded myself Agnes T. Ritter was a member of the Persian Pickle Club, so I had to like her and be her friend.

37

"I don't seem to get the hang of it," Rita said. "I keep pricking my fingers."

"Put rubbing alcohol on them. It'll toughen them up."

Rita ironed the patches with her hand, then put the thread hanging down from the back of the patch through the needle. The thread was dirty. "The needle's as sticky as that awful fly-paper Mom hangs in the kitchen. Well, I say it's spinach, and to hell with it," Rita said, wadding up the patchwork and throwing it between us on the bench.

Instead of letting Rita know I was too dumb to get what she said about spinach, I picked up the quilting and said, "There's nobody who can sew in this weather except Ella Crook."

"She's a funny one. I can't exactly figure her out. She looks like she'd fall down if you blew on her, but she walked all the way up here for a visit in the awful sun yesterday and didn't even work up a sweat. She hardly said two words when she got here, just handed Tom a plate of fudge and muttered something about remembering how much he liked it. I thought she didn't like me, but Tom says she's as shy as anybody he ever met. Is that so?"

"Yes. Even when you get to know her, she doesn't say much."

"How come she takes in sewing? She couldn't make much money at it, what with everybody in such a pickle about money just now. Who can afford to send out sewing?"

"She's alone, kind of a widow. She has to make do. We all help her out a little when we can."

"Does she live with that busybody?"

"Mrs. Judd? No, but Mrs. Judd looks out for her. We all do." I pressed my finger on the main seam of Rita's sewing so that it lay flat. "It helps if you iron the seams open before you start the next row," I said, changing the subject. "Do you have a thimble?"

"I can't use one," Rita said, and I could tell I had my work cut out for me in making Rita a quilter.

"What do you mean, 'kind of a widow'? Where's her husband?" Rita asked.

38

"Whose?"

"Ella Crook's?"

With Ben Crook, it was best to let sleeping dogs lie, as Nettie put it. I wanted to change the subject again, but Rita was looking at me with such curiosity, I knew she wouldn't let me. "Nobody knows," I said. "If you don't use a thimble, you'll poke a hole in your finger.

"You mean she's a grass widow?" Rita reached into her pocket and pulled out a thimble, putting it onto her middle finger.

"This one," I said, taking the thimble from her and putting it on the correct finger of my right hand. "What's a grass widow?"

"That's when a woman's married but her husband's ditched her or something. Is that what happened?"

I shrugged. "I personally think it was hard times. Ben Crook thought the sun rose and set on Ella. He was the best husband in the world, but he lit out a year ago, and nobody's seen or heard from him since. I try not to think about it. Farming isn't easy for men these days."

"I think it's worse for the women," Rita said. "I hate housework. The only time I ever agreed with Agnes was when she said we ought to wear wrinkled clothes and not waste our time with those flatirons." Rita looked down at her quilt square. "This goes so slow. It's enough to put me into a blue funk."

I'd never heard of a blue funk before, but I had an idea what it meant. "Why don't you turn it into a baby quilt? It won't take any time at all."

"Why that's a swell idea. You're a true friend, Queenie." She looked up as the screen door banged and Mrs. Ritter came out with a pitcher and two glasses.

"There's the true friend," I told Rita. Then I called, "Mrs. Ritter, I think I'd sell my soul for a glass of lemonade."

Mrs. Ritter tried to frown, but it didn't work because she was such a jolly woman. "My stars, don't let Dad hear you blaspheme, dearie, and call me Sabra. You know we always use first names for members of the Persian Pickle Club."

"Not for Mrs. Judd. I think God would strike me dead if I called her Septima," I said, and Mrs. Ritter laughed.

She looked down at Rita's little mess of sewing. "Don't you think she's getting the hang of it, Queenie? It's nice, isn't it?" Then she turned and went back to the house.

"This is real tasty," I called, then told Rita, "She cares a lot about you. Lemons must cost ten cents each."

"I'd trade lemonade any day for a real drink. Bourbon. Yum," Rita said, adding, "Tell me about those women at your club."

"At *our* club," I corrected her, because whether she knew it or not, she was a member, too.

There wasn't much to tell about us, because we were all pretty ordinary. Mrs. Judd was the richest, which anybody could tell from the Packard, even though it was old. The Judds owned the biggest farm in Wabaunsee County, and Prosper Judd was the president of the bank in Eskridge; Mrs. Judd had inherited it from her people. But rich didn't always mean lucky. Their only child, Wilson, who was a few years ahead of me in school, caught infantile paralysis, and the members of the Persian Pickle Club had exercised his legs every day for a year so that he could walk again. Then he walked right out of Harveyville and never once wrote to his mother.

Ada June was every bit as nice as she was the day she was the hostess for Persian Pickle, I told Rita. Buck raised horses, but people weren't buying horses anymore, and since the Zinns had more kids than nickels in their pockets, they were hard up. Still, it didn't bother them much, and they were as happy a couple as I ever saw. I liked Ada June a lot, but she was almost forty. Opalina Dux was the one with white hair so long, she could sit on it, I explained. You could always tell where she'd been by the trail of hairpins. Sometimes, she was as crazy as the crazy quilts she worked on, carrying on conversations with her chickens. There was no harm in that, however. Most of us talked to chickens at one time or another. But Opalina brought them inside the house so she could talk to them while she did her work.

Nettie Burgett had a goiter, so she always wore a scarf

around her neck, which made her look like her husband, Tyrone, who didn't have a neck at all. Tyrone ran a numbers game at the billiard hall over in Blue Hill, leaving Nettie and Velma, who was the only Burgett kid still at home, to do most of the farming. He'd turned to gambling after the government got rid of Prohibition, and his bootleg business went to heck. Of course, being on the wrong side of the law didn't keep him from being almost as righteous as Foster Olive. We all knew he was a trial to Nettie, although she never complained. We also knew he was years behind in his mortgage payments, and the Eskridge bank would have foreclosed if Mrs. Judd hadn't told Prosper to let it ride for Nettie's sake. Nettie's daughter, Velma, never came to Pickle, so I skipped her.

I told Rita that Forest Ann was Tyrone's sister, but you wouldn't know it, because she was so much nicer than he was. In fact, Forest Ann kind of made up for Tyrone being such a dope. She and Nettie were more like sisters than sisters-in-law. When Nettie turned fifty, Tyrone didn't give her so much as a pin, but Forest Ann drove her into Topeka to see *Captain Blood* at the picture show and have lunch at F. W. Woolworth's, where they drank Nehis and ate weenies that were cooked on hot rollers in a glass case. Nettie said it was the best birthday she ever had.

Forest Ann was a widow woman because of the untimely death of her husband, Everett Finding, who was dumb enough to drown in a glass of water. He was sitting on top of a reaper one day, reading a girlie magazine, when something spooked the horses, and Everett toppled over into the machinery. The horses ran away, dragging Everett and leaving pieces of him all over the field. Being fertilized by Everett, the next year's crop was the best that farm ever harvested.

"Forest Ann's kids had all grown up and moved away by the time Everett died, and she said spending the evenings by herself nearly killed her. Sewing kept her from going crazy. She says a woman without a needle is like a man without a plow." I didn't explain to Rita that Dr. Sipes was the real reason Forest Ann kept her sanity, because he stopped at the Finding house every

41

night for a glass of buttermilk. Or maybe Dr. Sipes drank the bootleg that Everett had received in payment for helping Tyrone with his still. Forest Ann had as many jars of hootch as tomatoes in her root cellar.

"A woman without a needle is like a man without a needle," Rita said, and I laughed, even though I didn't get it. "Who is that real old lady?" she asked.

"Ceres Root. She came out here from Ohio when she was a bride, marrying Cheed Root after she'd known him for only two weeks. She was about to get hitched to a fellow her parents picked out, even though she didn't think much of him because he hadn't gotten off his horse when he proposed. Then Cheed came along, and they ran off to Kansas and have been sweethearts all their life, just sweethearts. Quilting helped her, too, when she lived in a dugout and had no neighbors the first year. All she had was her quilting, and she went to sewing during the day instead of housework. Once, she looked under her bed and found grass growing eight inches high.

"Cheed was so happy she'd married him that he'd do anything for her. When he went to town one day, she asked him to bring her back a piece of fabric she'd admired. Instead of a length, he brought her the whole bolt of cloth. It was Persian pickle, what some call paisley. Ceres still has a few yards of it left because it's so precious to her. She's particular about what she uses it for or who gets the scraps. Of course we all have pieces of it in our quilts. That's how come we're called the Persian Pickle Club.

"Now, I've told you about all of us, except for Agnes T. Ritter and Mrs. Ritter, and you know them already. Of course, there's Ruby. She'd still be a member if she came back to Harveyville. Ruby and Floyd lost their farm last year when the bank in Topeka took it over, so they piled everything into their Chevrolet truck and went to California."

I stopped a minute, remembering my last look at Ruby and Floyd waving from the truck, with the kids in back, playing on a mattress. The Persian Pickle had gone over to see them pull out, and I cried and cried, until Mrs. Judd said, "Hush, up,

Queenie Bean. Don't make Ruby feel worse than she does already. They've got no choice. In times like these, it's root, hog, or die."

"Ruby was my best friend, but I haven't heard from her yet. Nobody has. Grover said they're too busy eating oranges." I knew Grover missed Floyd as much as I missed Ruby, but that was partly because he'd cosigned a loan on a tractor for him, and when they left, we'd had to pay it off ourselves.

"Don't you mind that all those women are so *old*?" Rita asked. She was right about them being old. Everybody in Harveyville seemed to be old nowadays, because all the young people had gone off to look for jobs.

"That's why I'm glad you've come. We're the same age, twenty-three. Of course, Agnes T. Ritter is only twenty-five, but she acts like she's thirty. Forty, even."

"I think she was born old and cranky," Rita said.

I nodded at that, then took off Rita's thimble, which I still had on. It made a sucking sound as it came loose from my sweaty finger. "I don't care how old the Persian Pickles are, because they're my friends. When my mama died, they saw me through it. The Pickles are family."

Rita clucked her tongue to show she was sorry about my mother. "Do you have a father?"

"I'm an orphan now. Same as Grover," I said. I told Rita about Grover and me, how my father passed when I was in high school, and Mama just wasted away from grief.

"Grover's mother was a member of Persian Pickle, just like mine, but I never knew her. She died when Grover was born, and his dad raised Grover and David, who is Grover's big brother. He lives in Oregon now. After we were married, Grover and I lived with Dad Bean until he died two years ago. David inherited half of the farm, but he said he'd never be a farmer like Grover, and he sold us his half cheap. The Beans are real nice people."

I started to tell her how Dad Bean had brought me that bunch of meadow flowers stuck in a milk jug when I lost the baby, but it wasn't right to tell a pregnant woman about a baby dying, so I put the thimble back on and finished Rita's quilt square in silence. When I was done, I smoothed the seams with my fingers and turned it over. "Now, this looks just fine. The Persian Pickle will quilt it for you after you make the rest of the patches. You can do it of an evening, when you're listening to 'The Bob Hope Show' or 'Fibber McGee and Molly.'"

"I read," Rita said.

I thought about that for a minute. "Reading's all right, I suppose, but with quilting, when you're done, you have a quilt. When you finish with a book, you don't have anything."

Rita looked at me kind of funny, as if she hadn't taken in the wisdom of what I'd said. Then, I thought she had something else on her mind and was deciding whether to tell me about it. "I read all the time because I want to be a writer," she said at last. "I've applied for a job at the *Topeka Enterprise,* and I'll write stories about Harveyville. They want somebody they can call in case we have a bank robbery or something here. It's called a correspondent."

"Harveyville doesn't have a bank," I said. When Rita frowned, I added quickly, "Still, I think that's wonderful." I looked down at her stomach. "But how can you be a newspaper writer when you're going to have a baby?"

"Somebody else will just have to look after it. I can't miss my chance."

I wanted to tell her that if I had a baby, I wouldn't trade it for all the newspapers in the world, but it wasn't my place to do so.

"Here comes trouble," Rita said, looking up at Agnes T. Ritter, who'd just opened the screen door. She started toward us, with Tom behind her. The two of them were almost the same height, but Tom had inherited all the good looks.

"It appears you drank all the lemonade," Agnes T. Ritter said, scowling at Rita. "So much sugar's not good for someone in your condition," she added, as if Rita had a disease. "At least Mom doesn't get the sugar mixed up with the salt, like some people." Tom rolled his eyes at me, and I figured Agnes T. Ritter would throw that salt and sugar mix-up at Rita for the rest of her life.

Rita grinned at Tom and said, "Hi, ace." Then she winked at me and looked over at Agnes T. Ritter and added, "Hi to you, too . . . Agnes T. Ritter."

❧

Before I left, I invited Tom and Rita for supper the next evening. That didn't give me much time to dust and Hoover the house and put out my best quilts and cook the supper, but with Agnes T. Ritter picking on Rita the way she had, I'd gotten an idea.

At noon, after I told Grover about our guests, he told me to serve pickled pigs' feet and sauerkraut, which was his favorite as well as Tom's, but I wouldn't do it. After all, Rita was from Denver and ate in restaurants where the food was cooked by Mexicans and Chinamen. Grover suggested fried chicken, but I told him Mrs. Ritter fixed it better than I did. So he said to make up my own mind, and finally, I decided on ham and red-eye gravy.

Grover approved. "There's nothing better than redeye gravy and mashed potatoes," he said. "Put plenty of bourbon in the gravy so Tom can drink it. You know how Howard Ritter is. Tom told me his dad's farm is the driest place in Kansas, and he wasn't talking about the weather. Why don't you make a pie for dessert?" I knew Grover would ask for that.

"Okay. How about rhubarb?" It was Grover's favorite.

"Rhubarb's a little past its prime, isn't it?"

"I found some late stalks that haven't gone stringy yet," I said, hoping Grover wouldn't ask me where.

He didn't. "I got chores to do before the old dog barks," he said, leaving me in the kitchen as he headed out to the barn. That was just the way I wanted it. Men didn't understand how much work there was in a supper invitation. It took me all the rest of the afternoon to do the cooking and set the table. There wasn't a minute to spare.

In fact, I barely finished in time to go stand in the screened-in porch with Grover to watch Tom and Rita walk down the the road, stirring up the yellow dirt that was as dry as ashes. It rose waist-high and stayed there, so you could see only the top half of them. The wind was blowing, too, not hard, just enough to get that darn dust all over my clean house. I ran back inside to close the windows, but they were already shut, with towels shoved into the cracks. Even so, little lines of dirt were forming near the openings.

Rita and Tom weren't in any hurry and fooled around as they walked along. Every now and then, Rita bumped into Tom on purpose, and they laughed. Watching them reminded me of Grover and me when we were first married and liked to walk around the fields at dusk, kicking at the clods of dirt and jumping over the ruts that the rain had cut into the road.

Tom went off into our east field and picked up a handful of dirt and held it to his nose, then stood up and let it sift out of his fingers. It was powdery, like the dirt on the road. I saw him shake his head and frown and say something to Rita, but by the time they reached us, they were laughing and holding hands again, and so were Grover and I. Rita hugged me, and Tom kissed my cheek, and that was the start of just about the best evening we ever had. Tom and Rita said so, too.

Boy, were they glad to get away from Agnes T. Ritter. "I don't care if you burn dinner, Queenie. Just don't give me anything white," Tom said. "If Agnes isn't serving creamed onions or cottage cheese, it's rice or chicken boiled so long, there isn't any taste left, and custard for dessert. I never knew there was so much colorless food a person could eat."

"Since she's so crazy about eating white stuff, I told her to serve popcorn the next time she and Mom had club meeting," Rita said. "Buttered popcorn."

I didn't understand. "You can't quilt and eat buttered popcorn."

"That's the idea, silly."

Tom sat down on the arm of the davenport, putting his arm around Rita, who stood next to him. "What's that you're drinking, Grover?"

"Popskull," Grover said. "Darn good stuff, too. It's Tyrone's leftover bourbon, which is better than what you buy legal these days. Sometimes, I think Franklin Delano Roosevelt was wrong about putting an end to Prohibition."

"Tangleleg suits me. How about you, morning glory?" Tom put his arm around Rita, who wore a pretty yellow sundress, a yellow silk ribbon around her hair, and a tiny gold wristwatch on her arm.

"Is that stuff really bourbon?" she asked.

"It's awfully strong," I warned her.

"Well, hot dog, then! The bigger the kick, the better," she said.

"I'll just see to dinner," I told the men after Grover brought the drinks, expecting Rita to follow me into the kitchen the way women did. Instead, she went out on the porch and sat down with Tom and Grover. I made the gravy and put dinner on the table, hurrying so I wouldn't miss anything. When I was finished, I called everybody to come inside. Tom and Grover said things looked good enough to eat, but Rita forgot to say, "My, you shouldn't have gone to all this trouble," the way you're supposed to. I guess they have different manners in the city.

"Tom applied for a job with a copper-mining company in Butte, Montana," Grover told me, after he'd returned thanks, being especially grateful for friends and asking the Lord for rain.

"Me and about a thousand other men. There's not much call for engineering graduates these days. I guess Rita will be a famous newspaper reporter before I even get the notice that I've been turned down." Tom took an extra big helping of mashed potatoes. "You know, I'd kind of looked forward to coming back to Harveyville, but I'd forgotten how damn hard farming is. Toots over there's been game, but she wasn't brought up to slop pigs. This life is even harder on her than it is on me." Neither Grover nor I could think of anything to say. We knew farming was hard, but it was the best life we could think of. We were silent until Tom said, "Queenie, this is the finest gravy I ever tasted."

I nodded to accept the compliment. Then I said to Grover, "Maybe you didn't know Rita's going to write articles for the *Enterprise.*"

"You writing up stitch 'n' cackle?"

I kicked Grover under the table. "For your information, it's called the Persian Pickle Club." Grover and Tom broke out laughing, anyway. Rita chuckled, too, and even I had to smile because "stitch 'n' cackle" really did describe Persian Pickle sometime.

Rita cut her ham into little pieces before she answered Grover. "I'm going to write about the school-board election." She put a piece of ham into her mouth and chewed it. "Tom's dad says the way people vote in it will tell whether good times are coming back. The new people running for the school board want to build a grade school, and that'll make taxes go up. So if they win, I'll say people believe good times are around the corner and they don't mind paying more to the government. But if the old school-board members are reelected, it means voters think hard times are here to stay and they want to keep taxes low. That's called a slant."

"You see those better times, Tom?" Grover asked.

"Maybe," Tom said slowly, using his spoon instead of his knife on the butter. It had been as hard as ice when I'd put it on the table, but the heat in the room had melted it, and Tom could have scooped it up with his slice of bread. "Not personally, I haven't. I guess I can't complain, since we've got a roof over our heads and something to eat. It could be a lot worst. I could be one of my creditors."

"Yeah, things are so tight here, they ought to call this place Hardlyville." I noticed that Grover's napkin was still folded on the table. We never used napkins except for company. "Had any luck finding work here, Tom?"

"You bet. I've made all of fifty cents this summer." He chuckled, but the rest of us didn't. "Edgar Howbert hired me to do a day's plowing for a dollar, but I finished in half a day, so all I got was fifty cents. If Rita sells this article of hers, she'll make twenty times what I did, and she won't have blisters, either."

"You spend the fifty cents in one place?" Grover asked, which was so funny that we all burst out laughing.

"I thought about taking it over to that place at Blue Hill and putting down a bet with Tyrone Burgett. You know, easy come, easy go. But it's too far to walk, so I guess I'll buy a farm with the money instead."

"It's not fair," Grover said, getting serious again. "Work like a nigger and what do you have?" He looked at me and said, "Negro."

"Hell, those Negroes have got it even worse than we do," Tom said. "Edgar offered Hiawatha Jackson fifty cents a day to do some work, and Hiawatha took it. I don't know if I'm madder that Edgar cut wages 'cause Hiawatha's a colored or that he didn't offer the job to me at the same price." Hiawatha and his wife, Duty, lived on Ella's farm and kept an eye on her.

"Edgar Howbert's a cheap bastard," Grover said.

"Hiawatha was glad for anything. He told me his oldest boy's been all over the state looking for work and that western Kansas is so dry, you couldn't grow a bone there. He came home with dust pneumonia."

"I've heard some of those farmers out that way are packing up and heading for the Sahara Desert because it's got more water," Grover said. "How are you holding up, Rita?"

Grover meant did she want any more food, but Tom misunderstood and said, "She ought to take it easy. Little Agnes there doesn't let her sleep."

"Agnes?" Grover said. "You aren't going to name it Agnes, are you, Rita?" I'd told Grover about the baby as soon as I'd gotten home.

"I'd rather eat goldfish."

"Agnes sure can get on your nerves, all right. Maybe we should have let her drown that time she fell in the creek. I told Tom to let her lie," Grover said.

"Aw, if I hadn't pulled her out, Floyd would have, and I'd have gotten a licking," Tom said.

"Why would Floyd do a thing like that?" Grover asked.

"He was sweet on her. Didn't you know?"

"Floyd?" I asked, looking at Grover. He was just as surprised as I was.

"Sure, but Agnes had her heart set on going to college. She wouldn't marry a farmer, and I guess that was just as well," Tom continued. "If Floyd had married her instead of Ruby, Agnes'd be an Okie now."

"Ruby and Floyd are not Okies!" I said fiercely.

"Call 'em what you like. There are plenty of us who are fifty cents away from being Okies," Tom replied. We were all silent for a minute, thinking that over. Then Tom said, "I was smelling the dirt in your east cornfield. I bet it's dry all the way down to China. It hasn't rained since we came here."

"We had a cloud last week," Grover said. "But I think it was just an empty on its way back from Kentucky."

"This bourbon tastes like it came from there, too." Tom swallowed the last little bit in his glass. "I sure miss the days when Rita and I spent Saturday nights drinking rye and playing cards."

"Your dad would have a fit if we did that here." Rita chuckled. "Sometimes, I feel just like that old lady in your club who lives off by herself without even electricity. What's her name again?"

Instead of answering, I got up and began to clear the table.

"Ella, isn't that it?" Rita asked.

"I'd rather be lonesome than live with Ben Crook. I can tell you that," Grover said. "Remember him, Tom?"

Before Tom could answer, I said, "Speaking of remembering, did you remember to save room for pie?"

"I remember Queenie's pies, all right. That's for sure," Tom said.

I asked Rita to help me clear, and Tom and Grover started talking about the weather again.

Rita and I took everything off the table and stacked it in the kitchen. Then I sent her back to the dining room while I got out the pie, stopping for just a minute to admire it, because it was the prettiest pie I'd ever made. The top crust was the palest shade of brown, sprinkled with sugar. A line of crimson oozed out of the vent I'd cut. I sliced it into four pieces, then whipped the cream and put it into a serving bowl with a big spoon and carried it all in.

Tom gave me a big smile when I set his piece in front of him, and he told me even his mother's pies weren't as good as mine. I passed around the cream, and we all waited until everyone had spooned it out before we picked up our forks.

As they cut their pie, the men discussed corn. Tom asked Grover how many bushels he figured he'd get from an acre, but instead of answering, Grover put up his finger to tell Tom to hold off a minute. He put a big bite of pie into his mouth before he said, "The way I see it—" He swallowed, stared at his pie a minute, then gave me a questioning look.

Tom tried his pie, and got the very same expression on his face. He didn't swallow, however. Instead, he pinched in his cheeks, keeping the pie in the middle of his mouth "Queenie . . ." Tom said, moving the food in his mouth from side to side.

"What's wrong?"

"What kind of pie is this, anyway?" Grover asked.

"Rhubarb," I said. "Don't you know rhubarb pie? I thought it was your favorite."

"It doesn't taste like rhubarb," Tom said. He finally swallowed what was in his mouth and made a face.

"I picked it today, on the north side of the barn," I said. Then I cut my own piece, but I couldn't bring myself to eat it.

Rita tasted hers and spit it out onto her plate.

Grover studied what was left of his pie, moving the crust aside, then picking at the filling. "This is not rhubarb, Queenie." Grover grinned at me. "It's Swiss chard! You made a rhubarb pie out of red Swiss chard!"

"Swiss chard!" Tom roared.

"No such a thing!" I insisted.

But Grover was right, and I turned as red as the chard while Grover laughed so hard, he almost fell over backward—which would have served him right, making fun of me like that. Tom tried to be polite and put his napkin over his mouth, but he sputtered behind it and shook his head while tears came into his eyes.

Rita laughed, too, after she wiped the red off of her little white teeth. "You're worse than me with the salt and sugar. Even I know the difference between rhubarb and Swiss chard."

"Well, they look a lot alike. They're both red, and they have green leaves and stalks. . . ." There was no use explaining.

"Honey, you won't live this down for a hundred years," Grover said, when he caught his breath, and I knew he was right.

I was so embarrassed that I was glad to gather up the plates and escape into the kitchen. The three of them were still laughing when I took in the plate of cookies I'd made that afternoon and served them for dessert instead.

I left the dishes in the sink, where I could do them the next morning, and after we'd eaten the cookies, I went out onto the porch with the others. Grover poured out some more liquor, then said, "I sure am glad I bought Tyrone's bourbon instead of his rhubarb wine." Tom and Rita laughed, but I gave Grover a poke, and he didn't say anything more.

We sat there a long time, talking and laughing, and I could tell Tom and Rita didn't want to go. Before they left, we asked them to sign our guest book on account of it was Rita's first time in our house. Tom wrote, "Next time, I'll take pie in the sky, if you don't mind."

As they started across the lawn, Rita called, "See you in the funny papers." Grover and I watched them walk down the road in the starlight. Once Tom turned back and sang,

"K-K-K-Queenie, Beautiful Queenie, you're the only B-B-B-Bean that I adore."

After a while, his singing faded and was drowned out by the racket from the crickets. Then Tom and Rita disappeared into the night. Grover smelled for rain, but we both knew there wasn't any in the air. A coyote howled a long way off, and Old Bob barked. Grover put his arm around me and said, "Time to hit the shucks," and we went inside.

"You're pretty nearly the best friend Rita could have in Harveyville, even if she might not know it yet," Grover said, hooking the screen door and following me into the bedroom.

I raised my eyebrow to ask what he meant, but in the dark, he couldn't see the gesture.

"I know Tom appreciates what you did."

"Fixing dinner isn't so much trouble. I liked doing it," I said, pushing up the bedroom window as far as it would go. The air was still hotter outside than in, but before morning there might be a breeze to cool us off, and I didn't want to miss it. You couldn't be a farmer without being an optimist about the weather. I stared into the night sky, but there were no clouds.

"I don't mean inviting them for supper. I'm talking about your pie. That was a real nice thing to do, Queenie." Grover took off his clothes and sat down on the edge of the bed to wind the clock, even though he always woke up long before the alarm sounded. As he turned to read his watch in the moonlight, checking the time against the clock, the light coming through the window into the dark room caught the bald spot at the back of his head, making it gleam like a silver dollar. Grover reached over and set his watch on the bureau, got into bed, and held out his hand for me to come to him. "Both Tom and I know there isn't a farmgirl alive who can't tell the difference between rhubarb and Swiss chard."

chapter
4

I'd taken dinner out to Grover in the field, and we ate it sitting on a wall of the old adobe house that somebody had built way back in history. The house had all but blown away —dust to dust, but then, what wasn't dust in Kansas these days?

We were in the shadow of a big cottonwood that must have been set out by the people who built the house. There's a special kind of man who plants a tree when he knows he'll move on before it's big enough for him to sit in its shade. Grover was that kind of man, and I told him so, but he wasn't listening to me. He was looking out across the field.

I took a piece of gooseberry pie from the dinner basket and looked at it with pride before I held it out to him. The crust was golden, and the berries were as plump and pretty as jade beads. "It's better than what we had at Persian Pickle yesterday," I told him. This had not been a bumper year for refreshments at club. Instead of the popcorn Rita had suggested, Agnes T. Ritter dished up tapioca pudding, and the time before that, Nettie served her fruitcake, which she mixes up every few years in a five-gallon drum. She said it would last for fifty years, and I told Ada June it had twenty more to go. The only good thing was that Nettie had soaked it in some of Tyrone's bootleg. When I whispered to Rita that it was a shame we couldn't just lick the whiskey out of it, she replied Tyrone must be a real pip to make booze that good. I meant to remember the word.

54

"You want this, honey?" I asked Grover, who still wasn't paying any attention to me.

"Who's that coming?" he asked.

I shaded my eyes and looked over the field. "He's in a real pip of a hurry, whoever he is."

Grover turned and gave me a funny look. "It might be Blue." The Massies had become so much a part of our lives that it was hard to remember when they weren't living in the shack. Grover would come across sticks laid in a strange pattern in the field and know Blue had left them as an omen. Or I'd look up from my work in the kitchen and see Zepha standing in the door with Baby, both of them silent as Indians. Sometimes I'd come home and find an old scrap of home-dyed goods tucked in the screen and know she'd sent Sonny with it. Every now and then, I caught Sonny sitting in the Studebaker, pretending he was listening to the radio. At first, I felt queer when these things happened, but now we were used to the Massies' ways.

"Maybe he's going to let us know he found a snake up in a cottonwood," I said. Blue had told Grover that if we saw a black snake in a tree, we'd have rain in three days.

"That's crazy. I've never seen a snake in a tree," I said when Grover told me.

"You've probably never seen rain, either." We'd both been checking trees ever since.

I moved out from under the cottonwood while I watched the man disappear into a gully. When he came out into view and started down the rise, we saw it wasn't a man at all.

"It's not Blue. It's Zepha," Grover said. "Why do you suppose she's moving so fast?" I didn't have any idea, but it couldn't be anything but trouble, so I wrapped up Grover's pie and put the dinner things back into the basket. Grover wouldn't be eating his dessert. By the time I was done, Zepha was within hailing distance.

"Hey, you, Zepha. We're over here. Is everything all right?" Grover yelled. Sometimes Grover isn't so smart. If everything had been all right, Zepha wouldn't have been running in the heat without her sunbonnet.

55

"Miz Bean," Zepha called as she slowed down. She didn't say anything more until she reached us. Then she had to catch her breath before she could speak. While she did that, I tried to think what could be wrong at the house. Then I realized she hadn't come from home, but from the direction of the hired man's shack. I hoped Sonny and Baby were all right.

I held out a hand to her and led her into the shade, then reached into the basket for the jar of lemonade and held it out, but she shook her head. Instead, while she gasped for breath, she picked at a thorn in her bare foot.

"There's a woman come along," she said after what seemed like a long, long wait. "She was in a Model A. A skinny woman with a face like a lizard and no lips. She said to tell you to come a runnin', Miz Bean. Her sister's time's come."

"What's that?" Grover asked. None of what Zepha said made sense to him, but it did to me.

"That was Agnes T. Ritter. Zepha means Rita's gone into labor," I told him. "She's early."

Zepha nodded her head up and down. "She couldn't find you at your place, so she come to the shack to ask if us'ns knew where you was. She sez it's bad. I wondered if maybe that baby's sideways. I knew of that happening to a woman onct. I can't think who 'twas. She got bloated up when the baby wouldn't come and screamed for two days and went crazy from the pain. When that baby finally got borned, Granny Grace, who ketched it, she couldn't save it. The woman died a-yellin', and her old man went around the rest of his life with his hands over his ears to keep out the sound. Now, what was her name?"

My stomach felt queasy, and I looked over at Grover, who was pale. "There was another woman," Zepha started, but I shook my head and pointed to Grover. Zepha understood and didn't tell the story, but she said fiercely, "Your man ought to hear about it. Men need to know the trouble they cause us'ns. They ought to have a baby just one time, and have it through their nose, too. That'd teach 'em."

Zepha looked at Grover as if a woman's trouble was all his

56

fault. Then she turned to me. "You tell her be careful. I heard a bird peck at the window three times last night. That's bad luck for sure."

I didn't hold with such things, even though Nettie and Forest Ann swore they were true, but I shivered, anyway. Grover took the basket out of my hands and said, "Go on, Queenie. You can run to the Ritter place 'cross fields faster than we can go home for the car. I'll take the dinner basket on back to the house and be along as soon as I can. Tom'll need somebody with him. Run, Queenie." He gave me a little shove.

"Tell 'em to put a knife under the bed," Zepha said as I started off. When I paused to ask what she meant, she called, "A sharp knife under the bed cuts the pain." I hurried as fast as I could, stopping only to take off my shoes and stockings. Then I ran like a field hand all the way to the Ritter farm, while Zepha called, "Don't you forget that knife!"

Half the Persian Pickle Club was already there ahead of me. After she'd come for me, Agnes T. Ritter went back home and called Ada June's, and all up and down the party line, women picked up the phone and listened in, including the members of the Persian Pickle, who knew they were needed.

As I ran across the Ritter's barnyard, I saw Ada June's Hudson and Forest Ann's old Dodge truck. The dust in the air behind Mrs. Judd's Packard hadn't even settled yet. She stood next to the car with a paper sack in her hand, talking to Tom, and when I came up, I heard her say, "It's not going to do you a bit of harm, and a little nip might relax you. I knew your dad wouldn't have any, so I brought you a bottle of Prosper's. You put it where Howard Ritter won't see it and take a swallow when you feel the need. I don't hold with drunkenness, being a good member of the WCTU. But the Lord has His reasons for everything He puts on this earth. Shut your mouth, Queenie Bean. I keep it around for fruitcake."

Tom looked relieved when he saw me. "I'm glad you're here, Queenie. We tried to call you everywhere. Then Agnes thought your hired man might know where you were, so she drove down there."

I put my arms around Tom and hugged him. "Is she all right?"

Tom's eyes went wild for a minute, and he shook a little. Then he got ahold of himself and said, "I don't know. The pain hit her all of a sudden. The doctor's in there now, along with Mom and Agnes. She's only seven months."

"Seven months," Mrs. Judd said. "Seven months is plenty of time, boy. The fact is, a smaller baby means an easier birthing. Rita won't get tore up so bad. Why, you've got nothing to worry about, Tom."

"Grover's coming as fast as he can," I said.

"You share that bottle with him. Just don't tell Howard where it came from, and you don't need to mention it to Nettie and them, either, since Prosper won't take his business to Tyrone. He says Tyrone's tangleleg tastes like Esso gasoline. Queenie, you go on inside. Rita would rather see your pretty face than mine." I started for the porch, then glanced back and saw Mrs. Judd with the bottle halfway to her mouth.

The members of the Persian Pickle Club had taken over the Ritter kitchen, which still had the spicy smell of plum butter that Mrs. Ritter had been making the day before. Nettie's butterscotch pie was on the table next to Ada June's bread pudding, and Velma, Nettie's daughter, was slicing tomatoes. Ada June built up the fire while Nettie filled the kettle. You'd have thought we were getting ready for a church supper if it hadn't been for Mr. Ritter, who was walking back and forth, muttering and bumping into everyone.

Finally, Nettie said, "Howard, would it trouble you too much to chop some wood for the stove? We might need us a whole tree by the time this is over." He nodded, looking glad that somebody had given him a job to do. He went outside, and before anyone thought to stop him, he'd chopped enough wood to last until Christmas.

"How's Rita?" I asked, and Nettie and Forest Ann looked at each other and back at me, making me remember the time I had lost my own baby. The two of them had sat with me all one afternoon, patting my shoulder and rubbing my back and feeding me bites of food that I didn't want. They'd told me all the superstitions they could think of about how I'd get pregnant again in no time. Of course, they were wrong, but the doctor hadn't told me yet that he'd cut out so much of me, and they made me feel better. I hoped Rita would draw strength from the Persian Pickles, just as I had.

"Queenie, you can do more good with Tom than you can in here," Nettie said, tying a Boy Scout knot in the scarf around her goiter. She didn't tell me old wives' tales anymore because we both knew I would never get pregnant again. Maybe Nettie wanted me outside because she thought if I wasn't in the same house with somebody in labor, I'd forget that I couldn't have a baby myself—as if I could ever forget that.

"I'll stay," I said, then glanced at Velma, who looked a little peaked. Who could blame her? It wasn't right for a single woman to have to listen to childbirth sounds. So I told Velma to go out and keep Tom company. She'd be glad for a swallow of Prosper Judd's liquor.

"She's to stay," Nettie said sharply, but Velma went outdoors, anyway.

Agnes T. Ritter stepped inside the kitchen just then, and I thought Zepha was right. She has no lips. Her eyes were little slits, and I couldn't tell if she was scared for Rita or mad that Rita was causing so much trouble. I touched her hand and asked, "Is Rita all right?"

Agnes T. Ritter shrugged. "How would I know? I never saw a baby born before. But I'll tell you this, Rita being almost as small as a midget doesn't help her any."

We heard a cry from upstairs, and I bit down so hard on my lip that I tasted blood. "Is she in pain?"

"Well, of course she's in pain," Agnes T. Ritter said, as if I were as much of a dummy as Charlie McCarthy.

"You forget about the pain," Ada June said, to herself more than to Agnes T. Ritter, who wasn't listening, anyway. "I don't know why. You just do. Rita won't remember it."

"Zepha, the hired man's wife—" I said, then stopped. I'd sound as foolish as Nettie if I repeated what Zepha had said.

"What?" Agnes T. Ritter asked. Her eyes were so narrow that I couldn't see any white through the slits.

I looked at the floor and said, "It's just a superstition. She says if you put a sharp knife under the bed, it cuts the pain."

There was silence for a minute, then Nettie said, "I heard that."

"I heard it, too," Ada June said. "Of course, I never knew of anybody who did it."

"It's stupid," Agnes T. Ritter said. "Quack medicine. Just what you'd expect from a squatter."

I wanted to tell her it wouldn't do any harm, but I never came out ahead arguing with Agnes T. Ritter. So I licked the blood off my lip and turned to the window to watch Grover, who was just getting out of the car. He slapped Tom on the back, and the two of them went across the yard. Then Mrs. Judd came in, dragging Velma back with her, and flopped down in Mrs. Ritter's kitchen rocker.

"I hope those two don't forget what's going on inside," she said, looking at Velma, who was slouched on a kitchen chair. Everybody knew that when Nettie went into labor with her, Tyrone got so drunk, he passed out and forgot all about the baby until he climbed into bed and almost squashed little Velma.

"I thought Velma might like to be outside," I said. Velma was pouting, making it clear to everyone she didn't want to be here at all. She was a real pretty girl, and she used to be a nice one, too, but lately she'd turned more sullen than Agnes T. Ritter. Maybe Tyrone took a strap to her. He always threatened to do that, and I didn't think either Velma or Nettie could stand up to him.

"I don't know anything about babies," Velma muttered.

"Well, I wouldn't brag about it," Mrs. Judd said, twisting her head to look at Velma. "I never thought being dumb about a thing made any sense." She turned to the rest of us. "It's time she knew about the wages of sin."

"Septima!" said Nettie. "Velma's *my* daughter. Anything she needs to learn about sin, she can learn from me." Ada June's

60

eyes twinkled as she turned away, and I looked down at the table so Nettie wouldn't see me smile. I rubbed my hand over the worn oilcloth, which had been scrubbed so many times, I could hardly see the pattern of tulips and Dutch girls. The cloth was cracked in places, and the backing showed through.

"Did anybody brown the flour?" Mrs. Judd asked.

"What for?" I asked.

"To rub over the baby, of course."

I went to the stove, pried off the stove lid with the lifter, then popped in a few sticks of wood to build up the fire. When they caught, I took out the skillet and poured in enough flour for a loaf of bread. At just that minute, Opalina and Ceres came into the kitchen. Opalina set down a little jar of piccalilli. It was a joke with the members of the Persian Pickle Club. The only thing Opalina ever brought to any gathering was a little jar of piccalilli, but that was all right with us, because Opalina was a terrible cook. I wondered who on earth would want to eat piccalilli after having a baby.

Ceres put a hamper on the table and took out a bottle of peaches and another of rose-hip jam. "Does Ella know?" she asked. Ella was the only one of us who didn't have a phone.

Mrs. Judd swatted the side of her head with the palm of her hand so hard that she must have felt like she'd been hit with a shovel. She hefted herself out of the rocker. "I must have left my brains on the car seat with my hat. I never thought to get her. I'll go now. Ella'd never forgive me if she missed out." Mrs. Judd went outside and fired up the Packard. Ella loved babies every bit as much as I did, and it was odd that the two of us who didn't have them were the ones who wanted them the most.

Since there wasn't anything left to do but wait, we unpacked baby clothes from a box Mrs. Ritter had set out, and Ceres got the Ritter family cradle from the parlor and began scrubbing it. "Lookit there," she said, turning it over. "It must have been made from an oats box. There's that Quaker man with his hair as long as Jesus'."

"That's a good sign, him looking like Jesus on the box," Nettie said.

61

We all found something to do, except for Velma, and were working away when Dr. Sipes came down from Rita's room on his way to the privy. "Afternoon, Forest Ann. Ladies," he said. Forest Ann gave him a silly smile, until Nettie cleared her throat, and Forest Ann turned back to the sink.

"The baby won't be here just yet. You can take that flour off the stove, Queenie," Dr. Sipes said. Outside, he stopped to exchange a few words with Tom and Grover, and when he came back, Forest Ann handed him a glass of lemonade. He took a swallow and said, "You womenfolks do all the work, and I get the credit."

"And send the bill," Nettie said. We heard a cry from above, and Dr. Sipes handed Forest Ann the glass, then took the stairs two at a time.

"I always liked that man," Ada June said.

"You always liked any man," Nettie told her. Before Buck Zinn showed up in Kansas, Ada June had so many boyfriends that she'd had to beat them off with a stick.

"That's not true," Ada June retorted. "There's one man I could name that I hated from the first time I ever saw him."

Before any of us could reply, Mrs. Judd's big Packard pulled up outside, and Ella jumped out, holding a box almost as big as she was and a bouquet of summer roses. I held the screen door open for her, and she rushed through and asked, "Is the baby here yet?"

"Not yet," I said.

"Rita could be in for a difficult time, but don't you worry. Doc Sipes is real good," Ceres told Ella.

Ella filled a canning jar with water from the kitchen pump and arranged the roses in it. "She'll be fine. She's got us."

"She's got too many of us," Mrs. Judd said, coming through the door and letting the screen bang shut behind her. She looked at her father's old pocket watch that hung from a ribbon around her neck. "Now I'm going home, and Nettie, you better take Velma back. Forest Ann, you go on, too, even though I guess you won't be having any visitors this evening." She looked up in the direction of the sickroom, where Dr. Sipes was with Rita, just in case Forest Ann didn't get her meaning. Then she looked over at the rest of us, deciding who else should go home. "Opalina—"

But Opalina wasn't going to let Mrs. Judd order her around, and she said quickly, "If nobody minds, I'll just run along and fix supper for Anson."

I wouldn't let Mrs. Judd send me home, either, but she didn't try. Instead, she told me, "If Lizzy Olive shows up with that slimy chocolate pudding of hers, you feed it to the pigs. Don't let Reverend Olive pray over Rita. He'll tell her that hog-wash about childbirth pain being her natural punishment on account of she's a daughter of Eve." Mrs. Judd shoved her big handbag under her arm and pushed at the screen door, letting it hit her behind so it wouldn't bang.

Before Mrs. Judd reached the porch stairs, Mrs. Ritter came into the kitchen and looked around like she didn't know who we were. "It's Queenie . . . and the Persian Pickle," I said.

"Yes, of course, dearie," Mrs. Ritter replied. Then her eyes came into focus and she smiled a little. "I came for . . . My stars, my mind's gone." She looked around the room until she spotted the teakettle. "That's it. The water. And a basin."

"Mrs. Ritter, the hired man's wife said if you put a knife under the bed, it cuts the pain. I told Agnes T. Ritter, but she said it was stupid. You could try it. I don't think it would hurt, anyway."

Mrs. Judd, who had stopped on the porch when Mrs. Ritter came into the kitchen, opened the screen and stuck her head in. I expected her to tell me I was a fool for holding with old wives' tales. "It helped with Wilson." I turned to stare, and she added, "If you keep leaving your mouth open, Queenie Bean, you'll swallow a fly. Now, get out a knife and go on upstairs with Rita. You being closer to her than the rest of us, you ought to be there with Sabra and Agnes."

I did as she ordered, pausing to snatch up a sharp knife, and followed Mrs. Ritter up to the sickroom, standing next to the doctor at the foot of the bed. He was telling Agnes T. Ritter what to do, and for the first time in her life, Agnes T. Ritter was doing a thing without talking back. I wanted to tell that to Rita so she'd laugh, but I didn't. When Agnes T. Ritter wasn't looking, I slid the knife under the bed. Then I moved around so I could stand beside Rita. I squeezed her hand and brushed back her hair, which was frizzy and damp. Little prickles of sweat stood out all over her face, so I dipped a cloth in a basin and sponged her off.

"The baby's coming faster than I thought. It won't be more than a few minutes," Dr. Sipes said as Rita stiffened. I clutched her hand and made little clucking noises until the pain passed. "That's good. That's real good, Rita. You just grab on to Queenie when you need to," Dr. Sipes said, as calm as if he was telling her how to spread chicken feed.

A car drove up, and through the window, I saw Lizzy and Foster Olive get out and go to the front door, just like they were company. I guessed Lizzy Olive had been listening in on the party line when Agnes T. Ritter called the Persian Pickle. Nobody answered the front door, so the two of them went around to the kitchen, which is where friends go when they call. We heard Reverend Olive's voice come up the stairs, although we couldn't make out the words. Then Ella said, "No! You stay away from her. We'll take care of her." Ella never talked above a whisper, and her voice was so loud, I jumped.

"Well, I'm glad for that," the doctor said. "I can't abide that man prattling around a sickroom." The car started, and Dr. Sipes winked at me. He was a real nice man, and I wished for Forest Ann's sake that he wasn't married to that ill-tempered woman. Dr. Sipes and Forest Ann deserved to be together, but he was too good a man to leave his wife, so the two of them carried on, thinking nobody knew.

Just then, Rita cried out, and Dr. Sipes told her to push hard. In our minds, all of us pushed right along with her, working up as much of a sweat as Rita did to get that baby born. I never knew how long it took, maybe five minutes, maybe thirty. All the time ran together. When it was over, the doctor was holding the tinest baby I'd ever seen, scrawny, like a new duck, and he said, "Why, Rita, you've got a little baby girl." Now that her job was over, Rita closed her eyes. At first, the tension went out of her. Then her knees shook, and the shivering moved all over her body, although the room was as hot as the kitchen. Agnes T. Ritter put a blanket over her.

"Oh, the flour," I said. "I'll get the flour," and I hurried down the stairs.

"It's a girl, a fine baby girl," I told the women in the kitchen. They'd known the baby was coming when I went upstairs, so they'd stayed right there instead of going home.

"Is Rita all right?" Ella asked.

"Why, she's fine." I told them. "I think." But I wasn't so sure of that. I grabbed the flour and rushed back to the sickroom.

Rita was asleep, and the doctor was working over the baby, who lay on a clean towel on the dresser. "How is Rita?" I asked.

Dr. Sipes didn't look up from the baby. "Rita'll be fine, but I don't know about the baby."

"She's a mewly little thing. She doesn't have a chance—" Agnes T. Ritter began, but her mother interrupted her.

"Somebody better tell Tom. He'll want to be here. Go get him, will you, Queenie?" Her face was damp from tears or perspiration, probably both.

Before I went downstairs again, I reached under the bed for the knife I'd put there, and discovered two of them lying on the floor. I never knew who left the second one, but I know it wasn't Mrs. Ritter, because she hadn't brought one upstairs with her. I slipped both of them into my pocket and set them on the kitchen table on my way outside. I told Tom he had a daughter and sent him up to see Rita, but I stayed outside and put my head on Grover's shoulder. "It's too little. It doesn't have a chance," I cried.

Little Wanda, which is the pretty name Tom and Rita picked for their baby, lived only two days, and I grieved as if that child had been my own. Rita kept her sorrow to herself, and I told Grover I thought she was a fine person not to trouble others. Grover replied he didn't think Rita was as upset as I was about losing the baby.

"That's the awfullest thing you ever said, Grover." He was sitting at the table eating brownies, and I picked up the plate and set it on the counter where he couldn't reach it.

"Honey, I know you like Rita, but you see her the way you want her to be, not the way she is. She's not a country girl any more than Tom's a farmer. He as much as told us that. Rita's looking over a different hill than you are, and I have an idea she's not going to be a friend to you the way you want."

"Grover, that's just not true."

"I know how much you still miss Ruby, but you can't expect Rita to take her place."

"She'll be as good a friend as I ever had, Grover Bean, and I won't hear a word against her!" But since he wasn't such a good judge of character, I forgave him and kissed the top of his big, fat head, the spot where the hair's the thinnest, and put the brownie plate back on the table.

Rita and Tom had a service for little Wanda. Reverend Olive preached, and Mrs. Ritter told him before the service that if he said a word about that baby being born in sin, the Persian Pickle would never sew a stitch for the church again.

Tom and Grover made a little coffin, and the members of the Persian Pickle lined it with pink satin. Then we dressed Wanda in a gown that Ella had made. The dress was three feet long, embroidered all over with roses. We put a matching cap on Wanda's head and tied it under her chin with a silk ribbon.

When we talked about Wanda later, Rita said she always pictured her wearing that dress and cap. "I can't believe Ella would give me an heirloom like that for burying," she said.

"It wasn't an heirloom. Ella has trunks of baby clothes just as pretty as that one. She made them all herself. She still makes them," I replied.

"I didn't think she ever had any kids."

"She didn't."

"Why, isn't that the oddest thing?"

Sorrow wasn't finished with the Persian Pickle Club. We were still mourning Wanda's passing when the death angel, which was how Nettie put it, came calling again, right at club meeting.

We had Persian Pickle at Opalina Dux's that day, and it looked like it would be a real nice quilting, even though Opalina's parlor was the most uncomfortable room in Wabaunsee County—and you always had to look where you sat because of Opalina letting the chickens inside the house. Of course, she cleaned up after them, but Opalina's eyesight being poor, it was a good idea to be careful.

Opalina had that old-fashioned horsehair furniture, and if you didn't slide off it, then those sharp little hairs that stuck out poked the backs of your legs. Opalina's house looked fifty years behind the times with all the embroidered mottoes hanging on the walls and the wax flowers that had melted a little under their glass dome so that they looked like tobacco chaws.

On the library table in the middle of the parlor, Opalina kept a candy Easter egg with a little scene inside it, but the candy flowers looked as if somebody had tried to lick them. There was a stereopticon lying next to it, and when I looked inside, I saw an Indian lady who wasn't wearing her blouse. I bet Opalina put in that picture just to shock Nettie, who could be every bit as righteous as Tyrone sometimes. Nettie was too smart for Opalina, however, and never once looked into the stereopticon.

Opalina had shut all the windows to keep the dirt from blowing in, and I thought we might suffocate. The room was cold in winter and hot in summer, and today, it felt like midsummer even though it was harvesttime. No wonder we always had the most absences on the days when Persian Pickle was held at Opalina's. This time, it looked as if Mrs. Judd and Ella weren't going to make it, the first time I could remember that Mrs. Judd had missed Persian Pickle. She hadn't called to let anyone know she wouldn't be coming, however, so there was a good chance the two of them were only tardy.

"It's that machine of hers. I fear to drive on the same road with her. I bet it's broken down out by Ella's, and her with no telephone," Nettie said. "Forest Ann and I will swing by on our way home and make sure they're all right."

Rita asked if we ought to go look for them right now. She wanted to get out of Opalina's parlor. "I'll drive," I volunteered.

"Septima can wait till after club. If nothing's wrong, she'll give us 'Hail, Columbia' for thinking she can't take care of herself," Nettie said. She was right about that.

Without Mrs. Judd, I felt jolly, like I did in school when the teacher was out sick. Even Opalina's quilt, which was set in the frame, waiting for us, couldn't get me down. It was another of her crazy quilts, made from old funeral ribbons, the ones they gave out at buryings long ago in memory of the dead. Who else but Opalina would have saved them? I whispered to Ada June that I'd go cold before I slept under that quilt, and she whispered back that maybe that's what it was for—to cover a cold body. Every time somebody admired a ribbon, Opalina told us about the person it represented, giving all the details of the death.

"I never saw a summer that promised so much in June and delivered so little in September," Forest Ann said, cutting off Opalina, who was explaining that the ribbons that were lined up like sausages were for the members of one family that had been killed by a twister.

"It didn't promise me a thing in June," Nettie said. She was down-in-the mouth that day, maybe because of Velma. Forest Ann had told me that Velma had taken up with a combine salesman out of Coffeyville, which upset Nettie because he was a married man. She was afraid that Tyrone would find out, and I couldn't blame her. Talk about catching "Hail, Columbia!" He'd thrash Velma within an inch of her life.

"Would you like to read, Queenie?" Opalina asked. The only book in Opalina's house was the Bible, and I did not want to read Scripture. The last time I did, Opalina had me read the *begats* in Genesis.

"Oh, let's not. Let's just talk and tell Mrs. Judd when she gets here that we already read."

"That would be a lie," Nettie said.

I blushed and felt one of those horsehairs poke right into my back as punishment. "It'd be just a little fib," I said, defending

68

myself. If fibs were so bad, then I ought to tell Nettie that the goiter on her neck made her look like a frog.

"Queenie, why don't you bring us up-to-date on the Celebrity Quilt," Mrs. Ritter said. "We won't wait for Septima and Ella."

Mrs. Ritter always had a way of finding something enjoyable to talk about. The Celebrity Quilt was the reason I'd expected such a nice quilting that day. It was just about the most important thing that had ever happened to Persian Pickle, and I was the one who got to tell about it, because it had been my idea.

The Persian Pickle Club hadn't been in any hurry to begin sewing on the Celebrity Quilt, of course. The longer that quilt took us, the more time we'd have before Reverend Olive came back to us with another project. Still, we'd started planning for it right away by making a list of people whose autographs we wanted to include—people such as Mrs. Eleanor Roosevelt, Ronald Colman, Babe Ruth, and Aimee Semple McPherson. When I put down Mae West as a joke, Nettie got so riled up that Mrs. Judd said, "Let her stay. It's men that bid on these quilts, and men'll pay more for Mae West than Sister Kenny."

We asked Rita to write the letters to the celebrities because she was the writer in the group. She's also the only one with a typewriter, but I know how to type, so I helped her. The two of us made a special trip to the library in Topeka to look up addresses of movie studios and radio stations and the White House. Then we went to lunch at the Hotel Jayhawk and paid fifty cents each for tuna-fish sandwiches with the crusts cut off. I had as much fun with her that day as I ever did with Ruby.

Nettie and Forest Ann cut out the squares of muslin for the people to autograph. Mrs. Judd bought the stamps to mail the letters, but she was against enclosing stamped return envelopes because she said celebrities were rich enough to spend three cents on stamps for a good cause. We'd put the last of the letters in the postbox on Monday, but that wasn't what I was going to announce.

When Mrs. Ritter brought up the Celebrity Quilt, everyone stopped talking, except for Ceres, who didn't hear very well. So

I cleared my throat as loudly as I could, and she looked up and smiled and asked, "Yes, dear. Are you ready to roll?" That's what we do when we finish the exposed part of the quilt. We roll it over so we can work on the next section.

"Roll out the barrel," Rita muttered.

"I have an announcement to make," I said, ignoring them both. I looked around the quilt at all my friends smiling at me, except for Agnes T. Ritter, who was being her ornery self and still sewing. I'd thought ahead of time how I was going to put it, and I said, "Our first square has been returned to us." When everybody clapped, I got so excited that I forgot the nice way I'd rehearsed it, and I blurted out, "It was Janet Gaynor—can you beat it?—and she wrote, 'Happiness to you' on it. Now, isn't that just like her!"

I took the square out of the envelope and passed it around so everybody could admire the handwriting and the sentiment. "Imagine that. The last person who touched this before us was Janet Gaynor," said Nettie. "I wonder who'll send the next one."

"Zane Grey," Rita said. "I forgot to tell you, Queenie. We got another one yesterday." She reached into her purse and pulled out an envelope.

"Lookit there. He drew a dog on it," Ada June said when Rita handed her the muslin.

"That's not a dog. It's a coyote," Agnes T. Ritter said, peering across the table at it.

"How can you tell?" Ada June asked.

"I expect I know the difference between a dog and a coyote."

"Maybe Mr. Grey doesn't," Mrs. Ritter put in. "Rita, do you want to tell the rest of the news?" I didn't know what that news was, so I turned to stare at Rita with everyone else.

Rita blushed a little, and I wondered if she was pregnant again, but somehow, I didn't think that was it. Besides, having a baby wasn't something you announced, even at Persian Pickle, until you showed. Rita strung us out just a minute before she said, "I'm going to write an article for the *Topeka Enterprise* about the Celebrity Quilt, and they might even send out a photographer to take a picture."

"Oh!" we all said, and Opalina touched her hair as if she was already primping for the photograph.

"Naturally, they'll have to see the article first. I mean, they might not like it," Rita said, and Opalina took her hand down. Agnes T. Ritter smirked at that. Nettie wasn't the only Pickle who was out of sorts that day.

"I'm sure they'll buy it. Your story about the school-board election was about the best thing I've ever read, and it didn't make a bit of difference that the names were mixed up," Forest Ann said, and we all nodded. None of us mentioned Rita'd misspelled most of them, as well.

Even if some of the club members were off their feed that afternoon, quilting went fast. We had barely finished talking about the Celebrity Quilt when Opalina said it was time for refreshments. "I'll put the kettle on. I'm serving scones," she announced, as if it was a surprise.

"I'd hoped you would, Opalina," Mrs. Ritter said.

I had hoped she would not, but fat chance. Opalina always served scones, just like Nettie always served fruitcake. The scones weren't as old as the fruitcake, but they were just as dry, with none of Tyrone's bootleg to help them go down.

I slid off my chair, scratching my legs, and went into the kitchen to help Opalina, since the big tin tray she used was the size of a kitchen table. Sometimes things slid off it, not that anybody would miss her refreshments. I made tea while Opalina piled the scones on the tray, dropping one on the floor. It chipped, but it didn't break, and Opalina brushed it off and set it back with the others. Then she carried the tray into the parlor herself.

"Oh, Opalina, what a treat," said Mrs. Ritter. I was amazed that she could be so enthusiastic about those scones, which she must have eaten for forty years. "Might you be English?"

"French. Dux is a French name."

"Dux is Anson's name. You were born a Cooper," Agnes T. Ritter said.

"I became French when I married Anson. That's the way it works. Don't you know that Agnes?"

71

Rita winked at me while Agnes T. Ritter moved her mouth back and forth for a few seconds, but instead of talking back to Opalina, she caught sight of something out the window and said, "There's Mrs. Judd."

It didn't sound like Mrs. Judd. You could always tell her car because Mrs. Judd turned off the motor and coasted to a stop to save gas. The car outside was parked with the engine running.

The rest of the Persian Pickle realized Mrs. Judd was not acting normal, and we all stood up to look outside. Forest Ann even went to the window and peered out past the red glass plate Opalina kept there to catch the light. With the afternoon sun shining through it, the plate glowed like fresh blood. "It's Septima, all right. She forgot to turn off the motor, and she's running," Forest Ann said. "Anybody ever seen Septima run?"

I took a step toward the window to get a better view, and it was not a pretty sight. Mrs. Judd moved like a runaway thresher. I knew something was wrong.

"Ella's not with her," I said, shivering. Even with Hiawatha and Duty to watch after her, Ella might have taken ill. Or she could have fallen or been burned by the cookstove. A dozen things could happen to a person who lived alone.

"I'm sure there's a perfectly good explanation," Mrs. Ritter said quietly, but she clasped her hands so tightly, the knuckles turned white. Only Agnes T. Ritter acted unconcerned. She bit down on a scone, and in Opalina's parlor, which had grown quiet, the crunching sounded like a cow in dried cornstalks.

Mrs. Judd lunged through the door, flinging it so hard that it banged the wall and then came flying back and hit her on the fanny, bumping her forward into the living room. Her eyes, behind the thick glass of her gold spectacles, opened wide in surprise, and I would have laughed if I hadn't been so worried.

"Ella?" Forest Ann whispered, asking the question for all of us. "Is something wrong with Ella?"

"Ella's fine," Mrs. Judd said. She caught her breath while the rest of us let out ours in unison.

Mrs. Judd gasped for air again. She looked pale and old as she slumped into one of Opalina's horsehair chairs and slid into

72

a corner. She looked around at the members of the Persian Pickle Club. "Ella's fine," she repeated. "It's not her, thank the Lord." Mrs. Judd gulped down a mouthful of air. "It's Ben Crook."

Nettie gasped and put her hands to her face. The blood rushed to my head, and I gripped the back of a chair to keep my legs from sliding out from under me.

"I said it's Ben Crook," Mrs. Judd repeated. "He's been found. Hiawatha dug him up in Ella's far-north field right before dinnertime."

chapter
5

Mrs. Judd slowly looked around the room, stopping for a few seconds to exchange glances with each one of us. Her eyelids flickered when she came to Rita.

"How's Ella?" Forest Ann asked, breaking the silence with a jerky voice.

"Prostrate with grief. Awful broke up," Mrs. Judd said. "Just as you'd expect. She thought the sun rose and set . . . ?" Her voice trailed off and she looked at her hands a minute before she shook her head and told us, "Like I said, Hiawatha found Ben up north on the Crook place. Ben was out there by the road, where somebody'd buried him. Hiawatha came to Prosper and me to ask what to do."

"He's real smart for a colored," Nettie said. She hadn't approved of Hiawatha and Duty Jackson moving onto the Crook farm, but she'd changed her mind after she saw how well they took care of Ella. About the time Ben disappeared, Ella's hired man ran off, so Mrs. Judd had driven Ella up to Blue Hill, where the Jacksons were barely scratching out a living, and the two of them invited Hiawatha and Duty and all the kids to move into the shack behind Ella's house. They agreed to work the farm on shares and do chores for Ella. Even if they didn't make much money, they'd have a place to live and something to eat. The day they moved in, Ella told Persian Pickle she'd always wanted to hear the sounds of children on her farm and that the Jackson kids were just like having her own.

When she heard that, Nettie sputtered all over Ceres's Drunkard's Path, which is what we were quilting at the time. Later in the evening, just before suppertime, Tyrone drove into the Judds' yard and yelled from his truck, "Prosper Judd, the sun never set on a coon in Harveyville, Kansas, and it won't this evening. You get rid of them Jacksons or I'll run 'em off myself." Tyrone blamed Mrs. Judd for Hiawatha moving to Ella's, but he was scared to take her on, which is why he threatened Prosper. Besides, Prosper had driven the Jacksons from Blue Hill to Harveyville.

Mrs. Judd came out from behind the sawhorse where she'd been killing chickens. Wiping blood and pinfeathers on her apron, she told Tyrone the sun would set on Hiawatha and Duty in Harveyville as long as they wanted it to, but she couldn't be sure how many more Harveyville sunsets a gambling man who was behind in payments to the bank she owned in Eskridge was going to see. It would be a real shame not to have Nettie in Pickle anymore, but a person had to stand by her standards. If anybody else caused trouble about the Jacksons, she'd have to check the bank's records on them, too. Tyrone sulked for a minute before he said that maybe it wouldn't hurt for Hiawatha and Duty to spend one night, it being late in the day already. He'd have to think hard about letting them stay longer, however.

The Judds never heard from Tyrone again, and the Jacksons had lived at Ella's ever since. Now, most of us wondered why there'd been a fuss in the first place.

But I wasn't thinking about coloreds moving into Harveyville just then. I was being thankful that Hiawatha, instead of Ella, had found Ben's body. Stumbling over Ben Crook's bones would just about have killed Ella.

"Opalina, I could use a glass of hot tea—and one of your biscuits with the raisins in it. I missed my lunch," Mrs. Judd said. Opalina looked up, startled, since nobody but Mrs. Ritter ever asked for a scone. She bustled about fixing a cup and a plate while the rest of us waited for Mrs. Judd to tell us the story in her own good time. There were two things you couldn't hurry in Harveyville—the weather and Mrs. Judd. She crunched down on the scone and said, "Real tasty." Opalina straightened up and passed the plate around, but only Mrs. Ritter helped herself.

Mrs. Judd belched a little behind her hand and brushed the crumbs off her lap onto Opalina's carpet. Now that she'd had a chance to catch her breath and eat something, a touch of color came back into Mrs. Judd's face. She settled back in the chair and looked up at us, and we leaned forward, knowing she was ready to talk.

"Hiawatha was walking along the road that hardly anybody ever uses, the one that goes by the creek, and he saw a bone sticking out of the dirt. He went over for a look, and when he realized it was a leg bone, he got real scared. He didn't know whether to pull it out or push it back in. He had a presentiment who it was, so he came to our place to ask what to do. Prosper went for the sheriff, and I drove right over to be with Ella."

"Was it Ben?" Nettie asked.

"Well, of course it was Ben. It couldn't have been anybody else, could it?" Mrs. Judd paused a minute to consider what she'd said. "Well, I didn't know for sure, of course, but I had my suspicions. After he dug up the rest of the bones, Sheriff Eagles came around to Ella's, where I was waiting, and he said he recognized Ben's skull right off. You know how Ben had that big gap between his front teeth. And all the teeth on his right side were missing from the time he got smacked on the side of the head with a singletree at the Hollywood Cafe. Anybody would have known it was Ben just from looking at the skull."

"Oh," Ada June said, sagging against the doorjamb and putting one hand over her face.

"Dr. Sipes came along with the sheriff. He said Ben's skull had been bashed in. That's how he died," Mrs. Judd said.

Forest Ann put her fingers over her mouth and made a little gurgling sound. Nettie put her arm around Forest Ann and patted her.

"Was he murdered?" Rita asked. I shuddered at the question and exchanged glances with Ada June.

Mrs. Judd didn't answer right away. She studied Rita a minute. "I wouldn't know about that. But I do know that no man on God's earth ever smashed in his own head, then climbed into a grave and covered himself up with dirt." Mrs. Judd looked uncomfortable, and I hoped Rita would get the hint that she didn't want to talk about murder. Well, who would? It was bad enough thinking about Ben's body rotting away in Ella's field all these months without paying mind to how it happened.

Rita didn't get it, however. "Who did it?" she asked.

"If he left his calling card, I didn't see it," Mrs. Judd told her.

Rita was about to ask something else when Ceres interrupted. "What are we going to do, Tima?"

"Why, what we always do," Mrs. Judd said, reaching for another scone, then reconsidering and putting her hand down. "We will comfort our friend in her hour of trouble. Prosper's bringing Ella home to stay at our place for as long as she wants. There's the funeral to be got through."

"Ella won't hold a viewing, will she?" Nettie asked. She had to move her whole body to look at Mrs. Judd, because the goiter had gotten bigger, and her neck didn't turn at all. "I wouldn't want to have to look at a man with his head bashed in."

Mrs. Judd started to say something smart but thought better of it and shut her mouth for a minute before she said kindly, "You don't have a viewing for a skeleton, Nettie. That's all Ben is now—bones and overalls."

"Oh." Nettie shivered. "Oh, I didn't think about that." She was embarrassed for a minute. Then, to save face, she searched for something Mrs. Judd had forgotten. "Did you think about Reverend Olive, Septima?"

"Of course, I thought about him. That's why Prosper drove to town to get the sheriff. I didn't want Foster hearing about Ben on the party line and getting to Ella's before I did. I'm afraid we'll have to tell Foster now."

"I don't know why you're afraid," Nettie said with a self-righteous sniff. "He doesn't scare me."

"That's a relief. You go call him," Mrs. Judd said. "Tell him there's no need for him and Lizzy to tend to Ella's bodily needs. That's our job. He's to see to the spiritual."

77

Nettie glanced around to see if anyone else would volunteer to make the telephone call, but none of us met her eyes, so, looking trapped, she went into the kitchen and turned the crank on the phone.

"Would you sit?" Opalina asked Ceres, which made us all realize we'd been standing ever since Mrs. Judd burst through the door. One by one, we found chairs and sat down. I got a horse-hair seat again.

Nobody spoke while Nettie made the call. Every now and then, one of us glanced at Rita as if to offer sympathy that she was going through another death so soon after her own sorrowful loss. I wished Mrs. Judd would say she was excused and should go on home, but she didn't, and it wasn't my place to tell her. So Rita sat quietly with the rest of us, listening to Nettie's loud voice.

Nettie stood a foot away from the box and yelled into the mouthpiece. She was careful about how she put things because she knew she was announcing Ben's death to everyone on the party line. "Lizzy? This is Nettie. . . . What's that? . . . Nettie Burgett. There's not but one Nettie in Harveyville. Don't you know that? Put the Reverend on the line. . . . Fishing? That ain't a thing a preacher ought to be doing when a body's in need. . . . No, Tyrone's all right. It's Ben Crook. They found him this morning. . . . What's that? . . . He's not behind any veil that I know of. He's buried out by the creek road north of Ella's place. You have your husband phone up Septima about the funeral, and don't go calling on Ella, because she's got the Pickles to take care of her."

Nettie hung up the receiver before Lizzy Olive could reply. "I guess I told her," she said as she bustled back into the room. Nettie sent a triumphant look at Mrs. Judd and was so pleased with the way she'd dealt with the Olives that she took charge. "Here's another thing. We'll have to find something to lay him out in. I expect he's lost weight."

For the first time since Mrs. Judd drove up, I felt like smiling, but when I realized what I was doing, I covered my mouth with my hand and coughed. Rita coughed, too.

"It'll be a closed coffin," Ada June said, and she winked at me.

Nettie blushed, realizing her mistake, then glanced at Mrs. Judd, expecting to be rebuked. Mrs. Judd only nodded.

"Well, of course," Nettie said. "What I meant was, you can't send a man to his last reward in overalls. Ella would want him buried in a nice suit. She thought the sun—"

"Oh, we all know that," Mrs. Judd interrupted impatiently. She'd let Nettie be in charge long enough.

Nettie shut up and sat down, and it was quiet in Opalina's stuffy room. We were all thinking about Ella, I suppose. I know I was. She was such a fragile thing, with a mind like a little girl's sometimes. It would be awful to know your husband's bones were scattered around a cornfield.

Rita finally broke the silence. "What do you think happened?" I guess it was a natural question, but the rest of us didn't want to think about how Ben had died, so instead of replying, we shook our heads.

Finally Mrs. Judd said, "I haven't got time to think on it just now. That's why we've got a sheriff." She stood and picked up her pocketbook. "Prosper ought to have Ella at the house before long. I'll see that she gets a rest. You can make your calls after supper."

That was the end of Persian Pickle for the day, of course, because there was work to be done, food to fix, and Ella to call on that evening. So we hurried after Mrs. Judd, not even offering to help Opalina clean up.

Rita looked thoughtful as the two of us walked out the door together. "Why would anybody murder Mr. Crook?" she asked me.

I didn't want to talk about it. I shook my head and said, "Now, how would I know?"

Prosper, not Mrs. Judd, took care of the funeral arrangements. He insisted that the service be held outdoors, where Ella could sit in the sunshine and look at flowers instead of inside that dark, dank church. The Olives kept the church closed up so it always smelled like a root cellar. Prosper warned Reverend Olive just before the service to keep it short and not say one word about hell's fire. "You upset that sweet lady, bub, and you'll have to deal with me," Prosper told him.

Of course, Prosper, who looked like Porky Pig in the cartoons with his pink face and little piggy eyes, wouldn't have hurt anybody. What he meant was if Reverend Olive ran crosswise of him, he'd cut off the church. Since the Judds were the biggest donors in Harveyville, that was enough to make Reverend Olive stop preaching after only fifteen minutes, and he never once mentioned hell. It didn't matter what he said, however, because Ella was propped up like a rag doll between Prosper and Mrs. Judd and didn't seem to know what was going on.

Reverend Olive finished by reading a few verses out of the Bible, and we sang "Going Home" and "The Old Rugged Cross." Then the deacons lowered the casket into the ground while I thought of Ben Crook's bones rattling around inside. Grover whispered to me that they could have stuffed what was left of Ben into a feed sack and dropped it in the hole and saved the expense of the coffin. I was shocked and told him to behave, but Rita snickered.

After Ben's casket reached the bottom of that big hole cut into the weedy sod of the cemetery, Mrs. Judd gave Ella a rose, which confused her, and she tried to pin it to her dress. Mrs. Judd took Ella's hand, and together they threw it into the grave. Then Prosper and Mrs. Judd said Ella wasn't up to receiving people, and they took her home. The rest of us went inside the church, which was chilly even in the heat of the day, to drink coffee and eat cake. Rita asked if there wasn't someplace we could go for a real drink, so Grover spoke up and said he'd treat the four of us at the Hollywood Cafe.

I wasn't sure drinking in a public place was the right thing to do after a funeral. I felt self-conscious walking from the church to the Hollywood, past the Flint Hills Home & Feed, where all those farmers were gathered. Most of them stood with their backsides against the front of the store, each with one cracked high-top shoe against the wall, as if they were holding it up. Those who couldn't find room to lean against the store sat on the edge of the wooden sidewalk, whittling and taking sneaky glances at ladies' ankles. There was a lot of shifting around when Rita walked past.

"How do," Butch Izzo said, touching the brim of his cap. He wasn't any too nice-looking, with the hair growing half an inch out of his ears and the arms of his union suit hanging beneath his shirtsleeves. Rita wrinkled her nose and ignored him, but I'd known Butch all my life. So I took a licorice button from the paper sack he held out and told him I was sorry about his cow Bessie, who had gotten cut up in barbed wire and had to be shot.

"One of the family. It'd like to kill me when I done it. One of the family," he said.

"Is he talking about Mr. Crook or his cow?" Rita asked when we'd gone on past. She giggled, then put her hand through Tom's arm and said, "Come on, ace." I wished I could do that with Grover, but he'd cut off his arm before he'd hold hands with me in front of the Home & Feed crowd.

Not all the loungers were in front of the feed store. Some were in the Hollywood. It had been a saloon way back, then became a candy store and restaurant when Prohibition was passed. Of course, everybody knew that was just a front for selling illegal whiskey. In those days, you'd have taken your life in your hands to order food in the Hollywood. The fib about it being a cafe was just so the sheriff would have an excuse not to raid the place. He never did, except every once in a while when he had to to keep up appearances. Mostly, he liked having all the drunks in one place, where he could keep an eye on them.

Now that Prohibition was over, the Hollywood was a tavern again and had been brought up-to-date. In addition to the long walnut bar and the varnished wooden booths behind the door, where people sat when they didn't want to be seen, there were cocktail tables and a jukebox. Rita seemed right at home as she sat down at a silvery table in the middle of the room and told Tom, "Order me a Manhattan, will you, honey?"

She took a package of Chesterfields out of her purse. Tom struck a match for Rita, and she stretched her neck, lit her cigarette, and blew out a cloud of smoke. Tom lit his cigarette, then held the match out for Grover, who had rolled one of his own. "Three on a match," Rita said, shaking her head. I guess I looked stupid, because she explained, "It's bad luck."

The men at the bar turned to get a glimpse of Rita in her maroon silk dress and matching lipstick. One muttered, "Hey, kiddo!"

"If those mashers don't stop eyeing you, I'm going to give somebody a punch," Grover said to me, and I squeezed his hand under the table. He knew as well as I did that they weren't staring at me in my crepe funeral dress and my mother's felt hat with the cherries on it. They made me look like a dumpy black salamander.

I didn't know what a Manhattan was, but I wish I'd taken a chance and ordered one instead of a root beer, because it was so pretty. Hanging over the edge of the glass was a bright red cherry like none I ever saw growing on a tree. Rita took it out and bit off the fruit, which she rolled around inside her mouth before swallowing it. Then she wound the stem around her little finger. "This is the life," she said, and Tom grinned at her.

"Almost as good as a bottle behind the corncrib," Grover said, and we all laughed, although I knew Grover would rather sit next to a corncrib any day than in the Hollywood. He hated being inside almost as much as he hated dressing up. He'd left his suit coat in the car. Now he rolled up his shirtsleeves and loosened his tie.

When I looked at Tom, I remembered what Grover had said about him not being a farmer anymore. He wore a dark blue suit that hadn't come out of the Spiegel catalog and a hat tipped back on his head like Franklin Delano Roosevelt. "Remember when we used to sneak in here and buy a pint?" he asked Grover. "It's a good thing we were always too short on money to buy any more. A quart of that stuff and we'd have died a wicked death."

"Queenie always liked it," Grover said.

"I did not!"

"Just about as much as rhubarb pie," Tom said, nudging me in the side with his elbow and laughing.

Grover didn't laugh, however. He put his elbows on the table, which wobbled, so he fished some wooden matches out of his pocket and stuck them under the short leg.

"This is a swell place," Rita said. "It's like the cocktail lounge where I worked."

"I thought you were a waitress in a cafe, the Koffee Kup Kafe," I said. "With *K*'s."

"Oops," Rita said, giving me a naughty glance. "You caught me. I was a cocktail waitress at the Pair-a-Dice in Lawrence. Tom's folks would have had a fit if they'd known, so I had to make up a story." Rita used the tip of her maroon fingernail to get a piece of tobacco off her tongue. Then she finished her drink and said, "That hit the spot. Order me another, would you, Tom? Funerals are so damn depressing."

Tom called to the waitress and made a circle in the air over our table.

"I would have found a reason to stay home if the *Enterprise* hadn't asked me to do a story on the murder," Rita continued.

"You already did a story when they found the body. Why would anybody in Topeka care about what happened to Ben Crook?" Grover asked.

"Because it was murder. This is what's called a follow-up story. Murder in a wheat field is big news."

"Cornfield," I corrected her. "Ben was buried in a cornfield."

"I don't think that's an important detail." Rita kicked off her patent-leather slippers and stretched out her legs, resting her feet on the chair across from her. Tom slid his arm around her shoulder. I wondered if she was getting drunk, but I wasn't sure, because women I knew didn't get drunk, not even on New Year's Eve.

"Rita thinks this could be a major story, right?" Tom said.

"Right. My big break. It's called a scoop," Rita said, pausing while the waitress set down another Manhattan and a root beer. Rita bit off the cherry again, then tied the stem into a little knot and held it up to inspect it. "Who would have guessed when I started writing those dinky stories for the paper that I could become a star reporter?"

"Why would you want to stir things up?" Grover asked her.

"Because it's news. People have a right to know. Besides, he was a nice man. Everybody says so."

"Ben Crook?" Grover asked.

"Righto. Dandy-nice old Ben." I was pretty sure Rita was drunk.

"He thought the sun rose and set on Ella. Best husband in the world," I said.

"Ben Crook?" Tom asked. "You mean the Ben Crook they just buried?"

"He loved Ella," I said.

"For Christ's sakes, Queenie, Ben Crook was a son of a bitch," Grover said. "Ask anybody in this room. Ask Eli Broom over there. Don't you remember him telling us how he'd worked a month for Ben and then Ben wouldn't pay him his wages? Ben was so cheap, if suits were selling for a dime, he wouldn't buy the armhole of a vest."

"If anybody deserved to get his head bashed in, I'd put my money on nice old Ben Crook," Tom added. "He was the mean-est bastard in Harveyville."

"Ella loved him," I insisted.

"You keep saying that," Rita said. The waitress came over with more beers for Tom and Grover. I took the menu that was stuck between the salt and pepper shakers in the center of the table and opened it, reading the short-order list for hamburg steak and ham and eggs.

"You want something, honey?" Grover asked, but I didn't. I just wanted to change the subject, but there was no stopping Rita.

She took a sip of her drink and turned to Tom. "Tell me about old Ben."

84

Tom snuffed out his cigarette in the glass ashtray that had SMOKE OLD GOLDS on it before he replied. "There's not much to tell. He was one of three—no, I guess it was four brothers, and not a single one of them was worth a pinch of manure. Let's see. Wilton got killed by a runaway team. Dimick passed out drunk one night and froze to death. John got into a fight with Ben and took off, and nobody ever heard from him again."

Tom paused to shake a Chesterfield out of the pack. "Hell, if Ben was still around, I'd put my money on John being buried out there. It wasn't beyond Ben to kill his own brother. They were all mean and big and dirty. They scared the hell out of me when I was a kid, and I wouldn't care to run into any of them on a dark road, even now."

Tom lit his cigarette and shook out the match. Then he removed his hat and set it on the table, brushing a piece of dirt off the brim. "I remember Mom saying once that everybody told Ella she was nuts to marry Ben, but I guess she was crazy for him. You never can tell what a woman sees in a man." Rita cocked her head and caught Tom's eyes, and he put his cigarette into his mouth so he could put his arm around her again. "Maybe they did love each other like Queenie says. All I know is, he was as ornery a man as I ever met, and cheap, too. Grover's right about that. Why, I guess he'd skin a louse for hide and tallow."

"Remember that cow he sold Prosper Judd?" Grover put in. "Ben Crook sure lived up to his name that time. The cow died before Prosper got her home, but Ben wouldn't give him his money back. He said it served Prosper right for being the dumbest farmer he ever met. Prosper was mad enough to kill him." Grover stopped and thought about what he'd said. "I don't mean that literally. Prosper wouldn't kill anybody. He was just mad, that's all. I think the two of them made up eventually, probably for Ella's sake."

Rita tied and untied the cherry stem until it broke in half, and she dropped the pieces onto the floor. "I'll ask the sheriff about Prosper when I interview him. I'm going to do a bang-up job with this piece. Maybe I'll even solve the murder and get a job in Topeka as a reward. It surely would not make me cry to leave Harveyville. How about that, ace?"

"I think we better get home, because if Dad finds out we've been boozing it up in here, he'll get madder than Ben Crook ever thought of being," Tom replied.

"Well, I like that! Around here, we can't do anything unless we get Tom's father's permission," Rita said. "I made the mistake of telling him I liked beer, and now he thinks I'm wicked. That's what he told Tom, anyway."

Rita wasn't finished, but Tom said, "Aw, honey." Rita stopped talking and pouted instead.

The waitress returned and asked if we wanted more drinks, but Tom told her no and pulled his billfold out of his back pocket. Grover put out his hand and said, "Your money's no good here. It's my treat. You save that fifty cents for a vacation."

As we got up to go, Eli Broom waved at us. "Did you folks come from Ben Crook's funeral?" he asked. Grover nodded, and Eli said, "That Ben was a dead ringer for the devil. I'd like to shake the hand of the fellow that killed him and buy him a Pepsi-Cola."

"That so? Well, don't look at me," Grover said.

"I sure wish I knew who done it. Hell, I'd buy him a whole damn cardboard carton of Pepsi-Cola."

"If you've got any ideas, you tell my wife here," Tom said. "She's going to solve the murder. She'll bring in Public Enemy Number One." He let out a big laugh, and so did Grover.

Rita took her reporting seriously. So I thought their joking about it would hurt her feelings, but it didn't because Rita took my arm to steady herself, winked at me, and said, "Men, huh?"

She stumbled and said, "Hell, damn!" in a voice so loud that a woman sitting in the last booth, the one behind the door, looked up at us. The booths were high, and she'd had to raise her head to see over the top. When she spotted me, she scrunched down, and all Rita saw was the top of her hat. "That looks like a member of the Persian Pickle Club over there," she said, slurring her words. "She's with a member of the traveling salesman profession, no doubt."

We all laughed at the idea of Mrs. Judd or Opalina Dux sneaking into the Hollywood Cafe to make time with a drummer, although, to me, the joke wasn't funny. That's because the woman in the booth was indeed a member of the Persian Pickle Club. She was Velma Burgett.

chapter 6

I was seated at the kitchen table, watching Sonny eat cold pancakes, when I looked out the window and saw Velma far off down the road. I knew as sure as Monday was wash day that she'd be my second visitor that morning.

Every day just after breakfast, Sonny showed up with the cream can and an appetite for anything we had left over. I'd gotten into the habit of making extra just so there'd be plenty for him. This morning, it was buttermilk hotcakes with syrup.

"Did you see the dead man?" Sonny asked me. He poured syrup out of the can, which was shaped like the hired man's shack, into a spoon and let it run off the spoon onto the pancakes. He licked the spoon, then licked his hand where the syrup had dripped on it.

I shook my head and wondered how Sonny knew about Ben Crook. But I suppose everybody in Harveyville had heard about Hiawatha finding the body, so it wasn't a surprise that the Massies knew, too. "Did a turkey buzzard fly over your head? Is that how come you know about the dead man?" I teased.

"No'm. When the turkey buzzard flies over, it means you're going to find you a dead snake." Sonny looked at me as if I was feeble. "I heard Pa talking. That's how come I know. The preacher lady told him."

I'd begun clearing the dishes off the table, but I stopped at that and turned around. "Who?"

"The one with them spectacles that pinch her nose. She come

88

to the house 'cause she heard about Ma's quilts and was wanting to buy one. She offered Ma a five-dollar bill for her Road to Californy, but Ma told her it weren't for sale. Then she says to Pa, 'I bet you'd sell it if'n I was to give you seven dollars.' "

The Massies needed every penny they could get. Still, I thought it was hateful of Lizzy Olive to tempt them to sell Zepha's most prized possession. "Did your pa do it?"

"Sure is hot," Sonny said. He went over to the icebox and took out an ice cube and rubbed it over his arms. Sonny liked ice cubes better than almost anything. He put the ice on the oil-cloth and took another bite of his breakfast while I waited. I wouldn't have to repeat my question, since nothing ever got by Sonny, but he wouldn't reply until he was good and ready. "Pa said, 'She told you once, and I tell you again, that quilt ain't for sale.' "

I smiled at Sonny. "What did Lizzy Olive say to that?"

"She called Pa an old sinner and said it was a shame Jesus died for people like him. Pa got her back. Pa says, "Died? I never knowed He was feeling poorly." Sonny laughed, and I had to smile.

"Then she put her nose up high in the air and told Pa he'd end up like the dead man that nigger found. Pa never did like preachers much. Me, neither." Sonny didn't volunteer the reason why. Instead, he put his face close to the platter and shoveled another pancake directly into his mouth, then licked the syrup off his arm. He looked up when he heard footsteps on the porch, expecting to see Grover, I suppose, and when he spotted Velma, he rolled up the last pancake, shoved it into his shirt pocket, picked up the ice cube, and shot out the door so fast, he made Velma blink.

"Is that the squatter boy?" Velma asked, squinting at Sonny. He'd made it as far as the grindstone and was perched on the iron seat behind it, peddling, making the stone turn to beat the band. He stretched his neck like a goose so he could see us.

"That is our neighbor," I corrected her, then wondered if Velma would think I was on my high horse. Velma couldn't help it if she was as nosy as Nettie and Tyrone. She was their daughter, after all. Even if she had come to tell me some made-up story explaining why she was at the Hollywood Cafe with a married man, she was my guest. I had no right to treat her as anything but company.

Since I'd decided to be polite, I set down Sonny's dirty dishes in the sink and fluffed up my hair. "I'm glad to see you, too, Velma. I've been looking for an excuse to make another pot of coffee. If I'd known you were stopping by, I'd have made a coffee cake." I filled the kettle and turned on the gas.

Velma narrowed her eyes, considering whether I meant what I'd said or was being sarcastic. She didn't reply, but looked around the kitchen instead and said, "You've got it real nice here."

She was right about that. My kitchen was a great deal nicer than Nettie's, which had a smoky old cookstove and no water inside. She had to carry water from the pump in the yard. Club members didn't rub it in when they were better off, however, so I said, "It'll do," and measured out the coffee. "Of course, the dust gets into everything, even the inside of the refrigerator. Last week, when I churned the butter, it looked like I'd peppered it. Grover calls this the 'dirty thirties.'"

Velma didn't reply, so I stopped trying to make conversation while she wandered around the room, picking up things and looking at the bottoms as if she was hunting for price stickers. She turned over the salt cellar, spilling the salt on the floor, and said, "Oops," but she didn't apologize. I wiped up the salt to keep it from pitting the linoleum. This wasn't going to be the best visit of my life.

When the coffee was ready, I got out two mugs, then reconsidered and took down the good cups and saucers that I used at Persian Pickle. "Rita calls coffee 'java,'" I said, sitting at Grover's place at the table. Velma was already sitting in mine.

Velma didn't reply.

"Have you met her?" I asked.

"She's kind of stuck on herself, if you ask me."

"Why, she's no such thing. She's nice. She's my best friend."

"Lucky you," Velma said.

I shut my mouth and pushed the sugar bowl toward her.

"I guess you know why I'm here," Velma said.

"I suppose so." I looked Velma in the eye, because I wasn't going to let her wiggle out of this. Velma took a spoon from the spooner on the table and helped herself to the sugar bowl. When she leaned over, I noticed there was an inch of dark brown on either side of the part in her hair, before the bleached yellow started. Velma took a sip of coffee, and because I can't abide a silence, I said, "I don't carry tales, if you're worried about it." That wasn't exactly true. I gossiped as much as anybody else, but I made a point not to *start* the gossip.

Velma studied me over the rim of her cup. "You got it real nice," she said again, and this time, I knew she wasn't talking about my kitchen.

All of a sudden, I felt sorry for her. "I wish you'd come to Persian Pickle," I blurted out, meaning it. "We have an awfully good time. I think you'd like it fine if you tried it."

"Maybe if I was an old married lady living way out in the country like you, I would," she said.

"Why, we're not all so old. I'm twenty-four now, same as Rita. You must be almost twenty-one." It surprised me to realize that Velma was so close to my age.

"I'm not married and settled down. What's there for me to talk about at that dumb club?"

"I bet you will be before long. Married, I mean."

"Fat chance. He's already got a wife—the man I was with. He's not a four-flusher. He told me about her right off. I expect you know about him being married."

I nodded.

"Did Aunt Forest Ann tell you?"

"Married men have a look to them," I lied, since I hadn't seen any more of him than the back of his head. I didn't want Velma to know Forest Ann had told on her. "I forgot to offer you the cream. Grover and I don't take it in our coffee." I rose, but Velma put out her hand.

"Dad don't know about him," she said. "I hope you aren't going to tattle."

"I won't. Tyrone would blame Nettie, and I wouldn't hurt your mom for the world," I said, which was true. Except for Ella, Nettie had it the hardest of any of the members of the Persian Pickle. Tyrone wasn't mean, exactly, but he was dumb and shiftless and self-righteous.

Velma nodded, and I got up to get the coffeepot, studying Velma as I poured hers. She was hard around the eyes, but she was a good-looking girl, and I said, "Velma, with looks like yours, you don't have to take up with a married man. There are plenty of boys right here in Harveyville who would be crazy for you if you gave them half a chance."

"Name one."

I opened my mouth to do just that, but I couldn't think of a boy her age still living in Harveyville who wasn't married or a hired man. Finally, I remembered one. "If you can overlook him being a cripple, there's Doyle Tatum," I said. "He's real nice."

"I wouldn't marry no ugly man." Velma laughed, and her face grew soft for a minute. "You see what I mean? I had real hopes for Tom Ritter, but then he went off and married that Rita person."

I tightened my grip on the coffeepot and wondered just what Velma meant about having hopes for Tom, but I wouldn't ask about a thing like that. "Oh," I said.

"We were having a real good time last summer, and I thought . . ." Velma hunched over her coffee. "I don't suppose you knew about it. We didn't exactly go out to the Hollywood or even to the picture show, 'cause Tom didn't have any money. Maybe he didn't want his dad to know he was seeing me, on account of my reputation. We just talked and stuff down by the creek."

Velma waited for me to say something, but I was wondering why Tom hadn't told us about Velma. I was also trying to figure out what she meant by "stuff." Maybe she was making the whole thing up.

When I didn't reply, Velma added, "Well, I don't have much use for a man that doesn't even write me that he got married. I let Tom know that, too, the last time I had a word with him. At least Charley—that's the man I was with at the Hollywood—told me right off he had a wife, even if she is so crazy jealous that she'd kill him if he asked for a divorce. That's why I respect him. He's honest. He's going to get me a job in Coffeyville."

Velma was as dumb as Tyrone if she believed all that, but I knew I couldn't talk any sense into her, so I said, "It's none of my business." Then I changed the subject. "Your mom sure did make a good pineapple upside-down cake for Ben Crook's funeral. I'd like to have the recipe."

Velma opened her mouth to say something. I think she wanted to ask me to promise to keep my mouth shut about Charley. But she thought better of it and said, "Why do you think whoever killed Mr. Crook buried him out there next to the road?"

I shrugged. "Don't ask me. What would I know about the way murderers think?"

"Charley knew him. He told me Ben Crook cheated him out of fifty dollars once, and the first chance he got, Charley was—" Velma stopped and stood up. "I'm obliged to you for not saying anything." Then she paused to gulp the rest of her coffee and slipped out the door just as quick as Sonny had, leaving me to wishing I'd gotten a look at Charley.

2⋗

After Velma left, I hurried to wash and dry the dishes because I'd promised Rita I'd help her with her story for the newspaper. Like Grover, I didn't see why she wanted to write another one. It meant more heartache for Ella if people kept talking about Ben, but Rita was set on it. Rita didn't want to interview folks on the telephone for fear of somebody listening in, so I volunteered to drive her around, thinking she might mention my name in the newspaper, and wouldn't that be something!

Rita showed up before I'd finished drying the dishes, and I thought even people in a big city like Topeka didn't get as many visitors through the kitchen door in one morning as I did.

"You're a peach to do this, Queenie," Rita told me as I

93

poured her a cup of the coffee I'd made for Velma. In her blue suit with a long skirt that was just the latest thing, and a stylish little hat with a feather on it, Rita looked like she'd stepped right out of the Mrs. Newlywed's store in Eskridge.

"Good java," she added, tightening the screw on her double-decked eardrops. She took out a list from her pocketbook. "These are the places I want to go. I thought I'd write them down so you can plot our trip. No use wasting gas."

There were only three places written on the paper, so it didn't even qualify as a list. Rita could have just remembered them, but maybe that wasn't the way reporters worked. The three places were Ella's field, where Ben had been buried, Mrs. Judd's house, and the sheriff's office. I asked why she wanted to go to Mrs. Judd's.

"Ella's staying there, isn't she?"

"You mean you want to ask her questions for your story? Why would you do a thing like that?"

Rita put down her cup, which had a bright lipstick smudge on the edge, and looked up at me. "Don't be so surprised. Reporters always talk to the grieving widow."

"It doesn't seem very polite to me. We want Ella to get over Ben's body being found. I don't think it's a nice thing to ask a friend about."

"I'm a reporter, Queenie, and reporters don't have friends."

The remark sounded like something Rita had read in a book instead of a thing a real person would say, but I was shocked anyway. "That's the worst thing I ever heard. Nothing's more important than friends."

Rita laughed. "Oh, Queenie, it's all right. This is just business, as they say. I can't see any difference between me interviewing a friend and Grover selling Ella a cow."

That didn't sound right to me, either, but I wasn't sure why. "Grover would *give* her a cow if she needed it," I said.

"I know that, but it's beside the point. Are you ready to go?"

I scratched at a place on the linoleum tablecloth where Sonny had spilled syrup, then put my finger into my mouth.

94

"You won't make Ella talk to you if she doesn't want to, will you?" I asked without looking up.

"Well, of course not, silly. How could I make a person do that?"

Grover came into the kitchen just then, washed his hands, and dried them on the roller towel while I poured him the rest of the coffee from the percolator. There was just a drop, and he drank it standing up, before he said, "Morning, Rita. Sounds like you're going to make Harveyville famous." He must have been standing on the porch, listening. "Even if you could make Ella talk, you'd have to go through both of the Judds to get to her, and that'd be harder than skinning a live mule."

"You see?" Rita said to me. "Ella's safe." She put on her little white gloves and stood up.

"I'll just get my keys," I said.

Grover had gone into the bedroom ahead of me to change his shirt because he'd gotten oil from the tractor all over himself. I closed the door, and even though I knew Rita couldn't hear me, I whispered. "Grover, do you know anything about Tom fooling around with Velma Burgett?"

"You mean now?" Grover asked. I caught the dirty shirt before it landed on the floor, and I touched the stain with my finger. I'd never get it out.

"No, of course not, you dope. Tom's married. I'm talking about last summer."

Grover went into the closet.

"You already got out your clean shirt. Look at me," I said.

Grover wasn't any good at hiding a thing from me. "There was nothing serious between them, Queenie. They were just out for a good time, is all. Velma's not the kind of girl you marry."

"I guess I don't know what you mean," I said, hoping Grover would catch the edge in my voice. I knew what Grover meant, of course, but nobody, not even my husband, could criticize a member of the Persian Pickle Club that way.

"Hell, Queenie, you know what kind of girl I mean. She's a hussy."

I couldn't let Grover get away with that. "She's a Pickle!"

"What does that have to do with it? How'd you like Tom bringing Velma over for a wiener roast on Saturday night instead of Rita?" Grover buttoned up his shirt and slipped the straps of his overalls over his shoulders. "I don't think Tom sees her anymore." He sat down on the bed and looked up at me. "I didn't really mean that about Velma being a hussy. She used to be a real nice girl. She just went to town, is all. I expect she'll straighten out one of these days."

Grover reached out his hand, but I didn't have time for that foolishness. Besides, Rita was in the next room. I decided to forgive him, however. So after I fished the car keys out of the Whitman's box on the dresser, I kissed Grover on the back of his sunburned neck and went out to Rita.

↬

We stopped at Ella's farm first because I was not in any hurry to take on Mrs. Judd, who would blame me for not having the good sense to keep Rita away from Ella. She'd be right, too, but I couldn't think of a way to head off Rita.

The minute I stopped the car next to Ella's side porch and killed the engine, Hiawatha stepped out from behind the barn and stood quietly, watching us. Rita waved and said in a friendly way, "Hi there, Hiawatha. You're just the man I want to see."

Hiawatha didn't move, just stood there with a pitchfork in his hands, so Rita had to get out of the car and go over to him. I was right behind her.

"I'm writing a story for the *Topeka Enterprise,* and I want to see where Ben Crook was buried." Hiawatha didn't say a word. Instead, he looked at me, and I nodded to let him know it was all right to talk to Rita.

"Out there," he said, pointing north with the pitchfork.

"Well, let's go 'out there,' " Rita said.

"The dirt'll spoil them shoes you got on. You drive out on the highway. Go north half a mile and turn off on the creek road. I'll go 'cross the field and meet you."

Hiawatha started off, but he stopped when I called to him. "Don't you want to come with us, Hiawatha? There's no need for you to walk on a hot day when you can ride."

He waited to see if Rita would object to him getting into the car with us, but she smiled at him and called, "Hop in." So Hiawatha stuck the pitchfork in the dirt, brushed off his clothes, and climbed into the backseat, his hat in his hand.

Rita took out a little pad of paper and her fountain pen, although I didn't know how she could write with the car bumping along. "It must have given you quite a scare, finding that body out there," she said, smiling at Hiawatha again.

"Old bones don't scare me none."

"No, I wouldn't think anything would scare someone as big as you. What did you think when you saw that big bone sticking out of the ground?"

"I thought, There's a dead man here."

"And right you were. Did you know who it was?"

"Maybe."

"Did you know for sure it was Ben Crook?"

"I don't reckon I could tell a man just from his one bone."

"Weren't you frightened? I mean, weren't you afraid there might be ghosts and spooks hovering around?"

I turned around in my seat to look at Hiawatha, but I couldn't tell what he was thinking. He might have been mad or hurt that Rita had asked him something so silly. If he was, he didn't show it. I thought I caught a little smile sneak across his face, but when I looked sharp, it wasn't there. "I'm a Catholic, Miz Ritter. I don't hold with that Baptist booger stuff like you folks."

Even Rita had to laugh at that. She knew Hiawatha was kidding her, so she screwed the top onto her fountain pen and dropped it into her purse. Then she put her arm over the seat and asked, like she was just making conversation, "Why were you working out there, anyway?"

"Who said I was working there?" Hiawatha asked. Rita didn't answer. She kept staring at Hiawatha, so, after a minute, he went on. "All I was doing was crossing the field on my way home from the Sutter place. They give me a quarter to chop up

97

two trees that the wind blew over last winter. I saw that bone sticking up in the dirt, so I squatted down and brushed it off. The wind had blowed open the grave, I reckon, and if I hadn't walked past it just then, the wind would have closed it up again, and I never would have found that bone."

"Then it was a lucky thing you came by when you did," Rita said.

Hiawatha didn't reply. He just quirked his eyebrow like he wasn't so sure—just like the rest of us weren't so sure.

We rambled right along until we reached an old section road that was pretty good, considering nobody ever used it. I followed it, driving along the creek, which was dry, and over a rise to a field that had lain fallow since Ben disappeared. Hiawatha pointed toward a dip, and I pulled up. I could have found that place on my own, however, because of the tire tracks people had made through the weeds and thistles to get a look at where Ben had been buried. There were shoe prints all over.

"Kids has been coming here," Hiawatha said as he pointed out bare footprints. I could see the big hole that was Ben's grave. It hadn't been filled in yet.

"What are those?" Rita asked, pointing to two small holes just beyond Ben's grave.

"It looks like maybe this here's a graveyard," Hiawatha said, sending a glance at me out of the corner of his eye. Then he wiped his face with his sleeve to cover up a grin.

"You mean there was more than one body?" Rita took out her fountain pen and flipped open the notebook.

"I just found one, is all." Hiawatha shifted from one foot to another, then said, "Anything else you ladies want? I got work to do for Miz Ella."

Rita's smile turned into a pout. "Well, I have just a few more questions for you. For one thing, do you notice anything different today from when you found the body? I mean, except for the footprints and the tire tracks?"

"There wasn't two womenfolks standing here. Is that what you mean?"

I giggled, but Rita scowled. "No, that's not what I mean."

Hiawatha shook his head. "I got to go now. There ain't nothing more to say." He turned and started off across the field, in the direction of Ella's place.

Rita tried to call him back, but he kept on going. So she walked around the grave, writing down things in her notebook. "Damn it. I'm out of ink. Do you have a pencil?"

I got out a runty stub I kept in the glove compartment. "What are you looking for?" I asked as I handed it to her.

"Clues."

"Clues? Clues to what?"

"Clues to who killed Ben Crook. I'll let you in on a secret, Queenie. I wasn't kidding when I said I was going to solve this murder. The newspaper all but told me I can have a job if I do. Now, what do you think of that?" Rita looked as pleased as our dog, Old Bob, the time he killed a skunk.

"How can you solve any murder? For heaven's sakes, you never even met Ben Crook. How could you know who killed him?"

"Well, I don't know for sure, of course, but I've got some keen ideas. Oh, damn it. That pen got ink all over my gloves." She took off her gloves, wadded them up, and put them into her purse.

"That's the dumbest thing I ever heard. I knew Ben, and I was living here when he was killed, and I can't tell you who did it."

"It's called a hunch. Reporters get them all the time. I can't tell you who it is yet." Rita stooped down by the grave and picked up a handful of dirt and let it drop, just the way Tom had the night he first brought Rita to dinner, only Rita didn't smell it.

I wondered if the dirt had a dead-man smell, and I leaned over to sniff, but I didn't know the smell a body gave off after being under the ground for a year, so how could I tell? The earth smelled a little like a dead cow, however.

Rita brushed off her hands. "I'll tell you what, Queenie. Maybe when I come up with a good theory, I'll try it out on you to see what you think." She stood up and walked to the car, wobbling a little as she stepped over the dirt clods in her high-heeled slippers. "Do you think Hiawatha did it?"

"He didn't move out here until after Ben died."

"That doesn't mean he didn't do it. Maybe he moved here to keep an eye on things. You know, to keep people from poking around and finding the grave."

"The reason Hiawatha's here is that Ella offered him a place to live. Besides, if he wanted to keep Ben's body hidden, he wouldn't have told the Judds he'd found it, would he? He'd have buried it again."

Rita frowned as she thought over what I'd said. "That's a good point. Still, he might have 'found' the body just to put everybody off. Like Nettie said, he's pretty smart for a colored, and he's strong. I bet he could kill a man just by swatting him in the head."

"So could Grover, but he didn't kill Ben Crook any more than Hiawatha did. Are you finished out here? I'll get freckles standing in the sun." I was wearing a sundress and wished I'd brought something with me to put over my shoulders. I was tired of the newspaper business.

Rita took another step toward the car, then stopped and tapped her lip with my pencil. She turned around and went back to the grave and peered down into it. "I know one thing for sure. Whoever killed Ben Crook had an auto."

Without thinking, I put my hand on the hot metal door handle of the car, then snatched it away and spit on the burn. "How do you know?"

"Because somebody drove down this road and dumped him here. That's how I know. Because he's next to the road. Now, think about it, Queenie. If you had to bury somebody as heavy as Ben, would you drag him off into the middle of the field? Of course not. It's too much trouble. You'd bury him next to the road."

"What if he was killed right here where he was buried?" I asked.

Rita thought that over. "Maybe, but what would he have

100

been doing out here with a killer? No, I think my first hunch is right."

"I guess that lets Hiawatha out. He doesn't have a car, and I doubt that he can even drive one."

"Maybe he had a partner. Maybe he was a hired killer and murdered Ben for somebody else. Then the two of them buried the body here."

Rita had gone too far. "Who would that be? Duty?" I asked sarcastically. "You'd better just forget about Hiawatha. I said I'd help you with your story, but I don't want to meddle in something that isn't any of my business, or yours, either, because you're liable to hurt somebody. There're some people like Tyrone Burgett who are looking for any little excuse they can find to drive Hiawatha and Duty out of Harveyville."

Rita came back to the car and used her hand to dust off the passenger-side running board, which was in the shade. She spread out a handkerchief and sat down. I had to walk to the front of the car just to see her. "Don't you want justice done? Don't you want Ella to know who killed her husband?"

"No, I don't."

Rita looked up in surprise and wiggled her finger back and forth at me. "Some detective you'd make." She sat looking out over the horizon, thinking, then stood up and wiped the dirt off her shoes with the handkerchief.

I went back to the driver's side, and this time, I used my skirt like a hot pad to cover the car door handle so I could open it. "I don't want to be some detective," I told her after I'd climbed in and started the engine. I wasn't sure I wanted to go through all this aggravation just to get my name in the newspaper, either, even though Ruby might see it and write me a letter.

As I backed down the section road and pulled out onto the highway, heading toward the Judds' place, I chatted about the weather and told Rita how nice she looked even in the heat, hoping I could get on her good side. Because I was so worried that Rita's story would harm Ella, I hadn't shown the proper enthusiasm for Rita's newspaper work, and I wondered if she thought I had let her down. If so, she didn't say anything. In fact, she didn't pay any attention to me at all, just sat and stared out the window, biting her lip.

So I stopped talking and enjoyed the scenery myself, thinking how nice it would be to make a quilt that looked like Kansas fields. I'd pick striped fabrics and cut them into squares and rectangles, setting some in crossways so they'd look the way our fields did when Grover plowed them at angles. Even though most of the fields we passed were brown, I'd use green material. I'd call the quilt Better Times, and I was so pleased with the name, I thought I'd tell Mrs. Judd. I pulled into her barnyard and switched off the motor.

Prosper stood beside the smokehouse, watching us, and I could make out Mrs. Judd, who was just a shape behind the screen door. To show sympathy for Ella, the Judds had tied a purple mourning bow on the door. Black crepe streamers hung from it, but in the heat, they looked like limp rags. I figured Ella was somewhere in the kitchen, blocked by Mrs. Judd.

Rita waited for me to get out of the car, but I wasn't in any hurry to face down Mrs. Judd, who'd be mad enough to chew my eyes out when she found out why we were there. So I fiddled with the key, pretending it wouldn't come out of the ignition, then stared at the barn as if something over that way had caught my attention.

Rita got out and faced the Judds by herself. "Is Ella around?" she asked Prosper.

"She's sleeping," Mrs. Judd answered from inside the door. "How do, Queenie." She didn't sound friendly, and I slumped down a little in the seat.

"I want to talk to Ella," Rita said.

"She's had about all the condolence calls she can take today, but thank you just the same. I'll tell her you stopped in. She'll appreciate the thought."

"Oh, I didn't come to tell her I was sorry. I came to ask her some questions." That didn't sound right, even to Rita, who added, "I mean, of course I'm sorry."

"What do you want to ask her questions for? Are you writing

another one of those stories?" Mrs. Judd's voice boomed out from the house like a radio that had been turned up too high.

"Rita thinks she's going to find out who killed Ben," I called out the window, and I could hear Mrs. Judd's snort all the way to the car.

Rita turned and frowned at me as if I shouldn't have told. Then she turned to Mrs. Judd with the same smile she'd given Hiawatha. "Of course, I can't promise I'll do it, but I'm going to try. It would be nice to know who the murderer is, don't you think? I imagine everybody would feel better, especially Ella, if they knew who killed Mr. Crook."

"Would they?" Mrs. Judd asked.

Prosper, who'd been staring at Rita, turned to look at his wife through the screen door.

"Of course they would. Everybody wants justice done, don't they?" Rita sounded cheerful, but she didn't cheer me up, and from the looks of the Judds, she didn't cheer them, either.

"I don't know about that. Around here, everybody wants to mind their own business. It seems to me, justice would be letting Ella alone. She doesn't want you or anybody else prying," Prosper told Rita. I'd never heard Prosper say that much at one time.

Rita had removed her pad and my pencil stub from her purse when she got out of the car, but she put them back and snapped shut the lock on the pocketbook. "What I don't understand is why everybody wants to cover this up."

Mrs. Judd came out from behind the screen, letting it slam behind her, making Rita jump. Before the door closed, I caught a glimpse of Ella sitting in a rocker in the kitchen. "What's that you said?"

I had to admire Rita for being braver than I'd ever been. She didn't flinch one bit under Mrs. Judd's frown. "I said it seems to me that everybody wants to cover up this murder. Nobody wants to talk about it," Rita replied.

Prosper took a step toward Rita and opened his mouth, but Mrs. Judd held up her hand. "Cover up!" she said, spit flying out of her mouth. "What's there to cover up? Ben Crook's death

103

is none of your business. None of my business—or Queenie's, over there, either. You're trying to stir up trouble with your newspaper stories. I don't know of anybody in Harveyville who wants their name in the newspapers." Even though Mrs. Judd couldn't see me, I blushed.

"If you keep on asking fool questions like you've been doing, people'll get suspicious of their neighbors and say things they don't mean. There're already kids out there digging up Ella's field, looking for buried treasure, because somebody said Ben was killed for money. Ben never had any money. Why, do you think he'd have let Ella live like they did with no electricity or running water if he'd had money? He thought the sun rose and set—"

Rita cut her off. "Well, somebody must have had a reason for killing him. And what if the murderer is living right here in Harveyville? Do you want to live with a killer? What if he goes after Mr. Judd? Or Ella? Or Queenie?" I shivered, even though it was so hot, I was sweating.

Mrs. Judd put her hands on her hips, stretched her neck, and puffed out her chest like a hen who's just laid an egg. "There isn't anybody going after a one of us that I know of."

"Tima," Prosper said. Mrs. Judd turned her eyes to Prosper without turning her face. The two of them looked at each other a long time, Mrs. Judd staring through her thick spectacles and Prosper looking right back with his beady pig eyes. I guess he was telling her something, the way married people do without talking, but I didn't know what it was.

After a minute, Mrs. Judd turned her eyes back to Rita. "If I let you talk to Ella, will you promise you'll never ask her another thing about Ben Crook? Ben's dead, and he's been dead over a year. It doesn't do her any good to dig up his memory, the way Hiawatha dug up his body. Ella's none too strong, and all these questions don't help her one bit. You promise you'll let her be?"

Rita nodded. "All right."

Rita started toward the door, but Mrs. Judd held up her hand. "I'll bring her out." She called inside in the sweet voice you'd use for a little child, "Ella, sweetheart, come out here, please, if you would. You've got you a visitor from Pickle."

The rocker scraped in the kitchen, and Ella, wearing her carpet slippers, shuffled out the screen door. She seemed smaller than ever since the funeral, and older, too. I jumped out of the car and ran to her and took her hand. "Why, Ella, you come and sit beside me on the swing. It's such a nice day. The fresh air will do you good. If I'd known we'd be stopping by, I'd have brought a kuchen. I make it just like my mother did. She said you were the only one who could make it better, and she always meant to ask you for your recipe." I chattered away as I led Ella to the swing, thinking Mrs. Judd would tell me to be still, but she didn't. Rita sat down in a chair next to us, and Mrs. Judd hefted her weight onto one of the porch steps. She motioned for Prosper, who came over and leaned against a porch post.

Rita slipped off her hat and laid it on the floor, running her hand through her damp curls, which were as springy as Shirley Temple's. I thought she'd take out her pad of paper again, but she didn't. Maybe it was because the pencil I'd given her was two inches long and had been sharpened with a knife. It was all right for putting down what you needed on a grocery list, but you wouldn't want to write a newspaper story with it.

"I don't want this to be painful, Ella. I'm just thinking that you might remember something that will help me find the man who killed your husband." Rita talked in the same little-girl voice Mrs. Judd had used.

"She already told everything to Sheriff Eagles," Mrs. Judd butted in.

Rita pretended she hadn't heard Mrs. Judd and kept on. "Maybe someone in Topeka will read the article and know who did it. Or perhaps something you say will give somebody an idea. Even the itty-bittiest thing could help."

"Why would anybody in Topeka kill Ben Crook?" Mrs. Judd asked. That wasn't what Rita meant, but Rita didn't answer her.

Ella looked at Rita for a long time. Then she gave her a sorrowful little smile and said, "Okay." Rita smiled back at her.

"When was the last time you saw your husband?" Rita asked.

"June twentieth of last year. Everybody knows that," Mrs. Judd answered for Ella. Rita raised her shoulders and sighed to show she was peeved at Mrs. Judd, but she kept looking at Ella. It became clear to me that Mrs. Judd's plan was to let Rita ask Ella questions, but Mrs. Judd would answer them. After all, Mrs. Judd had promised that Rita could talk to Ella. She hadn't said anything about Ella talking back.

"That was the day he disappeared. I asked when was the last time Ella saw him?"

"Are you asking Ella if she saw him after he disappeared?" Prosper butted in before Mrs. Judd could answer. Rita would have done a whole lot better if she'd gotten the Judds on her side in the first place instead of going against them.

"Did he mention he was seeing anybody?" Rita asked, and Ella shook her head. She made little bird scratches on her lap with her hands, then put them into her apron pockets. They wouldn't stay still, however, and in a minute, they were out of her pockets again. It was the first time I'd seen Ella sitting down without quilting or fancywork to occupy her hands. She played with a spot on the hem of her apron where the stitches holding the bias tape trim had come out. I wondered how she could have such dainty hands with all the heavy farmwork she'd done in her life.

"Did he ever have any fights with other men? Or did anybody owe him money or threaten him? Or did you ever see someone sneaking around your farm?" With the first question Rita asked, Ella shook her head no and kept on shaking it long after Rita finished. Mrs. Judd didn't have to stop Ella from talking, because Ella didn't have anything to say.

Rita realized that, too, and gave a sigh and was quiet. Then, to my surprise, she turned to Prosper. "I'd like to talk to you, Mr. Judd. Alone, if I may."

Mrs. Judd protested that anything Rita had to say to Prosper could be said in front of her, but Prosper put up a little pink hand. "It's all right, Mother." He and Rita walked over to the horse trough, which was iron and had green slime on the edges. Prosper stood with his back to the sun, and Rita squinted to see him. From what I could tell, she did most of the talking, while Prosper looked into the horse trough and ran his hand along the cool rim. His little eyes squinted until they were all but closed.

All of a sudden, Prosper gave a sharp sound. It wasn't a word really, just a sound that was like "huh" or "ha." I wasn't sure what it meant. He turned without so much as a glance at us and walked quickly into the barn, closing the door behind him. The barn was old, and long cracks had opened up between the wallboards when the big building shifted. I knew Prosper was standing in the gloom inside, watching us through one of those openings. Mrs. Judd stared at the closed door. Then she put a large hand on Ella's shoulder, and Ella's hands stopped scratching and lay still in her lap.

Rita called, "Thanks just the same, Mr. Judd." Instead of coming back to the porch, she took jerky high-heeled steps to the car and waited for me.

I stood and reached for Rita's hat, which she'd left behind on the porch, but before I could pick it up, Ella's hand shot out and grabbed it. She stroked the soft navy blue felt, then carefully brushed the dust off the feather.

Rita opened the car door and put a foot inside, but Ella was still playing with the hat, and I was no longer in a hurry to leave. Rita got tired of waiting and came back to the porch. "You think it'll rain?" Rita asked like some old farmer.

Mrs. Judd blinked at her without answering. Ella handed Rita her hat and said, "Pretty."

Rita put it on, fastening it with the hat pin, then took Ella's hand. "I don't want to hurt you, Ella. Honest I don't. It's just that I've got a job to do, and wouldn't you rather talk to me than some reporter you don't even know?"

That sounded like a threat, and Mrs. Judd pinched in her mouth while she thought it over. "Do you mean, if you weren't to write this up, somebody else would?"

"They'd send out a reporter from Topeka, probably one of those men who get people to confess to all kinds of things. They know how to do it," Rita told her.

Mrs. Judd mulled that over. "I don't want outsiders bothering Ella."

"That's why I'm helping Rita. She'll be nicer to Ella than somebody from Topeka," I put in.

Instead of looking at me, Mrs. Judd put up her hand to tell me to be still. She told Rita, "If they send one of those men reporters out, you let me know."

Rita and I went to the car, and I started the engine. Before I could put the Studebaker into reverse and back out onto the road, however, Mrs. Judd waved her arm and started toward us, calling my name. I stuck my head out of the window, waiting for her to reach us while I wondered if she'd scold me for my part in Rita's newspaper work.

"Queenie," Mrs. Judd said, puffing a little. "Queenie, I'd be obliged to you for a scrap of that nice red you have with the white stars—that is, if it wouldn't rob you. I'm making me a Dresden Plate, and the red'll look awful good in it."

I'd been holding my breath ever since Mrs. Judd called my name, and I was so relieved that I let it out in a rush. Asking for a piece of yard goods was Mrs. Judd's way of telling me she didn't blame me for Rita's prying, that everything between us was normal. "I'd be proud to see it in your quilt," I said. "I'll drop it off the next time I come this way."

When we were out on the road, Rita took her lip between her teeth and fanned herself with her hat. Then she asked what Mrs. Judd had meant by asking for a piece of my fabric.

I slowed down, thinking over my reply, before I turned to Rita. "She meant she wanted a scrap of my red with the stars in it for her Dresden Plate," I said. "That's all."

chapter
7

When we left the Judds', I hoped Rita was ready to give up and go home. I was tired of being a reporter's helper and didn't like people frowning at me, but she insisted we had to talk to the sheriff, so I drove us into Harveyville.

It was a Friday. No old bachelors leaned against the Flint Hills Home & Feed. Socializing was Saturday work, and the few people in town that day were hurrying to finish errands so they could go home and get their chores done and be back in town by dark. A sign on the door of the Home & Feed read: MOVIE TONIGHT. SUNDOWN. On Friday nights, the Home & Feed set up a big projector outside and beamed a motion picture on the side of the building. People brought their chairs from home so they could sit in the street and watch it. Tonight's picture was *Murders in the Rue Morgue.* I thought I'd had enough of murder that day, so I wouldn't ask Grover to take me.

Harveyville wasn't any "Gasoline Alley." Only one car was parked on the street, and it was in front of the sheriff's office— a Hudson Super Six with last year's license plate on it. The car had been there more than a year, ever since Pap Logan parked it in that spot, then walked into the street without looking and was hit by a farm kid in an old Willys Overland. Pap was laid up in bed for six months, and even today, he couldn't walk without crutches, so he never went back for the Hudson. He wouldn't let anyone else drive it, either. So it just stayed there. The tires were flat.

When I pulled in next to the Super Six, Sheriff Eagles was sitting on the running board on the car's shady side, whittling a stick with his pocketknife. I turned off the engine, and Rita and I got out.

"This is better than a front-porch swing," Sheriff Eagles said, not getting up, although he touched the brim of his hat to us.

"You know Rita Ritter?" I asked while the sheriff nodded how-do at Rita. "She's Tom's wife. She wants to talk to you."

He squinted at Rita. "You writing up another article about Ben Crook?"

"Did you read the first one?" Rita asked, smoothing the wrinkles out of her skirt. She liked it when people told her they'd read her newspaper stories.

"I guess everybody in Harveyville's read it," he said, and turned away to spit. "As least, everybody in Harveyville's told me you didn't spell my name right. It's Eagles with an *s* on the end of it, not Eagle. You know, not just one bird, a whole flock of 'em." Rita looked embarrassed and turned red, and Sheriff Eagles told her, "Oh, heck. That's all right, sis. Everybody spells it wrong."

"It doesn't matter what you say, just spell my name right," Rita muttered.

The sheriff looked at me, and I shrugged because I didn't know what Rita meant any more than he did. He asked, "How's that?"

"It's just an old newspaper saying," Rita explained. She put her elbow on the Hudson so she could get closer to the sheriff, but it slipped, and Rita nearly fell. She straightened up, then leaned over to Sheriff Eagles. "You don't mind being in the newspaper, do you, Sheriff Eagles?" She pronounced Eagles as if it ended in a whole string of *s*'s.

"Can't say it's any worse than a poke in the eye with a sharp stick."

Rita laughed hard, although I'd heard that expression a thousand times and didn't see why she thought it was so funny. She started to reply, then noticed that several people on the sidewalk had stopped to listen. So she said, "Why don't we go inside to talk."

"Suit yourself." Sheriff Eagles took his time, however, as he carefully folded the knife and put it into his pocket, then slowly got to his feet. He brushed the dirt off the seat of his pants but not off the back of his shirt, which was dusty from leaning against the car.

Rita and I followed him into the office, Rita whispering to me, "Where's his gun?"

Sheriff Eagles put his fists on his waist and turned to Rita. "What do I need a gun for?"

"I thought lawmen always carried guns," Rita said.

"This is Harveyville, Kansas, not Dodge City, Kansas," he said. "It ain't Abilene, Kansas, either," he added, but I think Rita had already gotten the point. "It's not . . ." He couldn't think of another Wild West place in Kansas and shook his head. "You don't need a gun to sit on the running board of a Super Six in Harveyville." Sheriff Eagles winked at me. I winked back, then decided he might think I was siding with him against Rita, so I reached up and rubbed my eye as if I'd gotten a cinder in it.

I'd never been in the sheriff's office before, and I was as disappointed with it as Rita was with Sheriff Eagles not carrying a gun. It was just a dusty room with an old wooden desk and a chair with an Indian blanket folded up for a cushion. Against the wall stood a rusty wood stove with dirty coffee cups on it. A row of upright bars like an iron fence marked off the jail end of the room, and you could see right through it to the two bunks and a slop jar. I wondered how anybody who was locked up in there had the privacy to go to the bathroom. I wished Rita would ask Sheriff Eagles about that!

The sheriff sat down behind the desk and leaned forward on his elbows, squinting at us. He didn't invite us to sit down, but Rita pulled up a chair, and I found one for myself.

"Rita—" I started to tell the sheriff, but she cut me off with a sharp look. I should have learned by now that she wanted to ask the questions.

Rita leaned forward and smiled at the sheriff. "I'm writing a follow-up to that story you read, and I'll make sure I spell your name right this time."

"You do that."

"You wouldn't have a pencil, would you?" Rita asked, and the sheriff rummaged around in the drawer and found a tiny pencil with a broken lead.

"You got a penknife so's I can sharpen it?" he asked.

I was about to ask what was wrong with the one in his pocket, but Rita said, "Never mind." She opened her pocketbook and took out my pencil stub and poised it over her pad of paper. The smile disappeared from her face, and she narrowed her eyes at the sheriff and asked, "Who killed Ben Crook?"

Sheriff Eagles looked at her as if she'd just asked him what day of the year we would get the next hard rain. "How the hell do I know, sis?" he replied. "Begging your pardon, ma'am." He said that to me.

"Don't you know?"

"I'm working on it. Ben Crook died more than a year ago. There ain't a lot of evidence left around. I didn't find anybody's name and address written down and stuck inside Ben's overalls pocket."

"Did you find any weapons?"

"Naw. Ben was killed someplace else and hauled there in an automobile. The man who done it most likely used a two-by-four or maybe a piece of cordwood to kill him. He did a right smart job of it, judging from the way Ben's skull was bashed in. It was a doozy."

Rita gave me an "I told you so" look before she licked the end of her pencil with her tongue, but she didn't write down anything. "What leads do you have?"

"Why would I tell you? You'd put it in the newspaper, wouldn't you, and the fellow who done it would run off. Ain't that about right?" Sheriff Eagles leaned back in his chair, looking pleased with himself. He glanced at me, but even though I thought he'd been pretty quick, I frowned. After all, I was on Rita's side.

"I'm betting you don't have any idea at all." Rita put the pencil down and stared at the sheriff. In a minute, he looked away. "Am I right?" Rita asked.

"No, you are not right," the sheriff mimicked, his chair squeaking as he leaned forward, his elbows on the desk.

"Then who killed him?"

"Sis, I'm not telling you anything. If you ask me, it ain't your business."

"It's my business if there's a killer loose in Wabaunsee County. After all, I live here, too. It's as much my business as it is yours—or Queenie's. I'm going to write that you don't know who killed Mr. Crook."

"That so? Well, I guess if you want to write lies, there's nothing I can do to stop you."

The two of them looked at each other for a full minute without saying a word, while I thought Rita would be better off if she knew that she could catch more flies with honey than with vinegar. She should have learned that from talking to the Judds.

"What about Hiawatha?" she asked, yanking off her earrings and dropping them into her pocketbook.

"Hiawatha Jackson?"

"How many Hiawathas are there in Harveyville?" She'd picked up that line from Nettie, the day she'd called Lizzy Olive, and I wanted to laugh, but I kept my mouth shut because the sheriff didn't think Rita was funny.

"What about him? Nice fellow, ain't he, and he don't fight like some of your coloreds."

"Do you think he did it?"

"Why would Hiawatha Jackson kill Ben? Was they acquainted? Hiawatha came down from Blue Hill after Ben disappeared."

"How did you know that?" Rita asked, but the sheriff only looked smug. I could have told Rita why the sheriff knew, but she'd made it clear that she didn't want my interference, so I didn't speak up.

The two of them kept at it like that, each trying to trip the other one up but not getting anywhere, and I stopped listening to look out the window. Being a newspaper reporter was a boring way to earn your living, not interesting like farming. I wondered if I should tell the sheriff about Velma's married boyfriend Charley having a run-in with Ben Crook. After all, I hadn't promised Velma I wouldn't let the sheriff know Charley had threatened Ben. Still, if I told, I'd have to explain how I knew about him, and that would make things even worse for Velma. I kept Charley to myself.

I turned back to Rita and Sheriff Eagles when he yanked at a desk drawer that was stuck and wiggled it open. He removed a sheet of paper and handed it to Rita, who turned it around and read it.

She cocked her pretty head and smiled at the sheriff. "You went over that site quite thoroughly, it seems to me. This list looks like it's got everything on it. It's as good a murder report as I ever read."

That didn't mean anything, because Rita had told me this was the first crime she'd ever written about, but the sheriff didn't know that. He looked pleased with himself and said, "I know a thing or two, I guess."

"I can see that all right." Maybe Rita knew about flies and honey, after all.

"How about tramps? Grover said back-door moochers started showing up about the time Ben was killed. Do you think one of them did it?" I asked, avoiding Rita's eyes just in case she was mad that I'd butted in.

Sheriff Eagles nodded his head up and down, which meant he was thinking, not agreeing with me. "Grover ain't as dumb as he looks, is he, Queenie? The fact is, Ella said there was a tramp who went through her place the day Ben disappeared. She thought it was odd, the way he showed up in the middle of the morning instead of at mealtime, when most of those fellows come looking for handouts."

Rita's eyes lit up, and I guess she was glad I'd asked, because she said, "Do you think he did it?"

The sheriff shook his head. "Ella said he had one leg gone and a hand that was all drawed up, so he couldn't have been

114

the responsible party. It took a strong man to kill Ben, to bash him in the head like that, then haul him over to that grave. Ben was a big man."

"Big like Skillet," I said.

The sheriff looked up at me quickly, then rubbed his chin with his hand. There were stubble patches on his face where the razor had missed his whiskers. "I already thought of that," he said.

"Who's Skillet?" Rita asked.

The sheriff and I looked at each other. Then he nodded at me to answer, and I replied, "Ben's hired man."

"Skillet who?" she asked.

I shrugged. "I never knew his last name. Did you, Sheriff?"

"Nope. Ella never asked. A man who goes by one name don't want you to know the other one. If Ella'd pressed him for it, he'd have made one up. I'll bet you a nickel his first name wasn't Skillet, either." The sheriff stuck out his chin as if he was waiting for one of us to tell him how smart he was.

"Do you think Skillet did it?" Rita asked.

Sheriff Eagles leaned back in his chair and put his fingers together. Then he stuck out his lower lip as if he was thinking. Rita fidgeted, which seem to tickle the sheriff, and he looked around the room, dragging out his answer. "Maybe so. Skillet was strong. I know he had a hot temper, 'cause he worked for a farmer over to Snokomo until a pig riled him and he killed it with a pitchfork. Skillet hightailed it over here and hired on with Ben. The farmer wanted me to get Skillet to pay for the pig, but I told him if Skillet had that kind of money, he wouldn't be a hired hand for Ben Crook. Hell, I wouldn't want to tangle with Skillet any more than I would with Ben. Each one of 'em was nastier than the other. All you had to do was look at Skillet to know you'd best keep your distance. He had a face ugly enough to clabber milk."

"Well, did he do it?" Rita asked one more time.

"Clabber milk?" The sheriff was enjoying himself.

Rita wasn't, however. She stared flint-eyed at the sheriff, waiting for him to answer.

"Probably not."

"How can you be so sure?"

"Because he took off before Ben disappeared, is how I know for sure."

"Where did he go?"

"Now, how would I know that? I got better things to do than stop every drifter that goes through Harveyville and ask for his traveling plans." The sheriff stood up. "I guess that's about all I've got to say. I don't get paid for talking."

"Can I say Skillet is a suspect?" Rita asked as she and I stood up.

"You can say everybody in Wabaunsee County's a suspect—including Queenie." He sent me a sideways look and rolled his tongue under his upper lip to show he was joking.

Rita and I went back to the car and got in. When I glanced over at Rita, she had a smug expression on her face. "You think Skillet did it, don't you?" I asked. I hoped if she put Skillet into her story, Rita would remember he was my idea.

But Rita shook her head, catching the feather of her hat on the car roof. She removed the hat to examine the feather, which was broken in half. "He just threw in that Skillet person to fool me, but I'm too smart to fall for it."

I was confused. "You mean you don't think Skillet did it?"

"I don't think he did it at all, but I've got a pretty good idea who did do it."

"Who?" I gasped.

"It's a secret. If I told you, you'll tell somebody." Instead of looking at me, Rita held up her right hand, the fingers spread wide, and examined her nails, which were freshly polished.

I turned my head away without a word and started the car. Rita had no call to insult me. I could keep a secret as well as anybody. Shoot, I could keep a secret from Grover if I had to. I knew I could even keep one from Rita.

2⦅

We didn't talk as I drove Rita back to the Ritter place. I suppose I was pouting while she was thinking about whoever killed Ben Crook. Neither of us opened our mouths until we came to the edge of Forest Ann's farm, and Rita grabbed my arm. "Isn't that Dr. Sipes's car parked there? I'd like to talk to him."

I laughed. "Of course not. It isn't five o'clock yet."

Rita turned to me with a puzzled look on her face. "What does the time have to do with it?"

I wished I hadn't been so quick. "Nothing."

"Oh, come on, Queenie. What do you mean about five o'clock?" Rita still held the broken feather in her hand, and she reached over and touched the tip of it to my cheek. "Tell me."

I shrugged.

"Queenie Bean, are you saying that Doc Sipes calls on Forest Ann every evening at five o'clock?" Rita patted her lips with the feather. She sure was smart at figuring out things—maybe not Ben Crook's murder, but other things.

"Not every day. After all, he's got sick people to see to."

"Well, I think that's kind of romantic, even at their age. We've had one birth and two funerals since I came here. Maybe next we'll have a wedding."

"No such a thing! Doc Sipes is married—" I stopped myself too late. I might just as well have dug a big hole and jumped into it.

Rita leaned back in the seat and giggled. "In Harveyville, Kansas, no less. Well, I'll be damned. This town's getting to be a regular Tobacco Road."

I didn't understand. "This is the Auburn Road."

"Oh, Queenie." Rita laughed again, as if I'd said something funny. "Maybe we ought to pay Forest Ann a friendly visit. We could say we were driving by and just stopped to chat. People around here are always stopping by without an invitation, whether you want them to or not."

"Forest Ann and Doc Sipes isn't something we interfere with. We pretend it's not going on," I said. "She's a member of the Persian Pickle Club, so we stand by her, even if we don't approve, which I'm not saying we do or don't. Forest Ann deserves a little kindness, and so does Doc. Mrs. Sipes is

117

meaner than Ma Barker, and Doc is a saint . . . just a saint. Nobody could blame him for taking up with Forest Ann."

I stepped on the gas just in case Rita was serious about stopping, but I wasn't fast enough. She leaned over and tooted the horn, and Doc stuck his head out from the porch and waved for us to turn in.

"Darn it. I guess we're calling on Forest Ann, after all," I muttered.

"We're not spying on them," Rita said. "This is kind of like a professional call. I want to ask Doc about Ben Crook's body. He's the coronor, isn't he?"

"The what?"

"You know, the man who cuts up the bodies to find out what people died of."

I shuddered. "I'd rather pick cotton."

Rita laughed, and although I was down on her for saying I couldn't keep a secret and then for honking at Dr. Sipes, when I heard the pretty sound that her voice made, I thought how much I liked her, after all. I loved Ruby, but being with her was like looking into a mirror. Ruby and I did things exactly alike, and sometimes I knew what she was going to say before she did. Rita was a surprise, and she made life interesting. Rita was what she would have called a real "live wire," and it was exciting to be around her.

When I turned off the motor, I saw Forest Ann in the shade of the porch, next to Dr. Sipes. She moved away from him as we came up. She didn't look glad to see us, and I tried to think of a way to let her know I wasn't the one who'd honked.

Dr. Sipes nodded as we got out of the car. Rita already had out her notepad and the pencil I'd given her. She only glanced at Forest Ann before she turned to Doc with the smile she'd used on the others she'd interviewed that day.

Before she could ask a single question, however, Doc said, "I'm glad you girls came along. I'd just stopped to tell Forest Ann about Tyrone."

I'd walked up next to the porch, and when I turned to Forest Ann to see what he meant, I saw tears on her cheeks.

118

"Doc thinks Tyrone's got the polio." Forest Ann sobbed.

"Oh no!" I said.

"Just like the President?" Rita asked.

"Albert told me just now. He left Tyrone only ten minutes ago."

"Who?" I asked.

"Dr. Sipes. Dr. Albert Sipes," Forest Ann said. I'd never thought about a doctor having a first name.

"It might not be polio. I don't know what it is for sure, so I'm not going to quarantine him just yet." Doc knew how hard a quarantine was on people. When her middle girl was quarantined with scarlet fever, Ada June said she thought she'd go crazy with no one to comfort her. Some people wouldn't even talk to her on the telephone, and when the Persian Pickles came with their cakes and potato salads, they had to leave them on a stump outside the house and yell at Ada June at the top of their lungs to come and get them.

"It might be just one of those sicknesses Tyrone gets this time of year," Doc said, glancing at Forest Ann. What he meant was that Tyrone always took to his bed at harvesttime. Doc removed his hat and used the back of his hand to rub the sweat off his forehead.

"Tyrone's never been a well person," Forest Ann said. Since he was her brother, Forest Ann had to defend him, but the rest of us knew Tyrone wasn't as sickly as he was lazy.

"I stopped to tell Forest Ann because Velma's off somewheres," Doc said. "Nettie's taking care of him by herself. Tyrone's not an easy man to deal with in a sickbed."

"Or anyplace else," I muttered, and Doc turned away so Forest Ann wouldn't see him smile.

"We'll all help," I told him. "I'll go home and call Opalina and Ceres and Ada June. Rita can let the Ritters know. We'll have to make do without Ella and Mrs. Judd." I tried to remember what I had at home that I could take over for the Burgetts' supper.

"Ella would want to help," Rita said suddenly, and Forest Ann and I looked at each other.

"She's right," Forest Ann said. "Ella'd never forgive us if somebody was in need and she didn't know about it. Helping Nettie will take her mind off her own troubles."

"It's just the ticket for her," Rita said. She looked pleased.

I was pleased, as well. Rita was thinking like a Pickle. Then I wondered if her real reason for the suggestion was she wanted another chance to question Ella. "Come on, Rita. Let's get going."

We were out on the highway by the time Rita remembered she had a pencil in her hand. "Oh, damn it! I forgot to ask Doc about Ben Crook." I thought that was about the only thing Rita had done right that day.

⁊

So there we all were at the Burgett place, just like we'd been at the Ritters' when Rita had the baby and at Opalina's after Ella's husband was dug up. It seemed as if we'd had more sorrow this year than sewing.

Tyrone was in bed in the parlor, which was where we gathered when Nettie was the hostess of Persian Pickle. With the lights turned off and the shades pulled down, it was the coolest room in the house, much nicer than the hot kitchen, where we sat. The parlor door was closed, but we heard Tyrone thrashing around in there. Every few minutes, he cussed from the pain or from feeling sorry for himself. Who knew which? He'd yell for Nettie to come in there, and when she did, he'd yell at her to get out.

"The only smart thing Tyrone ever did was marry Nettie. I wouldn't walk across the front porch for Tyrone Burgett, but there's not much a body wouldn't do for Nettie," Mrs. Judd said, taking the waxed paper from around her perfection salad, which sat on one of the Haviland plates she used at Pickle. "It's a pity we don't have a pesthouse anymore. That's the place for Tyrone." Nettie was in the parlor with Tyrone, but Mrs. Judd might have said that even if Nettie had been in the room. I was sure she'd have said it if Tyrone was there, especially after the dustup they'd had over Hiawatha moving to Harveyville.

Ella was right behind Mrs. Judd, the color back in her face. Helping people perked her up. She carried a mason jar filled with purple asters, set them down in the dry sink, and then dipped water out of a bucket into the jar.

"Tyrone doesn't care about flowers. They're for Nettie," Mrs. Judd explained. "We stopped at Ella's place on the way so she could pick them."

Tyrone let out a swearword, and Opalina frowned. "There's no need for him to blaspheme the Lord. Nettie ought to smack him when he talks like that. A good smack'd help his disposition."

"This is one time I wish Foster Olive would show up. We could send him right in to see Tyrone. It would serve both those men right," Ceres said. Even Ceres, who got along with everybody, found little to like about Tyrone Burgett.

Nettie came into the kitchen, looking tired and sweaty and smelling like a sickroom. She was startled to see that so many of the Pickles were there. Tears came to her eyes as she smiled at each one of us and glanced at the food we'd set out. The perfection salad sat in the place of honor in the center of the table, the celery and carrots sparkling like five-and-dime jewels, and when I moved aside, a beam of sunshine shot through the window, causing the clear gelatin to shimmer. It was so pretty that Nettie drew in her breath, then threw her arms around Mrs. Judd. "Oh, Septima, I never saw a thing as lovely as that."

Mrs. Judd looked surprised and a little embarrassed at the compliment as she patted Nettie's back. I'd never seen anybody hug Mrs. Judd before.

Just then, the screen squeaked, and the Ritter women came in. Mrs. Judd pulled away from Nettie, to nod at Mrs. Ritter and Agnes T. Ritter. When she came to Rita, she looked her in the eye but didn't nod or say hello. Rita met her stare and swallowed a couple of times. She was uncomfortable, and so was I as I wondered if Mrs. Judd was about to start something. Instead, she blew out her breath and said, "It's good you came, Rita. We always help one another." If Mrs. Judd was going to

121

have words with Rita, it wouldn't be in Nettie's kitchen in front of the other Pickles.

We visited as we set out food and made coffee. Agnes T. Ritter drew water from the pump outside. Opalina built up the fire in the cookstove to heat the water, and she and Ceres washed the dishes that were sitting in the sink. Forest Ann fed the chickens for Nettie while I carried out the garbage pail for the pigs. When we'd finished what there was to do, Mrs. Judd took charge and shooed out most of the Persian Pickles. She told Forest Ann to go home and rest, since she and Nettie would be taking turns sitting up with Tyrone. Velma, too, "if she got home," Mrs. Judd said, then corrected herself—"when she gets home." The rest of us sighed with relief, since we didn't want to tend Tyrone in a sickroom.

"Queenie, you and Rita stay till Forest Ann gets back. You're young, and you'll cheer Nettie," Mrs. Judd said, taking Ella's arm and steering her out the door.

Rita and I sat in the kitchen for a long time, making small talk, until Tyrone at last went to sleep and Nettie came out of the parlor, fanning herself with her hand. Tyrone couldn't have looked any worse than Nettie did.

"I'm taking you out on the porch to cool off," I said, putting my hand in Nettie's. I led her outside, being careful not to let the screen door bang and wake up Tyrone. Nettie and Rita sat down on the glider while I found a place on the top step of the porch. For a few minutes, we sat there, listening to the friendly squeak of the glider as we moved back and forth.

Tyrone made a noise, and Nettie rose and went to the door and listened, but it was just a sound in his sleep, so she sat down again and put her head in her hands.

"You've had your share of troubles, Nettie," I told her.

"Oh, you don't know the half of it, Queenie," she replied. Nettie might have said something more, but Rita put her hand on Nettie's arm to show she cared, and Nettie looked up in surprise, as if she'd forgotten Rita was there. Instead of continuing, Nettie squeezed Rita's hand and said, "I wonder where Forest Ann's got to." She didn't mention Velma.

"Forest Ann's resting. She went home for a while. Rita and I will stay until she gets here. I expect she'll be along presently," I said, getting up. I stood behind Nettie and rubbed her shoulders to soften the ache I knew was there, and to comfort her. We stayed like that for a long time, just listening to Kansas night sounds, which have their own way of giving comfort. Even I didn't feel the need for talking.

Finally, Forest Ann drove up, apologizing for being so late. She'd lain down to rest for a few minutes and had fallen fast asleep. When Nettie told her Tyrone was sleeping, Forest Ann wasn't in any hurry to go inside, and she leaned on the porch post while we said our good-byes to Nettie. Then Forest Ann walked Rita and me to the car and held the door open while I got in. She shut my door, and I rolled down the window to say the Massie boy would be over in the morning to do the milking and to help with chores. In their own way, the Massies liked to be neighborly, I explained, not telling her that Grover and I were paying Sonny five cents a day to help Nettie.

It was well after ten o'clock and as black as the inside of a barn when Rita and I left the Burgetts'. I told Rita I sure was glad for the fellow who invented headlights.

chapter 8

"It sure is dark," Rita said as I turned onto the section road. "Are you sure you've got your brights on?" She shivered a little and asked me to roll up the window part way.

I switched the headlights to dim and back to bright again. There was no moon, and we couldn't see the stars because of the clouds—not rain clouds, just those empties Grover talked about. The black Kansas night might bother a city person like Rita, who liked streetlamps and neon signs, but I was a country girl, so the dark was a friend to me.

I yawned. "It'll be eleven o'clock before we get home. What will Grover say?"

Rita turned on the radio and moved the dial around until she found a Kansas City station playing "Paper Moon." She put her head on the back of the seat and hummed along with it, then laughed. "If I live here for the rest of my life, God forbid, I'll never get used to going to bed with the chickens. Tom and I always stayed up until two or three on Friday and Saturday nights, and slept till noon the next day. Of course, with my job, we never got to sleep before midnight even during the week. If Dad knew how late we stayed up, he'd call us slothful. You know, he's even against playing cards. Imagine!"

"Most people around here are—cards and dancing. Grover's dad said it was just an excuse for a boy to hold a girl in his arms."

"Well, he's right about that." We both giggled.

I stopped and looked both ways when we reached the cross-roads, although I knew there wasn't a car within five miles of us. The people who'd gone to see the picture show at the Home & Feed had been in bed for hours, and I'd be surprised if we passed a single car all the way home. As I turned onto the highway, I finished rolling up my window, thinking I was glad for the chill in the air. I wouldn't miss this summer.

All of a sudden, Rita screamed, "My God! Look out, Queenie!"

I slammed on the brakes and skidded across the dirt, stopping no more than a yard in front of something big and black that was lying across the road. If Rita hadn't spotted it in time, we'd have run into it for sure, wrecking the car. This was indeed a time for troubles, and I shuddered when I thought of Rita and me lying there on the road, dead, with Grover at home waiting for me.

"Damn it!" Rita said. "That was close. What the hell is that?"

"Darned if I know!"

We got out of the car together and walked to a log as big as a telephone pole that was lying crossways in the road. "It must have fallen off a truck," Rita said.

I shook my head back and forth, getting madder with each shake as I thought how dangerous that log was. "Anybody who lost a load like that would have felt it roll off his truck. He should have stopped and moved it. Why, we could have been killed, Rita. Grover will find out who did it, and boy, will he be sorry!"

I leaned over to see if I could heft one end of the log and was about to ask Rita if she would pick up the other when she said under her breath, "Something's not right here. Quick, Queenie. Get back in the car."

I straightened up to ask her what the hurry was, and just as I did so, a man loomed up out of the ditch next to us. I opened my mouth to ask for his aid, but before I could utter a word, I knew he wasn't there to help us. That log hadn't fallen off a truck by accident.

"Rita . . ." I said. She'd dashed for the car but stopped when she heard me call. When she turned and saw the big shape in the dark, she froze. Rita hadn't actually seen the man until that moment. She'd just had a creepy feeling something was wrong.

I willed myself to run to the car, but my feet wouldn't move. As if to make up for it, the rest of my body shook, a little at first, then harder as I watched the man come toward me, real deliberate, like he was walking in slow motion in the movies. He stopped just as he reached the headlight.

I could smell him as much as I could see him, a moldy smell, like rotted manure, and his breath was as foul as old onions. I didn't smell any liquor, however, and even then, I thought it was odd that I'd notice such a thing. My mind was working even though my body wasn't.

He took a step closer, moving across the beam of the headlight, and I saw he was big, almost as big as Grover, with mean eyes and fat lips.

For a few seconds, I tried to convince myself he'd come to help, but Rita knew better. "Get away, you," she said. He waved a hand at her, the way a person does at a snapping little dog.

"Gimme your keys. Right now," he ordered me. He didn't act as if he'd been drinking, which scared me more than ever, because I'd rather humor a drunk than match wits with a sober man.

"Go to hell!" Rita said. "You go to fucking hell." I'd never heard anybody say that word, but if it worked, I'd use it myself.

"Shut up, you," he snarled at Rita. He was still looking at me, however.

"I don't have any keys," I whispered. What I meant was, I'd left the keys in the car.

The man took a step toward me and grabbed my hand, prying open my fingers to see if I was lying. The touch of his rough skin against mine felt worse than his fingernails digging into my palm.

"They're in the car," I said. My voice worked about as well as my feet. "The keys, I mean. I left them in the car."

126

The man didn't seem to be in such a rush now. With an ugly smile, he looked at Rita, then back at me. He held tightly to my hand, held it still while the rest of me shook so hard, I thought I'd fall down if he let go.

"Two women. Out here alone in a nice big car. Well now." His eyes gleamed in the car lights.

I glanced at Rita, who opened her mouth to speak but licked her lips instead. I was grateful she kept silent, because cursing him hadn't done any good.

"Our husbands are expecting us. They'll be here any minute," I said. "They're following us."

"I guess I don't see no automobile lights coming." His short laugh was like a coyote's bark.

I thought if I moved real slow, I might be able to pull my hand away, but when I tried, he gripped my wrist so hard that my hand went numb.

"You can have the car. It has a radio. Grover put it in," I said. "He's a real fighter. You better get going before he comes, because he'll beat you up."

By now, I didn't care if the man drove off and I never saw the Studebaker again. All I wanted was for him to take his dry, hard hand off my wrist and leave us, but he just held on to me.

"You got nice brown hair. I like that. I never was so partial to yellow-headed women," he said. He reached up with his free hand and stroked my hair. His touch felt like a hot iron pressed against my skull, and I yanked my head away. He slapped me across the face with the back of his hand, then hit me again with his palm.

"No!" Rita said. "Don't you hurt her!"

"Behave! Both of you!" he growled, rubbing his scaly fingers over my wrist. He made a fist with his free hand and shook it at Rita.

She watched him with hard little eyes. Suddenly, she yanked off her shoe and flew toward him, hitting his arm with the sharp heel. "You son of a bitch! Let her go!"

Her blows didn't hurt him any more than a horsefly bite. Still holding onto my wrist, the man slapped Rita, knocking her down in the road. "You stay there, blondie, unless you want a good kick," he ordered. I looked at his thick laced boots and hoped Rita would do what he said.

He turned back to me. "Okay, girlie, me and you are going for a ride now. Maybe we'll have us some fun."

Until that moment, I hadn't even thought about the man taking me with him. Now my stomach churned so hard, I was afraid I would throw up. "Oh no, please," I begged. "You can have the car. I won't tell anybody. My purse is in there. You can have it, too. There's four dollars in it. Take it. I won't tell anybody. Not even Grover. I promise."

The man didn't reply. Instead, he moved right up next to me and rubbed his stubbly face against mine. His whiskers raked across my skin, and as he turned his mouth toward me, I felt something cold. It was drool.

He pulled away and looked at me again, licking the wet out of the corner of his mouth. Then he yanked me toward the car door. I tried to reach up so I could scratch him with my free hand, but he batted it away. "I told you, behave!" he said, stopping to look me up and down again. All of a sudden, he reached over and squeezed my breast, wringing it so hard that I cried out from the pain. I prayed for Grover to come and save me or for God to kill me before he did what I knew he would do. Rita had moved to a crouch and was ready to spring at him, but he raised his foot at her and said, "You move and I'll hurt your friend bad."

"Don't," I whimpered to him. My teeth chattered.

Now he was angry. "What's the matter, girlie? Ain't I good enough for you? You rich ladies think you're better 'n me." He put his hand on the neck of my dress and ripped it all the way down to my waist. The tear made a sound like fingernails on glass, and it was so loud, my ears ached, so loud that surely Grover must have heard it. The man put his hand on my throat and moved it down over my body. "You're real soft. You be nice to me, and I'll be nice to you. Me and you's going to have us a real good time."

I began to sob, not just because I knew what he would do but because at that instant, I saw the shape of a second man coming out of the darkness. He would grab Rita. There was no hope that Rita and I would get away from two men. Both of us would be raped. I turned the ugly word over in my mind and felt it stick in my throat. "Please," I cried. "Oh, please. If you need money—"

"You'ns need help?" the shape in the dark asked softly. His voice was so quiet that the man holding me didn't even hear him.

"I asked if you'ns need help," he said a little louder.

The man dropped my wrist as if it were a hot stove lifter and spun around. My legs gave out, and I fell into the dirt next to Rita. As I sprawled there, relief spread over me as surely as if I'd been covered up with a soft quilt. "It's all right," I whispered to Rita, whose face was as white as flour. "It's Blue. Blue Massie." Rita grabbed my hand, the one the man had held, and I winced, but I held on to her.

"Mind your business!" the man snarled at Blue, flicking his hand at him to make him go away.

"By dogies, I reckon this here is my business," Blue replied in the same gentle voice. He talked as quietly as a person making mail-time conversation at the post office.

The man laughed at Blue, sizing him up. He must have thought because Blue was a head shorter and slight of build that he'd be as easy to overpower as Rita and I were. But Blue was wiry and strong. He was a dirty fighter, the way the hill people are. The man swung, but before he could land a single punch, Blue slammed him in the face with his fist, making a sound like a sledgehammer on a hog's head at slaughter time. There was the crackle of bone breaking. The man howled with pain and took a step backward.

Blue wasn't finished with him. When the man put his hands to his face, Blue kicked him in the groin. Blue was barefoot, but his foot was as hard as walnut, and the man doubled over. He dropped his hands to the front of his pants, and I saw the blood gush out of his nose. He turned to run, and Blue kicked him in the small of his back. The man made a *whoomp* sound and limped off into the dark. Blue let him go, and I was glad. I didn't ever want to see him again.

Blue watched, making sure he was gone for good, before he turned to me, his breath coming as easy as if he'd been out for a walk. "You all right, missus?"

"Oh, Blue, I prayed somebody would help us." I began to cry again and reached into my pocket for a handkerchief. I realized then that my dress was ripped open, so I clutched it closed. Blue looked away.

"Where did you come from?" Rita asked. Her voice was high and shaky, and she cleared her throat.

Blue took off his cap and held it in his hands, then squatted down next to us, sitting on his haunches. "Well, I tell you. Zepha, she's been itchy all day. She didn't know what it was, but she knowed it had something to do with you, missus. She tried to conjure it away, but it wouldn't go, so she knowed it was powerful. We was already in bed when she says go look over the Bean place. I didn't see nothing at the house, so I went down the edge of the field and chanced to see the lights of your car."

"My God, what if you hadn't come along!" Rita said.

"No such a thing." Blue chuckled softly. "I'd a come directly. Zepha knows her signs real good, that one."

I got up slowly, clutching my ripped dress with one hand and holding on to the car with the other. My wrist ached from where the man had held it, and my fingers tingled. My face hurt from the slaps, and where he'd touched it, my breast felt raw. Blue helped Rita up. She'd torn her dress when she fell down, and her hose were ripped. Her shoe was still in her hand, but it took too much effort to put it on. So she carried it. We held on to each other as we went to the car, because I don't think either of us could have stood alone.

"Thank you, Blue," Rita whispered.

Blue nodded, shifting from one foot to the other, not sure

what to do. "I'll move that log outta the road. Then I'll be gettin' on."

"No!" Rita and I cried together.

"What if he comes back?" Rita asked.

Blue shook his head. "No cause to worry. That one ain't going to bother nobody for a long time."

"I can't drive, Blue. My hands are shaking too much," I said. "Will you drive us to the Ritters'? I'll call Grover and he'll come and get me."

Before Blue ducked his head, I saw he was pleased to be asked. He maneuvered the log into the ditch. Then the three of us got into the front seat of the car, with me in the middle. Rita locked all the doors and moved in close against me. Tears ran down her face as we drove to the Ritter farm, and every now and then she let out a little hiccup.

When Blue pulled up by the back door, Tom heard the motor and rushed outside. He had just phoned Nettie to ask when we'd be home, and she'd told him we'd been gone for nearly an hour. Tom was wondering whether to call Grover. Then we drove up. When he saw Blue in the driver's seat, Tom jumped the porch rail, landing next to the car.

"What happened?" he asked.

"The women's all right, but they's sure had a scare," Blue said, getting out of the car.

Tom yanked opened the passenger door, and Rita fell into his arms. Tom picked her up and started for the house, then remembered me. "Queenie?"

"Help me, Tom," I whispered. I slid out of the car and clutched his arm with both my hands. I couldn't have walked to the house without him.

We had reached the porch steps before I remembered Blue and turned back to the car. He was not there. "Blue!" I called, but there was no answer in the darkness. Blue Massie was gone.

❧

Tom phoned Grover and asked him to come and get me, telling him I'd had car trouble. He said that so Grover wouldn't be alarmed, but he also didn't want people to know what had happened. A call that late at night got everybody out of bed to find out what was going on, and most of them had been listening in earlier when Tom called Nettie to ask where we were. Even if folks didn't know about the man on the road, Rita and I were going to be the talk of Harveyville for staying out so late.

After he hung up, Mrs. Ritter, who'd heard the commotion, came down the stairs to the kitchen, where we were waiting for Grover.

"My stars!" she said when she saw Rita and me sitting at the table, holding on to each other. Reaching across the oilcloth, Mrs. Ritter took the shoe out of Rita's hand and dropped it on the floor. She removed a sweater from a hook by the back door and handed it to me so that I could cover my ripped dress. Mrs. Ritter rubbed her eyes on the sleeve of her bathrobe before she stirred up the fire in the cookstove and put on water for tea. Then she bustled around the kitchen, setting out bread and a dish of butter. When there's trouble, women just naturally think of food, although there was no need for it this time. My throat was so tight, I couldn't eat a bite, and the way she kept swallowing, I knew Rita couldn't, either. By the time Mrs. Ritter sat down at the table with us, Grover was at the door.

The minute I saw Grover, I was embarrassed, and turned away from him, refusing to look him in the eye. I was glad the sweater covered up my torn dress, because I was so ashamed.

"Some man out on the road stopped them—" Tom started to explain. Rita and I had told Tom only a little of what had happened to us.

Grover put up his hand, and Tom stopped. "Are you all right, Queenie?" Grover asked. I nodded, my eyes on my lap, where my hands twitched, just as Ella's had earlier that day.

"Look at me, Queenie," Grover said softly. I raised my head as slowly as I could, glancing at him, then turning to the stove, where the teakettle was boiling. I couldn't stand to look at Grover while he studied me. He said a cussword when he saw my swollen face. I knew he'd already taken in my ripped dress

132

and the scratches on my legs. I waited for him to speak, hoping he wouldn't be cross with me for driving so late at night. Even though I could not have left Nettie's any earlier, I laid the blame for what had happened upon myself. After what Rita and I had been through, however, I couldn't stand to have Grover fuss at me.

"Queenie, are you sure you're all right?" Grover asked again.

"Yes," I said in a squeaky voice. "He didn't . . . He didn't have time . . ."

"Oh Jesus!" Grover said with what sounded like a sob, and grabbed me out of my chair. He hugged me so hard, I could barely breathe. Then he sat down and pulled me onto his lap, and I looked up at him. There were tears in his eyes. I'd never seen Grover cry, even when I lost the baby. "Are you sure he . . ." Grover swallowed hard and didn't finish, but I knew what he was asking.

"No. Blue stopped him," I said.

"Wait a minute. I forgot about him. Was that hired man in on this?" Tom asked.

"Oh, no," I said quickly. "Blue saved us. If he hadn't come along then . . . Isn't that right, Rita?"

Rita didn't answer. Instead, she put her head down on the kitchen table and began to cry. Tom patted her back, and Rita sat up and threw her arms around him. "I hate this stinking place, Tom. I hate it. I'll never feel safe here again after this ugly thing. I swear to God, Tom, I'd sell my soul to get off this damn farm."

I glanced at Mrs. Ritter, but there was nothing in her face except sympathy. She got up from her chair and filled the teapot with boiling water, let it steep, and poured the tea into four cups, which she set on the table. Then she hugged Rita and me and patted Tom's arm. "I'll let you young folks be alone. There's no need to tell Dad or Agnes till morning."

I waited until I heard the bedroom door close. Then I started at the beginning, telling Tom and Grover everything that had happened.

When I finished, Grover hit the table with his fist. "That son of a bitch. When I catch him, I swear I'll pull out his nuts with pliers!"

"Save one of them for me!" Tom told him.

Rita hadn't said a word since Mrs. Ritter went to bed. She'd just sat there, stirring her tea with her finger, Tom's arm still around her. "Honey, are you okay?" he asked.

Rita didn't answer or even nod. She licked her fingertip, and suddenly, she turned to me. "Was that Skillet? That man, was he Skillet?"

"Skillet?" Tom asked. "Who's Skillet?"

"Ben Crook's old hired man," Grover explained, a puzzled look on his face. "He hasn't been around in a year. Maybe more. Was it him, Queenie?"

"No. It wasn't Skillet," I said. "I'd have known Skillet. It was a tramp."

"Are you sure?" Rita asked.

"I'm sure. Skillet had a face like a wedge of pumpkin pie. This man's face was round." I shuddered when I pictured him. "He had a lot of hair, too. Skillet was almost bald."

"What made you think it was Skillet?" Tom asked. He let go of Rita long enough to sip his tea; then he put his arm around her shoulder again.

"Because somebody is out to get me. Queenie and me," she replied. "I'm sure of it."

I sucked in my breath. "He wasn't anybody I ever saw. He was a drifter. How would he have known we were coming along?" Even with the sweater on, I began shivering again, thinking that man might have been waiting just for the two of us.

"I don't think so, Queenie," Rita said slowly. "I think it has to do with Ben Crook's murder. Somebody's trying to stop us from finding out who did it, and whoever he was, he knew we were at Nettie's tonight. Who wouldn't with that party line? So he waited for us. He meant to kill us."

"Honey, it was just a coincidence. He was a tramp," Tom

134

said, squeezing her and giving her a kiss on the side of her head.

"Maybe so, but it wouldn't hurt to mention it to the sheriff," Grover said.

I was shocked. "Oh, no, Grover. We can't tell. I don't want anybody to know about this!"

I still sat on Grover's lap, and he put his chin on top of my head. "Queenie, if we don't tell the sheriff, then the man who tried to hurt you will go after somebody else, and you wouldn't want that to happen, would you?"

"But I can't talk about this, Grover. I just can't," I said. "I want to go home now." I tried to stand up, but my legs wobbled. So Grover picked me up, and after Rita and I hugged each other, Grover carried me to the truck.

"What if Zepha hadn't had a presentiment?" I asked him as we drove home. "What if Blue hadn't come along?"

"You can't worry about what didn't happen," Grover said, drawing me next to him.

"Do you think that man was after Rita and me because of Ben Crook, or maybe for some other reason?"

"Naw," Grover said a little too fast. "It was just bad luck."

He stopped the truck next to the back door, and our dog came out to greet us, wagging his tail. "You know, Queenie, it wouldn't hurt if you let Old Bob keep you company around the house for a while."

In the morning, Grover drove Rita and Tom and me into Harveyville to report to Sheriff Eagles.

"Rita believes this attack might have something to do with her investigating Ben Crook's murder," Tom said after we told what had happened to us.

"I think he wanted to scare us off, keep us from solving the murder," Rita added. "Maybe even kill us."

The sheriff mulled that over. "I thought you said Queenie was the one who got pawed." Sheriff Eagles turned red and looked down at his hands, which were folded in front of him like a little church. He was behind his desk, while Rita and I were on the same straight chairs we'd sat in during Rita's interview the day before. Grover and Tom stood because there weren't any more chairs.

"What difference does that make? Maybe he didn't know which was Rita and which was Queenie," Tom said.

The sheriff shrugged and told Rita, "If you think this has something to do with Ben, maybe you ought to back off and leave finding criminals to the law. It ain't worth you getting killed over."

"No sir! He's not stopping me!" Rita said, leaning forward and looking at the sheriff with fire in her eye. "Queenie and I are going to solve this murder, no matter what. Nobody's going to threaten us!"

She turned to me to agree with her, but I shook my head no. "Not me, Rita. Not now. I don't care who killed Ben."

Rita was disappointed. Still, she wouldn't give up. "Well, it doesn't matter. If I have to do it all by myself, I will."

"What do you think, Sheriff?" Tom asked. "Does it sound to you like this has something to do with Ben? Maybe the man was that Skillet fellow, after all."

"Nope," the sheriff said. He turned over his hands to see all the people, inspecting his fingers before he took out his pocketknife and cut off a dried blister. "Queenie knows Skillet. Besides, I already got a pretty good idea who it was stopped you ladies out there on the road."

"Then for God's sakes, why don't you arrest him?" Tom asked. "If you don't, Grover and I'll find him."

"You do that. It'll save me the trouble." The sheriff's chair squeaked as he leaned back and looked up at Tom and Grover. "I didn't say I had his name and his address. I just know there's a man who did the same thing over in Osage County last week and in Leavenworth a week or two before that. I got a report about him. You girls are lucky that hired man of yours came along when he did."

The sheriff licked his lips, but before he could continue,

Grover interrupted. "There's no need to go into the details. This isn't *Gang Busters,* you know."

"I was just going to tell you he was over in Missouri before that," the sheriff finished. "He moves around a good bit, so I expect he's hightailed it out of Wabaunsee County by now."

Grover nodded. "Whoever he is, he won't be coming around here for a long time. After what Blue did to him, I doubt if he can stand up straight." I wondered if Grover said that for my sake or the sheriff's.

When Rita and I got up, the sheriff stood, too, and came out from behind his desk to shake our hands. "I sure am sorry about this, ladies. A man's got no right . . ." He blushed and turned away. "If you catch sight of him again, you let me know."

"If they see him again, we'll let you know where to pick up the pieces," Grover told him.

On the way home, Grover said he'd treat the four of us to Coney Islands and a moving-picture show in Topeka that night, but I still couldn't eat and said I didn't feel like going to the movies, even if it was *Top Hat.* Grover was being awful nice to me, because he didn't like pictures with singing and dancing, but he knew I did. Rita said she'd rather stay home, too. She told us she had work to do, and when she said it, her eyes were as hard and as mean as those of the man on the road.

༜

Word got around about what had happened to Rita and me, of course, and the members of the Persian Pickle Club stopped in at our place with their potato salads and burnt-sugar cakes, their prettiest scraps of material and words of concern. I felt better, knowing how much they cared. And I felt safer, sitting in the rocker with Old Bob at my side while they clucked about me like I was a chick and they were biddies.

They called on Rita, too, and said how glad they were that she was all right, and when she explained to them the man had been waiting on the road just for us, they shook their heads and told her to forget about Ben Crook. "No matter who killed Ben, dearie, catching him isn't worth you and Queenie getting hurt," Ceres said for all of them.

That didn't deter Rita. She kept on trying to solve the crime. Sometimes she talked about it as we sat and stitched in the afternoon. I quilted because it was the most comforting thing I knew to do. Rita sewed, too, not because it steadied her nerves but because it kept her from biting her fingernails. We went over and over what had happened. We couldn't discuss it with the other Pickles because they changed the subject, saying we ought to forget. But Rita and I couldn't forget, and talking about the man and what Blue had done to him, wondering if he was still in a sickbed or maybe crippled for life, made him smaller, less scary.

Rita was at my house the day Forest Ann called with a pan of divinity. She told us she'd just heard some good news and had rushed over to tell us. "I can't think of anything that will cheer you more, so I came directly here," she said, cutting the candy into big pieces and setting them on a plate. Rita took a piece and nibbled at it, while I bit into another. With my mouth full, I raised my eyebrows to Forest Ann to show how good it was.

Forest Ann nodded to accept the compliment. She took a piece herself but set it down so that she could talk. "Just wait until you hear what I have to say. With all the bad that's been happening lately, we've had us at least one blessing."

"Did the sheriff find that man?" I asked.

Forest Ann wiped a crumb of divinity off her mouth with the heel of her hand. "No, not that. This is really good news. Tyrone's feeling stouter each and every day. Doc informed Nettie and me not more than an hour ago that Tyrone doesn't have the polio, after all. Now isn't that something to be grateful for!" Forest Ann gave us such a smile of happiness that we had to smile right back at her, even though we hadn't been worrying much about Tyrone lately.

After she left, Rita set her half-eaten piece of divinity back on the plate. I'd eaten all of mine and already had heartburn.

"Grateful? Grateful because Nettie's husband doesn't have

138

polio?" Rita's voice was so shrill that Old Bob, who was lying in the shade by the porch steps, got up and trotted over to me.

"Just think, Queenie, we almost got killed because that bootlegger Tyrone Burgett had an attack of rheumatism!" Rita snickered. After I thought it over, I giggled. Then the two of us laughed so hard that my divinity came up, and I had to swallow it back down. I think that's when I began to feel better.

chapter
9

I wasn't like Rita. I couldn't go running all over the county talking to people the way she did—not after what had happened to us. I was ashamed to show my face.

So Tom borrowed the Ritters' car, and he drove her instead. I know she was disappointed in me, but the farm was the only place I felt safe, and I refused to leave it, even to be with my best friends. I called Forest Ann to say I wouldn't attend the Persian Pickle Club, which was at her house that day.

Mrs. Judd stopped by for me, anyway. I heard her turn off the motor of the Packard and coast to a stop by my back steps, and I went to the kitchen door to see who it was. Ella peered over the big dashboard and fluttered her hand at me.

Mrs. Judd was already halfway up the stairs when I reached the door. Each step creaked in turn as she put her weight on it. She stopped at the door, breathing hard, the sweat on her face making her warts shine like little steel tacks. "I didn't know if you were feeling up to driving to Pickle this afternoon. Ella and I came to fetch you," she said to me through the screen. Old Bob got up off the floor and peered out at her, then wagged his tail. He was good company, but he wasn't much of a watchdog.

"I'm not going today," I told her. "Thank you just the same."

"Yes you are," Mrs. Judd said as she yanked at the screen door. It didn't open because I'd begun putting the hook on when Grover wasn't in the house. "Thunderation! You're living like a crow in a cage. Open this door."

I wanted to tell her it was none of her business if I locked up my house. Instead, I said, "I have a headache. I'm not going."

"You've never had a headache in your life, Queenie Bean. Now unlatch this screen." Mrs. Judd folded back the veil on her hat and pushed up her sleeves, ready to yank the door off the hinges if I didn't mind her. So I reached up and lifted the hook, and Mrs. Judd stepped inside. She was still puffing, not just from the exertion of climbing the stairs but from the strain of looking after Ella the past weeks. Ella had gotten even more childlike, and I wondered if she might live with the Judds forever.

Mrs. Judd settled herself on a kitchen chair, intending to stay there until she'd spoken her mind. "Now, Queenie, I know you've had a hard time of it. I'm not saying you haven't. But there're others less fortunate than you. You don't know the half of it." She stopped a minute and frowned, as if she'd said too much.

"You can stay locked up here feeling sorry for yourself like Lizzy Olive would have done, or you can put the bad time behind you like Ella did and think about all the good things the Lord gave you. And He'll keep on giving them to you if you'll let Him. But how can you take advantage of His opportunities if you're sitting behind the kitchen door with the hook on?" Mrs. Judd took a breath and leaned forward, resting her forearms on her thighs.

"Here's another thing. Forest Ann's already set in the Celebrity Quilt, and we're going to start stitching on it this afternoon. You ought to be there, because we're all so excited about it that we might stay and finish it up by evening, and wouldn't that be a shame if you didn't get one stitch on it? So you go put on that orchid dress with the yellow rickrack that makes you look so sweet, and then we'll be on our way." Mrs. Judd shifted her weight, putting a strain on the chair, whose joints squeaked in protest. "You got any of Ceres's burnt-sugar cake left for us to sample? I'll get it out of the fridge myself. Ella needs something that'll stick to her bones." As she got up to rummage through my refrigerator, she called through the door, "Ella, sugar pie, Queenie wants you to come on in here for refreshments while we wait."

The Celebrity Quilt changed my mind about attending Persian Pickle. I felt more comfortable going now that someone else would take me, because I was afraid that if I got behind the wheel of the Studebaker, I'd shake too much to drive. So I changed my dress and brushed my hair, and by the time I was ready, Ella and Mrs. Judd were rinsing off their plates in the sink. Grover came out of the barn as I got into the Packard. When I told him I was going to club after all, he just nodded, as if he'd expected me to. He and Mrs. Judd might have cooked this up between them.

If they had, I was especially glad, since Rita was there ahead of me. I was surprised, because Rita didn't like Persian Pickle the way I did, and I'd already told her I wasn't going. So I thought she'd stay home, too.

She came skipping out of Forest Ann's house when she saw me and whispered, "I'd think driving with Mrs. Judd would be as scary as . . . you know. . . ." I laughed.

Nettie overheard and was shocked—not because we'd said something against Mrs. Judd's driving. We all made remarks about that. Nettie acted as if it was blasphemous for us to joke about what had happened to us. Of course, it would have been if our husbands had, or even the other Pickles. But the jokes were a bond between Rita and me, and making fun of that night helped us.

Rita drew me off to one side. "I had a look at the coroner's report," she whispered. "Doc Sipes wrote there wasn't a thing about Ben's body that proved he'd been murdered. For all he knew, Ben had fallen out of a tree and somebody'd put him in the ground to save the cost of a funeral. Now, why would he say a thing like that?"

I shook my head.

"Why would he unless somebody paid him to?" she asked.

"And who's the only one in Harveyville who has enough money to spend bribing a coroner?" Rita glanced in Mrs. Judd's direction.

Mrs. Judd saw us looking at her and called me to come inside to see the Celebrity Quilt, and in my excitement, I forgot about Doc Sipes and who might want to pay him to put lies in his report.

The Celebrity Quilt was beautiful. Over the summer, as the autographs had come in, we'd embroidered them in red, but we'd waited until fall to put the quilt together, just in case some of the famous people we'd written to had been on vacation and hadn't gotten their mail. Forest Ann and Mrs. Ritter assembled the embroidered squares into rows, setting off each one with borders of red cotton. Then they stitched the strips together into a quilt. Where the corners met, they added tiny red-and-white nine-patch squares. It was as fresh and as pretty a quilt as I'd ever seen. Forest Ann had set it into the wooden quilt frame in the middle of her dining room, the big oak pedestal table pushed into the corner.

I stood at the edge of the quilt and fingered Lew Ayres's autograph. Then I ran my hand over "Good Luck, Eleanor Roosevelt," thinking I'd never met a woman who could look at a piece of material without touching it. I bet even Eleanor Roosevelt had pinched that fabric between her thumb and forefinger before she wrote her name. I looked over the rows of famous names and felt pride that they were all part of a quilt in Harveyville, Kansas—a quilt that'd been my idea.

We stood impatiently, waiting for Forest Ann to assign us places around the quilt, which it was her privilege to do, since we were at her house. Ella was the best quilter, so of course she'd work on the center, where the stitches showed the most. I was surprised when Forest Ann didn't put her there. She asked Ella to sit on the side. Then she placed Rita next to Ella instead of at the lower end, where the poorest quilter usually sat. That was a nice thing to do, even though Rita didn't understand what a compliment it was.

Then Forest Ann said, "Queenie, would you sit here, please,

where you can work on the center." Everyone smiled and nodded.

"Ella ought to be there," I protested.

"No, the Celebrity Quilt was your idea. You deserve the
honor," she replied. "Besides, you're a fine quilter."

I blushed and sat down on one of Forest Ann's dining room
chairs. Now I knew why Mrs. Judd had made me come to Persian Pickle. She and Forest Ann had planned this ahead of time.
I looked up and saw Mrs. Judd smiling at me, and I felt so
lucky to have such good friends that tears came to my eyes. I
didn't want anyone to see, for fear they'd think I was crying
over that night, so I picked up my pocketbook and searched
for my thimble. Then I threaded my needle and took a stitch,
carefully pulling the knot through the quilt top to hide it, and
began to make tiny stitches around Edgar Bergen's autograph.

With all the sorrows we'd been through, we hadn't had a regular Persian Pickle in the longest time. The last one, in fact, had
been at Opalina's, the day that Hiawatha found Ben Crook's
bones. Of course, with all the troubles, we'd seen plenty of one
another, but I realized as I stitched how much I'd missed all of
us sitting down and working together. There was something
homey and comfortable about the way we bent over the quilt in
Forest Ann's parlor. I had Grover, and I had the Persian Pickle.
Some made do with a lot less.

"This sure is a pretty quilt," Mrs. Ritter said. "Don't you think
so, Rita."

Rita muttered, "Uh-huh."

"Are you going to write another newspaper story about it?"
Mrs. Judd asked. Rita's first story about the Celebrity Quilt had
been only a paragraph, and it hadn't included any of our
names.

Rita shrugged without looking up. "I'm pretty busy right
now." She yanked at her needle, and the thread pulled out of it.
Rita licked the end of the thread, flattened it between her
thumb and finger, and pushed it back through the eye of the
needle.

Mrs. Judd stopped stitching to watch Rita. "Tell me why people's so crazy to read about a murder? It seems to me they'd rather read about what a body's doing for those less fortunate." Mrs. Judd looked over at Ella, who didn't seem to be paying attention. Sometimes I wondered if Ella heard one single thing we said anymore. Her mind had always wandered, but since Ben's funeral, she seemed more than ever to be living in some place that was far off from Harveyville.

Rita looked up and gave Mrs. Judd a smug smile, as if she knew a secret she wasn't telling. "Really?"

"It would be awful nice if they ran a picture," Opalina said.

"Of us?" Ada June asked.

"Of the quilt, of course," Opalina said, but Ada June and I exchanged glances. We both knew Opalina meant of us. I thought it would be awful nice, too.

"Maybe I'll write about the quilt later on," Rita said. "Right now, I can't let Queenie down. After what happened to us, I gave her my word that I'd solve . . . Mr. Crook's . . . you know . . ." She glanced at Ella and didn't finish. I put my needle down, wondering if I should protest. She'd never given me her word she'd find Ben Crook's killer for my sake. Nor did I ask her to promise any such thing, but I realized the club members knew that. So I kept my mouth shut.

Ceres took a couple of backstitches and bit off her thread with her teeth, then reached for her spool. "If you ask me, it was just your bad luck you getting stopped like you did. There wasn't anybody after the two of you. The man who did it was only a bum passing through," she said. "I meant to tell you, Cheed said that he heard a car got stopped over to Emporia last evening because of a stump in the middle of the road."

Rita and I looked at each other, and Opalina asked, "What happened?"

"Nothing. Two big men got out of the car and moved the stump."

Opalina cast a sidelong glance at Ceres, waiting for her to continue. When she didn't, Opalina said, "I don't get it. If nothing happened, what does that prove?"

"Why, that's the point of it, dearie. That stump didn't just

145

sprout by itself. Whoever's doing this doesn't have any idea who'll be coming along. It was an accident that two men were in the car last evening—just like it was an accident that Queenie and Rita were the ones who were stopped here. When that robber saw grown men get out of the car, he stayed hid. There's your proof."

"What I think—" Agnes T. Ritter said, but Mrs. Ritter had been watching Rita, who was getting fidgety as she listened to Ceres and Opalina. So she interrupted Agnes T. Ritter.

"I've been wondering. How many raffle tickets do you think we're going to sell on this quilt?" Mrs. Ritter asked.

Agnes T. Ritter was annoyed because she hadn't been allowed to tell us what she thought, and she opened her mouth to try again. But I didn't care what she had to say. Besides, like Rita, I didn't want to hear any more about the men in Emporia. So I piped up, "I'm going to ask Grover to sell the farm and buy all of the chances. That way, I'll win the quilt."

"My stars! To think a farm in Harveyville is worth that much," Mrs. Ritter said.

We talked about the price we'd charge for the tickets and how many we'd print and who would buy them, and before we knew it, Forest Ann called, "Ready to roll?"

"Ready," I said.

"Just hold your horses," Mrs. Judd told us. She'd tangled her thread and had to break it off. Then she cut a new length, put it through her needle, and took hurried stitches. As the rest of us completed our sections, we stood up and stretched and admired one another's stitching. We were making good time.

At last, Mrs. Judd snipped off her thread and said, "Ready to roll."

We stood back and watched while Forest Ann and Agnes T. Ritter rolled the part of the quilt we'd just stitched over the top of the frame, unrolling an unquilted section from the bottom at the same time.

While they did that, Ada June came over to me and put her arm around my waist. "I'm glad you came, Queenie. That's my

146

favorite dress of yours," she said. I thanked her, and she whispered, "Aren't you glad Mrs. Judd forgot about reading?"

"Oh, boy, am I!" I whispered back, although I wasn't so sure Mrs. Judd had forgotten. We all felt the need to visit.

As we took our places again, I saw Forest Ann pat Nettie's arm. Nettie moved her neck as much as she could to smile up at her sister-in-law. Then her mouth trembled, and I wondered if Tyrone's rheumatism was acting up again. I hoped not. I'd rather slop pigs than have to sit through another evening of tending Tyrone Burgett in a sickbed. Nettie looked worn out, and I thought that with all her worries, she'd been an especially good friend, calling on me with a molasses pie and some of her fruitcake after what had happened to me.

"I hope those pregnant girls appreciate all the work we're doing on this quilt," Agnes T. Ritter said after we'd gone back to stitching.

"Agnes! For goodness sakes!" Mrs. Ritter looked at Agnes T. Ritter and shook her head.

"I'm just saying we went to a whole lot of work, and for all we know, it's for a bunch of tarts. That's who stays in those homes, you know. Girls with no moral sense!" She pressed her skinny lips together.

Nettie drew in her breath so sharply that we all looked up at her.

"Well, maybe not every one, but I'll bet you most of them are. You can like it or lump it. I'm just saying what I think, which is girls who get in the family way when they're not married are no more than trash." Agnes T. Ritter sure was in a bad mood that day.

Mrs. Ritter reached across the quilt and touched her arm. "Agnes, that's enough. We're not here to pass judgment."

Agnes T. Ritter put her pointy nose in the air, but she shut up.

Nettie turned her face away, but not before we saw the tears running down it. She tried to get up, but her chair was wedged in between Ella's and Opalina's, and she couldn't move. So she put her hands over her face and began to sob, the tears running down her nose and dripping on the autograph of Bebe Daniels.

Forest Ann got up and stood behind Nettie, her arms around her. "It's all right, honey. Everything's going to be all right." Forest Ann sniffed back a few tears of her own. "Nettie's just concerned about Tyrone," she told us.

But we knew Tyrone wasn't the cause of Nettie's tears. One by one, as we remembered what had set Nettie off, we put our needles down and looked at Nettie with sympathy. No, it wasn't Tyrone. Except for Ella, who never did understand what was going on, Agnes T. Ritter was the last one to get it, and when she did, she sucked in her breath and said, "Velma's . . . Velma's . . . Oh, I didn't . . . Oh my God!"

"Be still," Mrs. Judd told her quietly. "Ella, sweetheart, do you have my scissors?"

"Oh," Ella said, looking around her chair.

All of us searched about our places for the scissors until Mrs. Judd held them up in the air and said, "Good heavens, they were right here in my workbasket all the time." Of course, she'd known they were. She wanted to give Nettie a chance to blow her nose and dry her eyes with a piece of toilet paper from her pocket. By the time we turned to Nettie again, she'd stopped crying, but her eyes were red and her face was blotchy. The scarf had slipped off her neck, and her goiter quivered like a piglet. Forest Ann, who was still standing in back of Nettie's chair, tucked the scarf into Nettie's collar.

"I guess you could say Velma's one of the less fortunates," Nettie said at last, giving a short, bitter laugh.

"It's her business," Mrs. Ritter said, taking three or four stitches in the quilt and pulling the thread through. "It's not ours."

"It'll be everybody's business before long," Forest Ann said.

Mrs. Judd picked up her needle and took a stitch, and the rest of us followed. Then Rita piped up. "We used to say in college that the first baby can come anytime. After that, it takes nine months." Rita failed to notice that the rest of us didn't think it was funny. "When's Velma getting married?"

Nettie sent her a quick look. "She's not."

"Oh!" Agnes T. Ritter said. "Oh, heavens!"

"He's a married man, if you must know," Nettie said, and began crying again.

We all made little murmurs of sympathy until Mrs. Judd cleared her throat. "What does Tyrone say?"

"He doesn't know. Velma's afraid to tell him. I'm afraid to tell him, too, if you want to know the truth," Nettie said. "You know how much he sets store by how a person keeps the commandments." She looked around the circle at each one of us— as if under these circumstances we'd point out that Tyrone Burgett's standards were always for the other fellow! As far as I knew, Tyrone didn't personally keep any of the commandments, apart from not working on the Sabbath.

"Nettie and Velma don't want to disappoint Tyrone. He'd be so hurt," Forest Ann put in. We all knew that wasn't it. They were afraid Tyrone would throw Velma out of the house, and maybe Nettie with her.

"Sometimes these young girls have accidents," Opalina said. We all knew exactly what Opalina meant, and I shuddered.

"No," Forest Ann said quietly. "I asked Doc Sipes. Velma's too far along. It would likely kill her."

I looked down at the quilt and saw how crooked my last few stitches were, and I pulled them out.

"I guess it's up to us to figure out what's to become of Velma," Mrs. Judd said. She was right. The others knew it and stopped talking to concentrate on sewing. We were women who turned to our needles when there were problems to be dealt with.

"If she needs a place to stay, she can always live with Cheed and me," Ceres said. "We'd welcome a young person—and a baby."

Nettie shook her head. "That wouldn't work because Tyrone would find out about it, and he'd give you 'Hail, Columbia' along with Velma and me. But thank you just the same, Ceres." Nettie put her needle aside and said in a voice filled with shame, "Besides, Velma doesn't want to keep the baby."

"Oh," I said, wondering why women like Velma and Rita, who didn't want children, got pregnant, while God denied me a baby even though I wanted one more than anything in the world. He even gave five at one time to that Dionne family in Canada. Was that fair? Maybe things like that happened because God was a man and didn't understand. I wanted to ask the others what they thought, but I was afraid Nettie would call me blasphemous.

Nettie glanced at me and continued. "I'm not saying Velma's wrong about that, but it would break my heart knowing there's a tiny baby out there someplace who's Velma's flesh and blood, and mine, too, and it's living in an orphan home with nobody to love it. The baby will end up in one of those places, just like corn in a crib, if Velma doesn't keep it, since nobody in times like these can afford to take in an extra mouth to feed. It's not right to leave a baby to be brought up an orphan." Nettie poked her needle into the quilt and took a single stitch. "Velma'll have to stay here in Harveyville to have the baby. We don't even have the money to send her to a home. They charge something, you know."

"We could all help out," Opalina said. "We could raise the money ourselves."

"We're women. All we have is egg money. If we ask our husbands, well, we'll have to tell them why, and then everybody will know," Ada June said.

That was true. Agnes T. Ritter began to say something but stopped before Mrs. Ritter could interrupt her. The rest of us thought hard but couldn't come up with any suggestions. Finally, when it seemed like there was no answer at all, Mrs. Judd spoke up, and it occurred to me that she'd had a plan all along. "I know one person who could pay, that is if he doesn't spend all his money trying to corner the market on this quilt," Mrs. Judd said.

I looked up quickly because it sounded like she meant Grover. He and I were better off than most. That was true. But we didn't have money to throw away, and if we had, Grover wouldn't give it to Tyrone Burgett's daughter. Mrs. Judd was staring at me, and I stared right back while the others looked from her to me. Then I had a terrible thought, and before I could stop myself, I blurted out, "Are you saying Grover's the father? Are you accusing Grover of committing adultery?" I heard one of the Pickles suck in her breath, but I didn't look because I wouldn't take my eyes off Mrs. Judd.

"Oh, no such thing!" Mrs. Judd said quickly. "Don't get your dander up, Queenie. I know well enough who Velma took up with, and so do you, I expect. What I'm saying is this: Velma's going to have a baby she doesn't want, and you want a baby you don't have. Now we can use one problem to solve the other. If Grover's willing to pay for Velma's keep in Kansas City, I'd guess she'd let you keep the baby. Isn't that about right, Nettie?"

"Well, I . . ."

"Oh course she would. It's a fact," Mrs. Judd told her.

My hand holding the needle began to shake. I'd been doing a lot of shaking lately, but this time it wasn't from fear. I tried to stop it with my other hand, but I jammed myself so hard with the needle that a drop of blood ran out onto the autograph of Mae West. I didn't feel the prick because what Mrs. Judd had said was running around inside my mind like a chicken without its head, and there wasn't room in there to think of anything else. I knew the club members had stopped talking and were staring at me, but I couldn't make their faces come into focus.

"What if Velma wanted it back?" I asked at last.

"She doesn't. I already asked her," Mrs. Judd said. "You and Grover'd have to adopt it legal, of course. If Velma ever did want it back, she'd have no way to prove it was hers. Still, she won't. She's got no way to support it, and the father won't have anything to do with it—or her, either, after she told him about the baby. Why, he said it wasn't even his. Besides, you know Velma. She's wanted to get out of Harveyville since the day she was born. She says after the baby comes, she'll stay on in Kansas City or move to Chicago or Omaha, anywhere that isn't Harveyville, Kansas."

"Harveyville's not so bad," Opalina said.

"That's beside the point," Mrs. Judd told her, glancing at Opalina just long enough to let her know she thought Opalina was crazy. Opalina ducked her head and returned to her stitching. Everyone else turned to me.

"I don't know if Grover would raise a foundling," I said.

"Velma's baby's not a foundling!" Forest Ann spoke up. "It's not a pig in a poke, where you don't know if it's got an inherited disease or foreign blood. Grover'll know it came from an American, Christian family."

Grover would also know that it came from Tyrone Burgett's family, because I wouldn't deceive him. Grover had no use at all for Tyrone, and he didn't approve of Velma, either, not after she'd gone to town. Still, he knew she'd been a nice girl once. Would Grover blame a baby for its mother? I didn't know.

The baby's parents weren't the only problem. There was another question, and that was, Would Grover want to raise anybody else's baby at all? We'd never talked about adopting. After Dr. Sipes told me I'd never get pregnant again, babies were a subject neither one of us ever brought up.

"Well?" Mrs. Judd asked me. All the Pickles were waiting for a reply.

I looked at her, then at Nettie, and back at Mrs. Judd. "I could ask him," I said slowly. "I'd have to tell him the truth. It wouldn't be right not to."

"Grover Bean'll do anything you say. If you ask him, it's as good as done," Mrs. Judd said. "I guess this settles it."

Nettie quivered a little and reached up to pat Forest Ann's hand, which was on her shoulder. "I won't interfere, Queenie. I promise you that. It would be your baby. But could I come visit sometimes? Would that be all right?"

"Well, of course you could! All of you can," I said. "Even Velma could come and visit."

"Oh, she wouldn't," Nettie said quickly.

The others went back to quilting, but I was too excited to continue my sewing, even if I was stitching Mae West's name. I stuck my needle into the quilt top and leaned back in my chair, shutting my eyes to recall everything that had been said. The conversation had happened so quickly that it made me dizzy. In hardly more time than it took to sew a thread length, I'd gone from a barren woman to a mother—that is, if Grover approved. But Mrs. Judd was right about that. Grover wouldn't say no. When I opened my eyes, I saw my friends glancing up at me as they quilted, and smiling. I was going to have a baby!

"When it's time for her to show, Velma'll just say she got a job in Kansas City," Mrs. Judd said, and we all nodded. "It'll be our secret, of course. Except for Grover, we won't tell a soul."

"That's crazy!" Rita blurted out. "I never heard of anything so dumb. Nobody can keep a secret like that. Someone will let it slip, and in five minutes, the whole town will know."

"No," I said.

"I'm sorry, Queenie, but somebody's going to tell."

Mrs. Judd held her needle still and peered at Rita over her glasses. She looked down at the square in front of her and ran her hand over it before she said in a flat, even voice, "The rest of us can keep a secret. Were you planning on telling?"

"No, of course not." Rita looked uncomfortable.

Mrs. Judd shrugged. "Then that's that. There's nothing to worry about." She looked over the quilt and asked, "Ready to roll?"

We stood up and stretched, except for Rita, who stayed in her chair, shaking her head.

Persian Pickle lasted late because we stayed to finish the Celebrity Quilt, just as Mrs. Judd had predicted, even though I was in the worst hurry to get home and talk to Grover. But I'd come with Mrs. Judd, so I had to wait while we took the quilt out of the frame and held it up for everyone to admire, then turned it over to look for places we'd missed. At last, Opalina got out her Kodak and took views of all of us standing on the porch, holding the quilt.

After that, I hopped from one foot to the other, waiting for Mrs. Judd to leave, and even walked over to the Packard, hoping that would hurry her up.

The club members carried the quilt back into the house, but

Rita remained outside, leaning against Forest Ann's cistern, watching the women. She ought to have felt comfortable at Persian Pickle by now. We'd all made such an effort with her. But she still seemed to be apart from us, and I wondered if she'd ever really be a member. Rita motioned for me to come over to her.

"Queenie, you're nuts if you go along with this. I know the female sex," Rita said.

"Maybe you do, but I know these women, and they won't say anything. I trust them." I watched Mrs. Judd come down the steps with Nettie, whose legs were lumpy under her flesh-colored cotton stockings, and wondered if Velma's baby would have sawdust legs like that. The idea made me grin.

Rita thought I'd smiled because of what she'd said. "I don't know why you think that's funny. If you knew what I know, you wouldn't trust Mrs. Judd any farther than you could throw her." Now Rita smiled. "Farther than you can throw her. That's pretty funny, huh? I bet even Grover couldn't throw her more than a foot." I didn't answer. After all Mrs. Judd had just done for me, I wasn't about to make fun of her.

Rita pushed out her lower lip when I didn't reply, then tossed her head back, sending her buttery curls bouncing. "I've found out some pretty interesting things, and like I said, I don't trust the Judds at all. You won't either when you know what I do. It makes me mad just to think about it. I'll come around and tell you."

She wanted me to ask her what it was, but I didn't care to know. "Don't bother," I said. "But I wish you'd come around and help me make a baby quilt."

chapter
10

Rita came around to see me one afternoon the following week, but Ada June was visiting then, so Rita couldn't tell me what she'd discovered about the Judds. I knew she was still busy with her story, because Grover said Tom drove her to the county courthouse at Alma and even took her into Topeka, although for what, I didn't know. Once I glanced out the window as Rita walked down the road past our place, wearing her reporter's suit. On an impulse, I decided to offer to drive her into town, and I called out, but she didn't hear me. I didn't go after her because, after I thought it over, I wasn't so sure I wanted to drive into Harveyville. Even though Velma's baby wouldn't arrive for a long time, I was too busy making plans for it to help Rita read through dirty old record books or ask questions of people who didn't want to talk about Ben Crook. In fact, I hoped I'd never hear Ben's name again. We'd put his body in the ground. It was time to bury his memory, too.

Mrs. Judd had been right, of course, when she'd insisted Grover wouldn't say no to me about the baby. As excited as I was, I waited until the next day to ask him. I fixed spareribs with the last bottle of the sauerkraut Dad Bean had put up, and I mashed the potatoes as fine as whipped cream. After I served sour cream–raisin pie, I said, "Grover, there's something we have to talk about."

"I thought so. We don't have dinner like this every day."

155

"We have a chance to have a baby," I said in a rush, forgetting I was going to lead up to it. Before Grover could even open his mouth in surprise, I told him about Velma and the married man, the unwed mothers' home in Kansas City, and Mrs. Judd's idea. "I didn't tell her yes. I said you'd have to agree, because you'll be the baby's father."

I held my breath waiting for Grover to reply, but when he spoke, he asked for another piece of pie. I cut an extra-big slice and watched him while he ate it.

"I just wish it wasn't Tyrone Burgett's grandchild," Grover said, using the back of his fork to take up the piecrust crumbs. He licked them off. "Nettie's all right, and what's wrong with Velma isn't something she would pass on to a baby. Shoot, if it's a girl, it might be real pretty like her." He took up a last crumb with his finger and popped it into his mouth. "Say, you don't think it'll have a goiter like Nettie's, do you?"

I looked at Grover in astonishment, until he said, "That's a joke, Queenie."

"We ought to know something about the father." I scraped my pie crumbs into a little pile in the center of my plate, where I left them.

"Oh, I expect he's all right," Grover said, so quickly that I looked up at him. For all I could tell, Grover knew who the father was. But more important, it sounded to me as if he had made up his mind to take the baby and was trying to keep *me* from having doubts. "If it's a boy, we're not naming him Tyrone. That's for sure."

"Can we afford the baby?"

"Hell no!" Grover grinned. "We couldn't afford to have our own baby, either, but that didn't stop us from trying."

I blushed, then grinned back at him like a ninny. "Grover Bean, what are you saying?"

"Well, Mama, I'm saying we better get that old cradle out of the barn."

I got up and stood behind Grover, my arms around his neck, and kissed the tip of his ear. He pulled me down on his lap.

"You won't mind so much if the baby isn't ours, will you?" I asked.

"It'll be ours."

⁂

A few days later, Sonny stopped by. When I turned around from the sink, he was sitting at the kitchen table, smiling at me.

I'd never get used to the way the Massies slipped in and out of our place as quiet as foxes. Once, I'd dropped a whole apronful of eggs from the henhouse when I looked up and found Blue standing in my kitchen garden, next to the snap beans. He was as still as a beanpole, and I half-expected the runners of the vines to curl up his legs. When I saw Sonny that morning, I barely managed to keep hold of the butter I was taking out of the churn and putting into a glass dish.

"You want some buttermilk?" I asked after I set the butter dish in the refrigerator. I wiped my hands on a tea towel and threw it over my shoulder.

Sonny made a face. "Buttermilk makes me puke. Cookies don't." I knew that, but I always asked because his answer tickled me so.

I put half a dozen snickerdoodles on a plate and set them in front of Sonny, then picked up one myself and took a bite.

"Hey, that ain't yours. You give it to me," Sonny said, putting his arm around the plate, drawing it to him so I couldn't help myself.

I reached into the jar and dropped another cookie in front of him. Still, Sonny watched me suspiciously as he held on to the plate and gobbled up the snickerdoodles. When he was finished, he said, "Missus, Ma says, you'ns come down this evening." It wasn't an invitation as much as an order, and it made me smile. Sonny never thought we might have other plans.

"I'll have to ask Grover."

Sonny frowned. "He best say yes. Where's them toothpicks?" I got out the little glass holder and set it on the table. I never

157

knew what Sonny did with toothpicks. He always took as many as he could get away with, but I never saw him pick his teeth with one.

"What does your ma want?" I asked.

Sonny shrugged. "She just said if you'ns was to home, I was to tell you to come calling right after supper." He slid from his chair and disappeared out the door.

With the harvest over, there wasn't much work for Blue, and I figured the Massies wanted to ask us about staying on. I hoped they would, anyway. Now that the hired man's shack was fixed up, I was afraid that tramps would break in and light fires. But that wasn't the real reason I wanted Blue and Zepha in the place. The Massies were neighbors now. I liked having them there. Besides, I owed Blue, after the way he'd rescued Rita and me. I felt safer with him in the shack. It would suit me fine if the Massies lived with us forever.

The Massies had their own garden, and we gave them milk and eggs because we had plenty. With prices as low as they were, it hardly paid to truck the stuff to market. In exchange, Zepha made us liver pudding and ash cake, which were not favorites of Grover's and mine, but the chickens liked them.

Sometimes Grover caught Blue out mending fences or repairing equipment. He told Blue to keep track of his time so we could pay him, but Blue never did, and Grover didn't push him, since it was Blue's way of settling with us on the shack. The Massies didn't want to be beholden. Often, Grover wouldn't see Blue working. He'd just notice that the pedal on the grindstone had been fixed or the shovels sharpened, and he'd know that Blue had been around.

"Maybe they'll tell us they're ready to move on," Grover said as we drove through the dusk to the shack. I didn't like walking across the fields in the dark anymore, so we went on the road.

Even though Grover was with me, I reached over and locked the door. Then I shivered under my heavy sweater. I didn't much like being on the road after dark, either.

"Cold?" Grover asked.

"Yes." I think he knew without my telling him that I was scared every time I got into a car at night. "Where would the Massies go if they left here?"

"Dunno," Grover said. "I doubt that's why they asked us to come down, though. Blue's fixed the stove to throw out more heat, and he's patched the shack to keep the snow from drifting in. With those quilts Zepha hung on the walls to keep out the cold, they couldn't find a warmer place." Grover steered the Studebaker around a spot where the road had eroded.

"It's my guess they'll ask to stay. If they were to leave, they'd pick up and go without a word. That's the way the hill people are. We'd go down to the shack one day, and they wouldn't be there. Besides, if they were going to leave, they'd have done it by now, gone someplace where there's still a harvest. With what Zepha's put up from the garden in those jars you gave her and the milk and eggs from us, they've got it real nice." Grover switched on the radio, but the stations were too scratchy, so he turned it off.

"You know, Queenie, if they stay, maybe Blue and I could put electricity into that shack. Sonny sure would like to have a radio for Christmas."

"Zepha, too," I added, squeezing Grover's hand.

We turned off the highway and drove down the old road to the shack in the soft dusk, past the fence where Blue hung the rattlesnake skins that Pup, the Massies' dog, killed. Grover said Pup wasn't much of a hunting animal, but he killed snakes deader than a Kansas Sunday night. The skins made me shiver, although I'd rather see the snakes dead on a barbed-wire fence than alive out in the field.

Sonny ran to meet us and hopped onto the running board, leaning over to listen to the engine. He knew as much about machines as his father did. I wondered if the two of them had ever fixed Blue's old car with the water pump Grover got for them. I'd never seen Blue drive it, but then, plenty of people walked places because they couldn't afford gas.

Blue was looking at the sky when we got out of the car, and Grover asked, "You spot a rain cloud up there, do you?"

159

"Cain't say's I did." Blue shook his head. "Sure wish there was one for Sonny's sake. I already seen rain onct."

Zepha sat on the steps, rocking back and forth and crooning to Baby, who sucked on a sugar tit. Blue'd built a little roof over the stoop. Next to Zepha were old lard cans filled with geraniums, grown from slips I'd given her. She took them inside at night to keep the frost from getting them, then set them back out every morning.

"It always feels like home when I see the stars. You never go so far away you can't see a familiar sky. I draw comfort from it," Zepha said as I sat down next to her and hugged my knees to my chest to keep warm.

"There's a harvest moon tonight." I pointed to the big orange circle in the sky. "Did you ever see anything so pretty?"

"Not never."

I put a brown paper sack next to Zepha. "I've been cutting out quilts. These are just a few old scraps that I can't use."

" 'Bliged." Zepha reached into the sack with her free hand and took out one of the scraps, fingering the cloth, knowing without looking that it was store-bought, the thread count high. She held the piece up to the light shining through the doorway and laughed when she saw the little sailor boys on it. "This'll make real pretty kivers," she said. "We got coffee on." She handed me the baby.

"Obliged," I said, then frowned in the dark. Grover said it took me less than five minutes to start talking like whoever I was with.

I followed Zepha inside, intending to set Baby on the bed. Then I noticed Zepha had put her Road to California quilt on it, most likely in our honor, so I put the baby on the hired man's bed that Sonny slept on. I lifted the Road to California to inspect the stitches and saw Zepha watching me.

"I never saw such small stitches or such a pretty quilt," I told her. "I sure am glad you didn't sell it to Lizzy Olive."

"That one!" Zepha sniffed and turned to the stove.

There was a cottony smell in the room that came from the

160

quilt Zepha was working on. Blue had rigged up a frame that hung from hooks on the ceiling and could be lowered and raised by ropes tied to the wall. "I see you got a quilt going," I said, looking up at the frame, which was snug against the ceiling.

"I always got a quilt going. Wouldn't be natural, not. At home, I picked the cotton for the stuffing and carded it till it was soft like clouds, but I cain't find none here. I used an old blanket for fill. I warshed it in hot water, and it all drawed up and weren't good for nothing but the inside of a quilt."

Zepha handed me two cups of coffee, which I took out to the men, returning to the shack for mine. As I glanced up at the quilt in the frame near the ceiling, I said, "A comfort like that will keep out the Kansas winter—that is, if you're planning on staying the winter."

Baby let out a cry, her tiny tongue moving in and out of her mouth and her little fists stretching up over her head. It wouldn't be long until my own baby was doing that very thing. Why, those two little ones might even be friends. Zepha picked up Baby and murmured a snatch of a lullaby I'd never heard. When Baby was quiet, Zepha set her back down on the bed. She didn't respond to my remark about staying on, and I didn't repeat it. The Massies would tell us their decision in their own time.

The wind came up, sending dirt through the door, and Zepha called, "You'ns come on in now and get out of that blow." She went to the stove and poured water over the old coffee grounds in the pot and put it back on the hot stove to boil. "We'll have us more coffee in a minute. Me and Blue make coffee from parched chestnuts. It ain't half bad. But we got us real coffee for company."

"Well, it tastes fine!" I said as Blue and Grover came inside. Sonny followed, standing in the doorway, one bare foot on top of the other.

"Shut that door, boy," Blue yelled, then turned to Grover and me. "Grab you a seat." Zepha motioned us to the place of honor on the Road to California quilt. When we sat down on it, Blue nodded with approval.

"That's the wife's favorite. She loves her Road to Californy more than a cat loves sweet milk. Of course, it was give to her. She didn't make it herself. Hers is made some better." Zepha ducked her head with pleasure and embarrassment.

"I told Blue I was thinking of getting a new manure spreader, but he says he can take the old one apart and put it back together as good as new," Grover told me when we were seated. He turned to Blue. "You know, I was thinking we could use that wrecked automobile frame out by the smokehouse to build you a windmill down here—that is, if you're staying on for the winter. We'd sure like you to. Isn't that about right, Queenie?"

"It's been real nice having you as neighbors," I said.

Blue and Zepha looked at each other a long time, then Zepha cast a sideways glance at us. She turned her eyes back to her husband but spoke to Grover. "Mr. Bean, there's something you got a right to know. You tell it, Blue." Instead of replying, Blue looked at his hands. Zepha said again, "Tell it, Blue. You know you got to say it."

Blue nodded. "The woman's right."

Grover and I looked at each other, not knowing what to expect. I felt a chill on my back as I wondered if Blue had had something to do with the man on the road, after all. We didn't know the Massies very well, and they did have odd ways. But the minute I thought of Blue being tied up with that man, I knew I was wrong. I trusted the Massies almost as much as I did the members of the Persian Pickle Club.

"We ain't told you the truth. We didn't just break down there on the crick last summer like we said we done. We come here a'purpose." Blue gave Grover such a look of remorse that I wondered if he feared he'd be struck down by lightning.

"I guess I don't follow you," was all Grover said. I took a drink of coffee, and the sound of my swallowing was so loud, everybody looked at me. Sonny sat down on the hired man's bed with Baby. The sun had set behind the deep blue fields, and the only light in the room now came from the yellow circle cast by the kerosene lamp on the table. All I could see of Sonny, sitting back along the wall, were his eyes, shining like a coyote's.

Blue opened his mouth to say something, but he was talked out, so he nodded at Zepha and leaned back in his chair in the shadows, which made his face dark.

"We heard about you'ns. We come here looking for this place. We heard you was good for a handout," she said.

I looked at Grover, but he wouldn't meet my eyes. So, he'd been helping back-door moochers without my knowing about it!

Grover wouldn't admit it, however. Instead, he asked, "Do you mean my neighbors say I'm an easy touch?"

Blue found his voice again. "No, sir." He drew himself up so he could look Grover in the eye. "It wasn't nobody around here. We heard it at a place where we was camped. Man said to go two miles north of Harveyville, past the yellow house on the left, and camp by the creek. He told us, 'The man'll help you, but stay clear of the woman. She ain't partial to drifters.' "

Zepha added quickly, "We say he's wrong about that, missus. You've been every bit as nice as your husband."

Grover grinned at me, then turned serious and said, "I don't blame you for it, Blue. When your family's hungry and you've got no place to stay, you do the best you can. It's no skin off my back why you showed up, and now that you're here, Queenie and me are glad of it, aren't we, honeybunch?"

"You bet!"

"There's nothing more to say, then." Grover stood up. "We'll be getting on—" Blue put out his hand, and Grover sat back down.

"Fact is, there is," Blue said, while Zepha nodded and gritted her teeth. "We wasn't going to say nothing about it. Then we heard about them finding that dead feller."

"You mean Ben Crook?" Grover asked. He put his hand over mine on the quilt.

"That's the name," Blue said. Zepha interrupted, but Blue tapped the table with his fist to stop her from talking. "You told me to tell them, so I'm doin' it. Now, hush up." He leaned back on the two legs of the chair and took a deep breath.

"I don't know that this means nothing, but that feller who told us about you did a good piece of talking. He said to stay away from the Crook place, since a poor widow woman lived there with not enough to share."

"That's true enough," Grover said.

"Then he told us her husband was buried out there in a field." Blue set the front legs of the chair down with a thump. That was the only sound for a full minute.

"How would anybody know last spring that Ben was buried out there?" I whispered to Grover.

" 'Xactly," Blue said. "When he told us, I thought the man was already dug up."

"This fellow who told you, do you remember what he looked like?" Grover asked.

Blue shook his head. "We tried, and we cain't. He was just a voice over the fire. Zepha says she recollects his head was shaped like a hoe, and he was narrow between the eyes. She remembers he had a beard like a feed bag, but she don't recall no more than that. He 'lowed as how he sneaked into this here cabin and lived a time, and you never knowed about it."

"Maybe Skillet," I said. "Did he tell you his name was Skillet?"

Blue looked at Zepha, who shook her head. "I don't recall that he said his name."

"If he did, I don't remember no name of Skillet," Blue added.

We all stared at one another until Baby cried. Sonny muttered, "Doggone," and patted her, and she went back to sleep.

"We don't want to cause no trouble," Blue said at last.

"It's our duty to tell you, that dead man being torn from the bosom of his family like he was," Zepha added. "We been talking about it ever since we heard. At first, we weren't sure we'd say nothing, 'cause we aimed to move along in the fall. But now that we're fixing to stay the winter . . ." She glanced at

164

me, then continued. "Well, I put it to Blue, 'We got to tell the folks.'"

"What are you going to do?" Blue interrupted her, and we all turned to Grover.

"We'll have to tell the sheriff, I expect," Grover said. Blue's eyes narrowed, and he glanced at Zepha, so Grover added quickly, "It doesn't mean whoever it was you met killed Ben. Maybe it was a lucky guess, since everybody knows Ben disappeared. It's a natural thing to make up a story like that over a campfire."

"That feller seemed sure enough about it," Zepha said. "The way he talked, it sounded like that Mr. Crook had already been dug up. We never thought nothing of it till the preacher woman spoke up about the nigger finding them bones."

"We'll have to let the sheriff know about it. I don't expect he'll do anything, since you don't know who did the talking. I'll drive you in tomorrow," Grover said.

Blue exchanged another look with Zepha, then turned to Grover. "I wouldn't be wanting to talk to no sheriff myself," he said.

"Oh, don't concern yourself with Sheriff Eagles. A man can't be responsible for what he heard somebody else say," Grover told him.

"There ain't going to be no trouble, is they?" Zepha asked.

"I shouldn't think so. The sheriff is liable to ask you the same questions I did. Come on up to the house in the morning. I'll go with you myself."

"We don't want no trouble." Zepha rocked back and forth, looking at Blue. "We's honest. That trouble back home, it weren't Blue's fault. There's those can tell you so, but they never spoke up." Then she added darkly, "I heard an owl hoot last night after supper. I know they's bad times coming. I told you that, Blue. I know the signs."

"Hush, woman," Blue warned her.

Grover stood up. "I wouldn't worry about it, Zepha. Sheriff Eagles is a nice man, and I'll tell him you're as honest as anybody I ever met in Harveyville."

165

"We cain't have no more trouble," Zepha said. "I never seed the like o' signs. I saw a hawk fly east across the moon—"

"Quiet," Blue said.

Zepha kept on rocking, muttering to herself. She didn't even notice when we left the shack.

"That one sure does take on," Blue said, shaking his head at Zepha. He walked us to the car and ran his hand across the hood. "Coming in, she sounded like she's got a rod loose," he said.

"Maybe we can take a look at it in the morning when we get back," Grover said, and Blue nodded.

Driving home in the dark with the headlights shining across the brown stubble on our fields, I locked the doors again and moved close to Grover.

"Are you thinking about Skillet—or whoever that was the Massies met—living in the shack?" Grover asked. I nodded, and even though he couldn't see me in the blackness, Grover knew I was. "Don't you worry. If it was Skillet living there, he won't come back now that Ben's body's been found. I never knew why he stayed on the Crook place as long as he did, the way Ben ragged on him."

"Did you give him permission to stay in the shack?" I asked. Grover didn't answer, so I knew he had.

Grover stopped when we reached the highway and turned to me. "Skillet told me Ben went for him with a pitchfork. There was no reason for it. Skillet was putting away a harness and heard a sound, and there was Ben right behind him, ready to stick him in the back. That's why he took off. I ran into him down by the creek. He was waiting until Ben left so he could sneak back and get his things."

"Did he get them?"

"I never knew. All I know is, he wasn't in the shack a few days later."

"Was he living in the shack after Ben disappeared?"

"I don't know. I've been trying to remember that all evening." Grover shifted the car into gear and turned onto the highway. "The fact is, I've been trying to recollect it ever since Hiawatha

166

found Ben's body. One thing's for sure, whether Skillet killed Ben or not, he's got no reason to come back to Harveyville."

Grover and Blue never went to the sheriff's office. Grover waited for Blue until almost noon, then went to the shack looking for him.

When he returned, Grover leaned his back against the kitchen sink and faced me. "They're gone, Queenie."

"What?" I asked.

"The shack's empty. The Massies must have packed up right after we left last night and took off. The place is as clean as a whistle. They even removed that quilt frame from the ceiling."

"I don't understand. They asked to stay, and we told them they could. Why would they leave?"

Grover took off his hat, hung it on the knob on the back of a kitchen chair, and sat down. "I suppose they were scared. Hill people don't much like lawmen. It took pretty near as much courage as they had just to tell us the story. I should have thought about that. It's my fault for telling Blue he had to talk to Sheriff Eagles." Grover went to the icebox and took out a pitcher of buttermilk. "You want some?" he asked, reaching into the cupboard for a glass.

"It'll make me puke," I said. We both laughed, even though it brought tears to my eyes. "I'm going to miss that little boy. I'll miss all of them. Maybe they'll be back next summer."

Grover shook his head.

"Did they leave a note?" I asked.

Grover took a swallow of buttermilk right out of the pitcher and wiped his mouth with the back of his hand. "Could they write?"

I didn't know.

"They left the cream can and some other stuff." Grover put down his glass and went to a cardboard box he'd carried in and left on the Hoosier cupboard. Inside were dishes and spoons I'd loaned to Zepha, along with some of Grover's tools that Blue had used. There was a pile of toothpicks, too, tied with an old

167

shoelace. Grover took out a bundle that was wrapped in newspaper and fastened with string. "They left this, too. It was sitting on the hired man's bed. You better open it."

I didn't have to open it to know what it was. I stared at the package in Grover's hands for a long time, blinking back the tears. I took the bundle from Grover and untied the string, putting it into my apron pocket to save. I carefully unwrapped the newspaper and took out the quilt, folded with the design inside so it wouldn't get smudged from the newsprint. "It's her Road to California quilt," I said, slowly opening it and staring at the tiny pieces, no bigger than postage stamps.

"That's a real shame. They sure set store by that quilt," Grover said. "They must have left in such a hurry, she forgot all about it."

I felt the homespun goods between my thumb and finger and rubbed my hand across the stitches. Then I held the folded quilt against my face. "No," I told Grover, "Zepha didn't forget it."

chapter
11

So much had been happening lately—first the excitement over the baby, then the Massies pulling out—that before I knew it, a week had passed and Persian Pickle had come around again. Club meetings were back on schedule, and so was I. Going out, at least to Pickle, didn't bother me anymore.

Mrs. Judd was the hostess. So I thought, surely, Rita would find an excuse not to come. Those "interesting things" that Rita'd found out about the Judds didn't sound very nice, and with the way she and Mrs. Judd felt about each other, Rita wouldn't be comfortable sewing in the Judd parlor. Women can't quilt when they're angry. It shows up in the stitches. Of course, even when Rita was in a good mood, her stitches weren't the best I'd ever seen. Despite my efforts, Rita, at heart, was not a quilter, and I'd begun to doubt that she ever would be.

To my surprise, however, Rita was at the Judds' when I arrived, waiting for me. She stood off by herself in the parlor, fidgeting and looking more ill at ease than she ever had. When she saw me, Rita grabbed my arm and said, "My God, Queenie. I sure am glad you're here. It makes me feel creepy being in this house." She bit the end of a fingernail. Most of her fingernails had been chewed off, and the polish was a mess.

"Oh, it's not so bad," I said, although the truth was, the Judds' parlor with its heavy walnut furniture covered with brown upholstery was as dreary a place as I'd ever seen. Paper with big tan feathers covered the walls, making me feel I was inside a pillow. The pictures were hung so high that you got a crick in your neck just looking up at them—although I don't know anybody who would bother to do so, since the same pictures were in every house in Kansas. They were *End of the Trail,* which showed an out-of-luck Indian about to fall off his horse, and another, whose name I never knew, of a bunch of dogs sitting around a poker table, playing cards. That one was a favorite of Grover's. We had the same picture hanging in Dad Bean's old bedroom, and I hoped Grover would let me throw it out when we turned the room into a nursery.

Rita curled her lip a little as she looked around the room, stopping at Mrs. Judd's prized Whig's Defeat hanging on the wall.

"Look at that quilt. There's a big hole in it," Rita said, touching a dark spot where the stuffing showed through.

"It's a bullet hole, and the red around it, that's blood," I told Rita, who snatched her hand away. "The quilt belonged to Mr. Judd's father. He carried it all through the Civil War and claimed it saved his life when he was shot by a Confederate."

Rita bit the end of her finger because there wasn't any nail left to chew. "If that rifleman had been a better shot, there wouldn't be any Mr. Judd." I smiled a little, only to be polite to her, because it wasn't a nice thing to say. Then Rita whispered, "Murder seems to run in the family."

I didn't know what she meant by that, but it reminded me I hadn't told her what the Massies had said about Skillet. "Come over here," I said, glancing at Ella to make sure she was out of earshot. I drew Rita into the dining room and looked around, because I didn't want anyone else to overhear, either. Of course, Grover let Sheriff Eagles know what Blue and Zepha had told us, but the sheriff kept it to himself, so I didn't care to upset the club members by bringing it up. They wanted to forget about Ben Crook's murder every bit as much as I did.

"Here's your killer," I whispered. I told Rita the story of the

Massies overhearing a drifter say a man was buried in Ella's field. "Blue and Zepha knew about Ben's body before Hiawatha found it. That hobo at the campfire just had to be Skillet. The way they described him, I know it was," I said.

Rita listened without interrupting, furrowing her brow as I finished. "Well, maybe it was, and maybe it wasn't." Rita thought a minute. "For crying out loud, Queenie, you know as well as I do that that Skillet person didn't kill Ben Crook." She tapped her front teeth with her thumb. "Of course, he could have been in on it one way or another. It sort of complicates things. I'll have to think about that."

"You're crazy!" I sputtered. "A man knows about Ben Crook being buried before the body's found, and all you can say is it's something to think about?"

Rita ran her tongue back and forth over her lip. "Hold your horses, Queenie. I'm not saying Skillet wasn't involved somehow, but I know for sure he didn't do it. Wait till you hear what I have to tell you. Do you know what a conspiracy is?"

"Well, of course. I'm not so dumb," I said, trying to remember what the word meant.

"What's this about a conspiracy?" Mrs. Judd had come up behind us, and neither Rita nor I had noticed her until she spoke. She wore a brown dress with tan stripes that made her look like a piece of her furniture. The dress was baggy, with spots on the front, and crumbs, too, which wasn't like Mrs. Judd, who'd always been tidy. She'd been a big woman once, but her bones seemed to have shrunk in the past few weeks, leaving her skin loose and saggy. Caring for Ella had taken its toll on Mrs. Judd, but she'd bite her tongue off before she'd utter one word of complaint. So would Prosper.

"Oh, we're just talking," said Rita, who was a lot faster with the comebacks than I was.

"Yeah, talking," I added.

"Well, come and quilt," Mrs. Judd ordered. "You can talk while you sew." She wet her finger and touched the crumbs on her bosom, then brushed her hands together.

Mrs. Judd went ahead of us into the parlor, and Rita drew her finger across her throat. "Whew!"

Mrs. Judd's Dresden Plate was ready for us in the quilt frame, which was propped up on the backs of four chairs. The club members gathered around it, telling Mrs. Judd how nice the quilt top looked, even though Mrs. Judd didn't have an eye for color. She'd picked orange for the centers of the design, which made the quilt looked like a field of pumpkins. Mrs. Judd had bleached the sugar sacks she used for the background, but I could still make out the writing on some of them. The stitches in the quilt were nice and even, however. Ella leaned over to inspect them, and her monogrammed brooch fell off, right onto the quilt, which was lucky, because the pin was made of china and would have broken if it had hit the parlor's linoleum carpet.

Rita picked up the pin and handed it back to Ella, first brushing her finger over the gold letters. "E.E.C. Ella Crook. What does the middle initial stand for?"

"Eagles. It's Ella's maiden name," Ceres said.

"Let's get started," Mrs. Judd interrupted. "Sit anyplace you like. I'm not particular." Even so, Mrs. Judd maneuvered Ella as far away from Rita as possible. She didn't trust Rita any more than Rita trusted her, and I wished now that I'd found out what it was Rita knew. I didn't want her to spoil our quilting by saying something rash.

"Ladies, the Celebrity Quilt's all bound," Mrs. Ritter announced as we took our places and began stitching around the Dresden Plate wedges. We all murmured our approval.

"We used red for the binding, the same fabric as the sashing. It's pretty. Awful pretty," Agnes T. Ritter said. Both Ada June and I stopped sewing to look at her. Agnes T. Ritter had never in her life said anything was pretty. "Well, it is," she sniffed.

"It will make us famous," Nettie said. She looked at me and smiled, and I smiled back. Neither one of us was thinking about the quilt. We were thinking about Velma's baby—

my baby. Still, I knew from the last club meeting that not one Pickle, including Nettie, would ever say a word out loud about the baby until it arrived, so Nettie and I only smiled.

"So famous, maybe somebody will ask us for our autographs for *their* celebrity quilt," Forest Ann said.

"Maybe so," Mrs. Judd put in. "Maybe Lizzy Olive will."

We laughed, and I was glad things were back to normal at the Persian Pickle Club. This was going to be as pleasant a quilting as I'd ever attended. The entire club had come, and except for Rita, who was still jumpy, we were all in a good mood. The room was sunny, and big enough so that we weren't cramped. We sewed with the windows open, since it was warm outside, but we didn't have to worry about chiggers because the first frost had killed them.

We stitched quietly for a minute. Then Opalina said she'd heard Blue and Zepha had pulled out, and I nodded. "I guess they just got itchy feet," I said. "Drifters do that. That's why they're called drifters."

"Did they steal anything?" Agnes T. Ritter asked. "People who sneak away in the night 'most always take something." Now she was her old self again.

"No, not unless you count the girlie calendar that the last hired man left behind a couple of years ago." I knew the Massies hadn't taken it, however, because Grover had removed it when he took the Massies to the cabin in the early summer, then tacked it up in the barn where he thought I wouldn't notice it. "But they left something behind. Zepha gave me her Road to California," I said, blushing, because the Pickles knew women didn't give you their best quilts unless you were special to them.

"Oh, a Road to California's a nice quilt," Ella said. She was following things better that afternoon than she had in a long time.

"Zepha's a fine quilter. She told me that in the hill country, they throw a cat on top of the quilt as soon as the last stitch is

173

in. If the cat jumps into your lap, then you're the next to get married." I glanced at Agnes T. Ritter, but she didn't look up. "I don't know where they went, but I hope the Massies headed for California. Zepha always talked about going there."

"Maybe she'll see Ruby," Ella whispered.

"Now, Ella, sweetheart, those people weren't the kind Ruby would be acquainted with. Besides, they don't even know Ruby's name," Mrs. Judd told her. "We'll get a postal from Ruby one day soon. Just you believe it."

We talked about Ruby, wondering where she was and whether she ate oranges every day, until we heard the Packard drive up, and Mrs. Judd said, "That'll be Prosper. He went to town for lemons. I forgot to get them yesterday. We'll have tea with lemons this afternoon."

Prosper came into the parlor with a paper bag clutched in both hands, and when he saw us, he blinked his little pink eyes, then ducked his head with embarrassment. Our husbands stayed away from the Persian Pickle Club, and if they didn't, we shooed them out. Prosper took off his hat and looked around the circle, nodding at each one of us. When he came to Ella, he smiled and said, "My, Miss Ella, don't you look pretty as paint."

"Oh, Prosper." Ella looked down at her needle and blushed.

Prosper kept on around the circle, and when he reached Rita, he didn't nod; he just looked away.

"Well, hello, Mr. Judd," Rita called, bold as brass. Her voice was high and a little out of control, which made me look up. So did the others, and Prosper backed out of the room.

"I'll set these in the kitchen, Mother," Prosper said. The back door slammed, and the Packard started up again. Mrs. Judd, who'd been watching Rita since Prosper left the room, continued to stare at her.

In a minute, Rita glanced over and caught Mrs. Judd's eye, and the two of them watched each other like sniffing dogs, not saying anything. Ella didn't notice, and she said in her tiny voice, "Prosper's the best man."

It was the second time that afternoon that Ella had spoken up. I was about to send her a smile of encouragement when suddenly Rita blurted out, "Like hell, Ella! Prosper killed your husband!" I don't think Rita had planned to say that. It just happened. Before she could stop the words, they were out. Rita froze, the point of her needle stuck in the quilt.

The room was so quiet, we could hear Opalina's needle go through the quilt. Opalina was sweating, as usual, and her sticky needle squeaked as she pushed it through the cotton with her thimble.

I finished my stitch at the instant I looked up at Rita, and I ran the needle into my finger. When I glanced down, I saw a little drop of my blood on the Dresden plate I was stitching around. I put my finger into my mouth.

Nettie and Forest Ann turned to each other with shock in their faces, and Mrs. Ritter grabbed Agnes T. Ritter's hand. Ceres, her eyes wide, put her knuckles into her mouth and bit down. Ella held tightly to the seat of her chair to keep from sliding off, her face even whiter than usual. We exchanged glances with each other before turning to stare at Rita, who had a look of horror on her face at what she'd said. Her open mouth was a round O, and a little line of perspiration appeared on her upper lip. Her hands shook on the quilt, and to steady them, she held fast to the edge of the frame.

At that very moment, before anyone spoke, a lazy winter fly buzzed in from the kitchen, made big swoops around the room, and landed on the light globe hanging above us. Mrs. Judd stood up slowly so she wouldn't disturb it, took a flyswatter off the wall, and slapped it against the light. The dead fly fell onto the quilt, landing on the bright orange center of one of the Dresden plates. Using the edge of the swatter, Mrs. Judd picked up the fly and carried it to the screen door, flicking it outside. She closed the door and hooked it, returned the swatter to its nail, and sat down.

"What's that you were saying about Mr. Judd?" Mrs. Judd's voice was quiet, but there was an edge of steel in it, the way it got when city people tried to talk her down on the price of her eggs.

We looked at her as she spoke, then turned to Rita for the answer.

Rita swallowed uncomfortably, looking as if she wished she could fall through the floor. After making an accusation like that, she couldn't back off, and I think she knew not one of us in that room was on her side. She opened and shut her mouth a couple of times before saying, "I told Ella your husband killed Ben Crook." Rita still didn't have control of her voice.

"That's what I thought you said. You as much as told Prosper that the time you caught him out by the horse trough, didn't you?"

Mrs. Judd waited quietly, but Rita didn't answer. The rest of us were too stunned to speak.

Ella broke the silence. "Not Prosper," she stuttered.

"He did, Ella." Rita gave her a pleading look, then turned again to Mrs. Judd. Her voice was firmer when she spoke this time. "You know he did it, don't you, Mrs. Judd? Why, I think you all know it, every one of you." She looked at each of us, even me. I lowered my eyes.

"No," Ella whimpered, but Rita didn't pay any attention to her. She watched Mrs. Judd instead.

"You know all about it, do you?" Mrs. Judd asked. "You think you know what happened?"

Rita gripped the edge of the quilt and leaned forward. "I know Prosper was making payments on Ella's mortgage. I know Ella deeded you a field by the river just before Mr. Crook disappeared. I found that out in the records."

I didn't know that. I glanced at Ada June, but her face showed she was as surprised as I was.

"So?" Mrs. Judd said. "So, you think paying a mortgage makes Prosper a mankiller?"

Rita leaned even farther across the quilt toward Mrs. Judd. "Prosper was"—she paused to find the right words—"romantically involved, I guess you'd say, with Ella. That's why he was paying off her mortgage. You found out about it, and Ella gave you that piece of land to keep you quiet. I think Mr. Crook caught the two of them together or something. So Prosper killed him. I'm not saying it was murder. It could have been an accident. I don't know how it happened, but Ella does. That's why you're keeping her here in your house, so she won't tell. I think the rest of you"—she stopped long enough to look around the circle at each of us again—"I think you all know about it, and you formed a conspiracy to keep it a secret."

So that was what a conspiracy was!

"Prosper didn't. No, Prosper never . . ." Ella mumbled, shaking her head back and forth. Mrs. Judd reached over and put her hand on the back of Ella's head to keep it from wobbling, and Ella was still.

So were the rest of us, sitting there as dumb as cows, unable to speak. I wished that fly would come back to relieve the tension in the room. Ceres moved her lips, but no words came out. Even Mrs. Judd seemed talked out. My mouth was as dry as Kansas dust. Why hadn't I found out what Rita was up to and kept her from saying these terrible things? It was my fault this was happening.

Rita took our silence to mean she was onto something, and she became bolder. "It's what newspapers call a 'crime of passion.' Prosper paid Doc Sipes to say Ben might have fallen out of a tree and been buried by somebody who didn't have the money for a coffin. That's what the doctor put in the coroner's report, and the sheriff would have gone along with it if I hadn't written up the murder for the *Enterprise*. I couldn't figure out why, unless Prosper bribed him. Then today I discovered he and Ella are family. He probably doesn't want the scandal." Rita turned to me with a pleading look, and I cringed. My loyalty was to the Pickles, not to Rita. I hoped the club members knew I hadn't encouraged Rita. "Prosper hired that man to stop Queenie and me on the road, and I think he was that Skillet person, even though Queenie says he wasn't. Why, he probably helped Prosper bury Mr. Crook's body."

If the Judds were paying off half the people in Wabaunsee

County, then no wonder Mrs. Judd was piecing on sugar sacks, but that wasn't what I was thinking just then.

I put my hands over my ears to shut out Rita's accusations, but I still heard them, although by now, Rita had stopped talking. I shook my head back and forth, hoping the rattling of my brain would drown out the sound. Instead, the terrible words exploded inside my head like Fourth of July firecrackers. I prayed one of the other Pickles would speak, but it was as quiet as death in Mrs. Judd's parlor, and I thought my skull would burst if I didn't say something to end the silence. "Stop it! That's not true, Rita!" I blurted out so loudly, the sound echoed around the room. "Prosper and Skillet didn't bury Ben Crook. We did!"

No one else spoke. The only sound in the parlor was Opalina drawing in her breath. Rita turned to me in shock, but even she couldn't say anything. I looked around at the other members of the Persian Pickle Club, then burst into tears. "Oh, I'm sorry. I broke our promise." I put my head in my hands and sobbed. Rita would put our secret in the newspaper, and we would go to jail, and Grover and I would never have a baby.

They watched me cry, too dumbfounded to say even a word of comfort. Then Mrs. Judd reached across the quilt with her hand, which was wrinkled and covered with liver spots as brown as the furnishings of her house. "It's all right, Queenie. One of us would have said it if you hadn't."

I glanced up, but she was staring at Rita. So were the rest of the Pickles. They weren't angry at me, but their faces were set against her, and when Rita saw that, she shrank away from them. I almost felt sorry for her, because Rita hadn't been out to hurt us. At that moment, I came to understand Rita.

She wasn't lazy like Agnes T. Ritter claimed she was. Rita had worked as hard at solving Ben's murder as I'd ever worked at farming, and it sure wasn't easy with everyone trying to stop her. She had courage, because even though I knew that man on the road hadn't been sent by Ben's killer, Rita didn't. She believed he'd come back for her if she kept on with her reporting. Rita stayed with it so that she and Tom would have their chance, just like everyone else in Harveyville wanted a chance at something. For Rita and Tom, it meant getting away from farming. No matter how much I wanted Rita to live in the country and be a Pickle, she didn't want that and never would.

"I don't understand," Rita whispered, looking at us like a cornered animal. "How could . . . I don't—"

"Prosper never did Ella anything but kindness," Mrs. Judd broke in. "Prosper paid the mortgage Ben took out with a Topeka bank on the farm, the old Eagles place, because Ben spent the money, and the bank said it was going to foreclose. If it hadn't been for Prosper, Ella would have been turned off her own land. Ella deeded me the only field she still owned free and clear, since Ben had it in mind to sell it out from under her. It didn't matter to him that the land was left to Ella by her people. Ben would have found a way. Many's the time Prosper risked his life going against Ben Crook for Ella's sake, did it to protect Ella, at the risk of his own precious life. Why, Ella wouldn't be alive today except for Prosper. You've no right to accuse him of being immoral with her. No right at all." Mrs. Judd's eyes flashed, and color came into her face, and she didn't look so tired, after all.

"That was an awful, awful thing to say," Ada June scolded.

"Nasty," Nettie added, rubbing one index finger down the other in a sign of shame.

Rita looked at each of us, but not a one of us showed her a friendly face—except Mrs. Ritter, of course. "It's not Rita's fault. Maybe we should have told her in the beginning," Mrs. Ritter said. "I think we'll have to tell her now." She looked around the circle for approval. "Do we have your permission, Ella?" she asked after the rest of us nodded.

Ella's eyes were wild, and she clutched and unclutched her hands. I wondered if she understood Mrs. Ritter.

"Ella, is it all right for Rita to know our secret about Ben?" Mrs. Judd asked her, saying each word slowly while the rest of us waited.

179

Ella shrugged her shoulders up and down, but at last, she muttered, "Yes. Okay."

Mrs. Judd nodded at Mrs. Ritter. "You tell her, Sabra."

"Ben Crook was as mean a man as ever lived. He was born mean, and no one knew that better than Ella," Mrs. Ritter began.

"Smacked her all the time. Crazy mad. Maybe Ella sat on a table when she was young. That's a sure sign you'll marry a crazy man," Nettie said. Agnes T. Ritter gave her a scornful look, and Nettie muttered, "Well, she could have. You don't know any different."

"Awfulest man," Opalina added.

"Evil. I believe to my soul, he was truly evil, even though I hate to say that about a body," Ceres said. "I know he's in hell, and I'm glad for it." I glanced at Ella, who nodded her head up and down but wasn't aware of it, because she continued nodding after Ceres finished speaking.

"We saw him close the car door on Ella's hand once," Forest Ann said.

"On purpose. You can see yourself how it's bent because Ben wouldn't let Doc Sipes administer to Ella," Nettie added. I looked at Ella's little twisted hands and felt that pain myself. "Ben took to sneaking around Forest Ann's place evenings after her husband got killed. She was afraid of Ben, so she asked Doc to start stopping by—" Forest Ann shook her head at Nettie, who didn't finish.

"I saw him—" Agnes T. Ritter said, but Mrs. Judd broke in.

"He was always after Ella. Just opening her mouth was an excuse for Ben to hit her. He used his fist or a poker, anything he could put his hands on. Who knows how she lived through it, or how she turned out to be the sweet thing she is. I think Ella goes someplace back in her head to hide, and that's what saved her."

I glanced at Ella, who seemed to hiding there now.

"Sometimes she'd run away and hide with us," Mrs. Judd continued. "Prosper would stand up to Ben when he came

180

looking for her, and there were times I thought Ben would kill him for it. Ben was a big man, and Prosper . . . isn't so big. But he's man enough. Don't you doubt it." Mrs. Judd paused to make sure we all knew how proud she was of her husband.

"There were other ways Ben was mean. He trampled Ella's flowers because she loved them so, and he'd hide her shoes so she couldn't come to Pickle. Once, when Ella had club meeting at her house, she baked a cake, got it all iced, too, and Ben threw it to the pigs. That was the day he died, and I've never been sorry for it. I don't suppose anybody else in this room is, either." As we nodded in agreement, Mrs. Judd took a deep breath and sat back in her chair, talked out.

"Septima knew everything, but the rest of us, we only saw a little of it. We never knew how terrible Ben was. Until that day," Opalina said. She reached over and put her hand on top of Mrs. Judd's.

"I remember when they were married. We didn't think Ben was much of a catch, except he was handsome, and oh, those hips! Hips'll do it. Ella was so happy," Ceres said. "Who would have guessed?" Ceres looked at Opalina and Mrs. Judd, who had known Ella in her youth, and both shook their heads.

Now, Rita spoke for the first time since I'd told our secret. "Well, why didn't Ella leave him? She could have gone to the sheriff. I suppose Sheriff Eagles is her brother, isn't he?" She'd stopped trembling, but her face was still pale.

"Yes, he's that. Ella was too ashamed to tell him—" Mrs. Judd stopped talking because Ella had put up her hand, and I knew she understood what was going on. "What is it, sugar pie? Did you want to say something?" Mrs. Judd asked her.

Ella gave a wistful little smile as she traced the circle of the Dresden plate in front of her with her forefinger. "I loved Ben," she said without looking up. "He promised, promised he wouldn't hit me again."

"Ha!" Mrs. Judd said.

"So Prosper killed him because he was mean to Ella?" Rita asked. "Then, after he did it, all of you buried the body?"

"I told you, Prosper didn't kill anybody," Mrs. Judd yelled, as though the loudness would get the words through Rita's head. I glanced out the window, glad no one was outside to hear. "Prosper didn't even know Ben was dead until Hiawatha found the body."

"Then who killed him?" Rita asked.

The question hung in the air as we all grew quiet again. We'd told Rita almost everything, but not that, not the final part of the secret. We looked around the circle at one another, avoiding Rita's eyes; then each of us turned to Mrs. Judd, just as we always did when there was a difficult decision to make.

Mrs. Judd sat with her elbow on her knee, her mouth in the palm of her hand, knowing without looking up that we expected her to speak. She blew out her breath, but before she could, Ella opened and shut her mouth like a little bird, then whispered, "I did."

Rita looked at that tiny woman with astonishment. The rest of us did, too. "I did it," Ella repeated, then shrank back against her chair. She would have toppled over if Ada June hadn't grabbed her.

"You?" Rita asked. "How?" Obviously, she didn't believe Ella.

Mrs. Judd snorted at the idea of Ella killing Ben Crook, but Ella replied quickly, "Snuck up behind him. I hit him with the fry pan. I said, 'Don't throw out the cake.' He hurt me bad." Tears rolled down Ella's cheeks, and she rubbed her eyes with her little fists. She was used to crying without making a sound, however, and the only noise in the room was the ticking of Rita's wristwatch, which seemed as loud as our alarm clock.

"That's a lie."

I didn't know who'd spoken. I looked at Ada June and Nettie and Forest Ann. Then, with astonishment, I turned to Agnes T. Ritter, who spoke louder this time. "That's a lie, and you know it is, Ella," she said. "I killed Ben Crook." Agnes T. Ritter stared at Rita with her lips pressed together so hard, they'd gone inside her mouth.

She had to breathe, however, so her lips came back out, and

182

she opened her mouth a crack. Agnes T. Ritter's eyes gleamed, almost as if she was having a good time, because, at last, her mother wasn't telling her to be still. "I was the first one to arrive for Persian Pickle that day because Mom had the car in town, and I walked. It didn't take as long as I'd thought. So I got there early and heard Ben screaming at Ella. He hit her with his fist, and when she fell down, Ben kicked her. I saw it through the window, and by the time I got to the door, Ben had a butcher knife in his hand. Ella was curled up in a little ball, and I knew if she wasn't dead already, she would be in a minute if I didn't stop him. I picked up the skillet from the stove next to the door and bashed Ben over the head with it. I didn't mean to kill him, but I'm not sorry I did." Agnes T. Ritter sat back in her chair, defiant.

Mrs. Ritter leaned over and put her arms around Agnes T. Ritter. "No, dear. You don't have to protect me," Mrs. Ritter said, then turned to Rita. "The stove isn't next to the door. You're smart enough to find that out, Rita. I got to Ella's in the car before Agnes arrived, and I killed Ben. I didn't use any skillet, either. It was the side of the ax that Ella kept outside for chopping wood. I never saw a mad dog go after a person the way Ben went for Ella. He was an insane man. I didn't have a choice—"

"You didn't either do it, Sabra," Nettie interrupted. "I did."

"We did," Forest Ann corrected her. "Nettie and I killed him dead. Nettie called out to him to stop, and I ran around behind him and bashed him on the noggin with a flatiron. I'm not one bit sorry. I sleep good at night knowing nobody has to worry about Ben Crook again."

"I'm an old woman, and I'm willing to take my punishment," Ceres told Rita.

Ada June shook her head. "I know you're trying to protect me, with my kids and all, but I'll own up to it. Lord knows, he deserved it." She looked Rita in the eye. "I struck him with a piece of kindling. I did it two or three times, until he stopped moving."

183

"The truth is," Mrs. Judd broke in, and everyone turned to her. "The truth is, I'm the only one strong enough to mash in Ben Crook's head. And I'm the only one mean enough to do it."

"Oh, no, dear, I stood on a chair so I could hit him," Opalina said. Mrs. Judd gave Opalina such an astonished look that I almost laughed.

"We all put him in Mrs. Judd's Packard and drove him out to the field to bury him. Then we swore a pact that if anyone ever brought up Ben's name, we'd say he loved Ella and thought the sun rose and set on her," I explained. "I guess we said it too much."

"With so many men walking away from their families these days, why, folks just naturally thought that's what Ben did," Ceres added.

"Ben didn't have any family, and Ella was the only one who cared about him. Everybody else in Harveyville was glad he was gone. Who'd take the trouble to look for him?" I said. The others nodded.

"But it was murder," Rita said, drawing out the word and shuddering.

"Murder? You think killing a crazy man who's about to beat his own wife to death is murder?" Agnes T. Ritter asked.

Rita didn't reply. No one else spoke, either. We were relieved when a car drove past to give us something to listen to besides the sound of our voices. I was more tired than I'd ever been in my life. I could have put my head down on the quilt right then and gone to sleep. The others were weary, too, especially Mrs. Judd, who had black half-moons under her eyes. The fire had gone out of her.

She knew this wasn't over, however, and when the sound of tires on the dirt road faded away, she asked, "Now that you know the truth, Rita, what are you going to do?"

Mrs. Judd question was the one we all wanted answered, although not one of us had had the courage to ask it. Rita frowned as she thought it over, and she wouldn't meet our eyes. I wondered if the others heard my heart pounding away.

"You won't put it in the paper, will you? Anson would lose his job, and they might chop off our heads, just like chickens," Opalina said. She began to cry.

Ceres reached over to hold Opalina's hand while Mrs. Judd said, "Hush. The state of Kansas doesn't behead anybody."

"We didn't tell you this to put in the newspaper," Agnes T. Ritter said slowly. "We told you because you are a member of the Persian Pickle Club, because you are one of us. We extended the hand of friendship to you, and there's nothing in this world that's stronger than friendship. You had the right to know our secret, because we trust you." I had never heard Agnes T. Ritter say anything so fine, and I wanted to hug her for it. The idea of doing that almost made me giggle.

Rita thought hard, her teeth biting into her bottom lip. She'd chewed off all the lipstick, and the skin was raw. I remembered that night in the Ritter kitchen when Rita had sworn to sell her soul to get out of Harveyville. She wouldn't have to sell her soul now. She'd just have to sell our story to the newspaper.

As I watched Rita twist her wedding ring around her finger, I saw how rough and cracked her hands were, not at all pretty like they were the first time I saw her. The thumb, where she'd torn off a hangnail, was bleeding onto the edge of the quilt.

"I promised to write one more article for the *Topeka Enterprise,* and I told the editor I was certain I knew who killed Ben Crook. He'd think I was stupid if I didn't come up with something," Rita said, choosing her words carefully. She put her hands in her lap and looked directly at me. I wanted to turn away, but knew I had to look her in the eye. Ceres put her arm around my shoulder.

"Just today, Queenie told me a story that happened before Mr. Crook's body was found. A man at a campfire said he knew somebody was buried in Ella's field." Rita paused, then gave a high little laugh. "Why, you'd have to be as big a dummy as Charlie McCarthy to think it was anybody but that Skillet. It's my duty to write a story about Skillet—you know, to warn people to watch out for drifters."

Rita looked a little pleased with herself as she finished and

185

winked at me. As each of us understood what Rita had said, we sighed with relief and smiled at her. I unclenched my hands to see that my nails had sunk through the flesh and drawn blood that had dripped onto the quilt in front of me. We'd spilled more blood on Mrs. Judd's Dresden Plate that day than the Whig's Defeat had gotten during the whole Civil War.

"That's a real good idea. You tell folks to start locking their doors at night," Nettie said.

"It would be what you call a service to mankind," Forest Ann added.

"And women," Opalina added.

The rest of us chimed in about what a help a story like that would be to people, especially those who live out in the country. Ceres said she knew Rita would do a bang-up job.

"Maybe you could run his picture," Opalina said.

"Now, who takes a picture of a hired man?" Mrs. Judd asked her, and we all laughed.

Ella didn't laugh. She didn't say anything, either, which made the rest of us grow quiet again. I wondered if Ella would object to Rita's story, but she didn't. In fact, she wasn't listening to us anymore. She smiled to herself and took up her needle, which had been lying on top of the quilt, and made half a dozen stitches, pulling the thread through as she hummed a little tune under her breath.

"Why, shame on us. We've hardly quilted at all today," Mrs. Ritter said. One by one, each member of the Persian Pickle Club, including Rita, picked up her needle and begin stitching around the Dresden plates.

We sewed quietly for a long time, no longer feeling a need to talk, until at last, Mrs. Judd stuck her needle into the quilt and took off her thimble. "Somebody tell me where's the time gone. I forgot all about refreshments." She placed her hands on the side of her chair and hefted herself up. "I'll put the teakettle on. Hot tea always hits the spot after an afternoon's sewing. Did I tell you I've got fresh lemons?"

Mrs. Judd took a few heavy steps toward the kitchen before stopping to place her hand on the back of Rita's chair and leaning over to examine the quilt in front of her. "Honey, those are real nice stitches. You're coming along just fine." She straightened up and added, "We've had an awful good quilting this evening, haven't we, ladies? Why, you might say it's the best Persian Pickle we ever had."

chapter

12

It was my turn for Persian Pickle, and I could hardly wait. I'd kept quiet for two days, ever since I found the package and the postcard in the mailbox, both of them on the same day. The other club members would be as thrilled as I was!

I checked the icebox pudding again and made sure that no dust had collected in the last five minutes on the dining room table. Then I leaned over the cradle and kissed Grover junior, who was sleeping under the Sunbonnet Sue and Overall Bill quilt that Nettie and Forest Ann had made for him.

He was the sweetest baby in the world, and pretty, too. He didn't look the least bit like Tyrone Burgett, although Grover said it would be a while before we knew whether he had Tyrone's beer belly. That was the one and only time Grover mentioned that our baby was Tyrone's grandson. After that, Grover forgot about it, and so did I. The Persian Pickles never mentioned Grover junior's parents, of course. He was our baby.

Things had gone just the way we'd planned. Velma turned over her little boy to us two weeks after he was born, then went on to Moline, where she found a job as a clerk in the house-wares department of a Kresge's five-and-dime. She'd never once written to ask about him. People in Harveyville knew we'd adopted, of course, but, except for the Pickles, no one ever suspected the baby's mother was someone they knew.

Of course, I'd have mortgaged the farm to pay for Grover junior, but Velma's stay in the unwed mothers' home in Kansas

City hadn't cost us much at all. That's because the folks there gave us credit for the $124 we raised selling raffle tickets on the Celebrity Quilt.

An old bachelor who lived north of Paxico won it. He wasn't at the drawing, so I volunteered to mail the quilt, but Opalina warned us not to trust the United States Post Office. Someone who worked there was bound to recognize the box and take the Celebrity Quilt home, she said, and how would we explain that to Mrs. Roosevelt? She was right, I guess, so I drove all the way over to Paxico to deliver the quilt in person, which tickled that old boy. Ada June, who'd ridden along with me, said what a pity it was he couldn't read and so didn't know whose names he slept under.

⚘

At last, I heard the first car turn into our yard, and I glanced out the window, to see Nettie and Forest Ann pulling in next to the balm of Gileads, which still glistened with water. It hadn't been much of a rain, but we weren't particular, being grateful for any amount of moisture. I watched the two women walk toward the house, arm in arm, with their sewing baskets in their hands. They came inside, letting in the smell of the earth that Grover had just turned for the kitchen garden, and went to the cradle to peep at the baby.

"He grows every time I see him. He'll be as big as Grover if you don't watch out," Nettie said. She patted the scarf around her neck, but these days, the gesture was only habit. Dr. Sipes had removed her goiter, probably for free, just to please Forest Ann. Nettie had gotten her hair marcelled, too, but she'd had to pay for that herself. Tyrone must have been doing some better in the gambling business.

"Him never fusses one bit. Him takes after Grover," Forest Ann said, smoothing Grover junior's hair.

The other members of the Persian Pickle Club arrived a few minutes later, talking softly so they wouldn't wake the baby. I told them they could speak up. "Grover junior could sleep through a thunderstorm."

"How would you know? We haven't had a thunderstorm since he was born—hardly since I was born," Agnes T. Ritter said. She and I had become closer, not best friends exactly, but good friends.

She'd stopped by right after that quilting at Mrs. Judd's in the fall to say we shouldn't blame Rita for trying so hard to leave Harveyville. Agnes T. Ritter confessed she'd wanted to get away every bit as much as Rita. She'd hoped to leave right after high school, but somebody had to stay on to take care of Howard and Sabra Ritter. So after finishing college, she'd come back home instead of looking for a job in Lawrence or Topeka. Her folks had hoped Tom would be the one to stay. They needed a man to help with the farming, and, well, Agnes T. Ritter sniffed, they thought Tom was smarter and better-looking and more fun to be around than she was, so who wouldn't rather have Tom? Even in her own home, Agnes T. Ritter wasn't anybody's first choice. Still, she knew Tom never would come back for good. So her folks were her responsibility. I came to understand Agnes T. Ritter after that talk, and I admired her for her sacrifice.

Rita had done just what she'd promised that day at Mrs. Judd's. She'd written one more article for the *Topeka Enterprise* about Ben Crook's murder, warning people to be careful of drifters, especially one named "Frying Pan."

Rita told about the Harveyville Masons putting up a ten-dollar reward for the capture and conviction of Ben's murderer. When I read that, I asked Grover if Ben Crook was a Mason in good standing. Grover said he wasn't because he'd never paid his dues, which was the second reason the reward was only ten dollars. The first reason was that nobody cared enough about Ben to pay more than a sawbuck to find his killer. Ben's murder had caught the Masons between the mud and the wagon wheel, Grover said. Some of them thought they ought to give twenty-five dollars to whoever had killed Ben. They never paid out a reward one way or the other, because Skillet never was caught.

Rita didn't get the job on the *Topeka Enterprise,* but she and

Tom moved away just the same. Not more than two weeks after the quilting at Mrs. Judd's, Tom was offered the engineering job he'd applied for at the Mountain Con copper mine in Butte, Montana. A day later, they were packed and gone. I think Tom was even more anxious to get away than Rita. A couple of weeks after that, Rita wrote to say she hadn't had any luck with the newspapers in Butte, but she'd gotten the next best thing, a typist's job at the Anaconda Copper Company. She was learning shorthand so she could get a promotion to steno, and one day, she might even be a secretary. "It's a humdinger of a chance, and it sure beats feeding chickens," she wrote.

After Rita left, the Persian Pickle made her an old-fashioned Remembrance quilt. We embroidered our names along with favorite sentiments on diamond-shaped pieces of fabric. I assembled the diamonds into a star and added a nice background. The club members stitched the quilt one day at Nettie's house, and we sent it off.

Rita wrote us a note by return mail, saying she'd never seen anything as gorgeous as that quilt, which she'd put on the bed as soon as she unfolded it, as a surprise for Tom. Rita turned into an even better friend after she moved away. She was my best pen pal, sending me a letter every couple of weeks, telling me about the funny people she met in Butte and the fancy restaurants where she and Tom ate.

When I wrote to tell Rita the baby had arrived, she and Tom sent Grover junior a telegram congratulating him on choosing us to be his parents. I framed it.

After the club members finished cooing at the baby, they sat down in the chairs I'd arranged around my quilt frame and admired my Christian Cross, which was made entirely of plaids and polka dots, each square a different material. I'd asked all the club members to search their ragbags for scraps so I'd have enough. I thought it was the prettiest quilt I'd ever made, and they did, too.

I assigned chairs around the quilt frame and waited until everyone began sewing before I announced, "I have a surprise for you." I tried to sound important.

"You see another rain cloud, did you?" Mrs. Judd asked, looking up from the stitches she was taking around the blue-and-yellow-plaid cross.

"It's something just as good and maybe better. Look at this!" I took a postcard out of my pocket and held it up. "It's from Ruby!"

"Oh, Ruby. Goody!" Ella said. Now that the Judds had arranged for a telephone and electricity to be installed at her place, Ella had moved back to her farm. Duty and Hiawatha kept an eye on her, and Prosper picked her up at noon every day so she could take her dinner with the Judds. I'd never seen her so happy.

"Are you going to pass it around, or are you just going to wave it in the air like that?" Mrs. Judd asked.

"Read it out loud," Ada June said.

I cleared my throat. "It's from Bakersfield, California, and in case you can't see it from where you're sitting, there's a picture of two little boys sitting on a giant peach."

"They'll squish it," Opalina said.

Mrs. Judd shot her a look. "Read the postal," she ordered.

"It says, 'I bet you never thought you'd hear from me again. I hope you haven't forgotten your old friend Ruby. Floyd is working for a farmer here, and we are living in a tourist cabin.' And it's signed, 'Love to the Persian Pickle. Ruby Miller.' "

"Well, that's just fine," Forest Ann said, and everyone nodded.

I handed the card to Ada June to be passed around. She studied the picture while the others went back to their sewing, but not me. I cleared my throat, and they looked up.

"What now, Queenie?" Mrs. Ritter asked.

"That's not the only thing that came in the mail. I got something from Rita, too." I went into the dining room and came back with a cardboard box. I set it on the edge of the quilt frame and folded back the tissue, then lifted out a baby's quilt and held it up. "It's from Rita. She made it out of the scraps we gave her at our quiltings. She took them with her."

"Why, we taught her to quilt, after all," Mrs. Judd said, taking the quilt and holding it up close to her spectacles. She passed it on.

"Did you ever see anything so cunning?" Ceres asked when the quilt reached her. "It's threads of all our lives, Rita's and ours, pieced together." Ceres handed the quilt to Mrs. Ritter.

"Lookit here. She's used the little sea horses in 'that green,' you gave her," Mrs. Ritter told Forest Ann. "And here's a dear little piece of Persian pickle from you, Ceres. I'd have thought it was all used up by now."

"Her stitches are getting better," Ada June said, although that wasn't true. Rita's stitches were as big and crooked as they'd always been. "I bet she's been practicing out in Montana."

Nettie traced her finger around the edge of one of the pieces. "This is real nice. What's the design?"

"It's Double Ax Head," Forest Ann replied when the quilt reached her.

Forest Ann passed Rita's quilt to Agnes T. Ritter, who looked it over and said, "No it's not. It's not Double Ax Head at all. Well, I mean, some might call it Double Ax Head, but that's not its real name, not the name on my templates, anyway."

I'd sat down and begun stitching around a dark blue square with orange dots, but something in Agnes T. Ritter's voice made me glance at her.

She was holding up the quilt and looking my way, waiting to get my attention before continuing. "When Rita wrote me to send her a pattern for a quilt for Queenie's baby, I went through my templates and picked the one I thought had the best name. Of course, I chose an easy one, Rita not being such a good quilter and all. But it was the name that decided me. This quilt is a Friendship Forever."

"Oh, Agnes T. . . . . Agnes," I said. She blushed, something I had never seen her do, and it was not a pretty sight, but I didn't mind, because I wasn't as critical of Agnes as I used to be.

"Fancy that. Of course it is. Could you think of a better name!" Ceres said.

"Was there a card?" Mrs. Judd asked. I told her there was and took it out of the box and handed it to her.

193

"It says, 'If you wonder who's responsible, I did it.' " Mrs. Judd frowned at me. "Does Rita think you wouldn't know she'd made it?" Grover had asked me the same thing.

"I guess not," I said, going back to my stitching. I knew that wasn't what Rita meant at all, and I smiled to myself.

The note was a kind of joke between Rita and me that I couldn't explain to the members of the Persian Pickle, even though it went back to Rita's last quilting, the one at Mrs. Judd's.

When the time had come to go home, Rita had left the house with me and walked all the way to my car, where we were out of earshot of the other club members.

"Queenie, there are two things I have to clear up, just in my own mind. I promise I won't put them into the article."

"Well—"

Rita broke in before I could object. "How did Skillet know Ben Crook was out in that field? It's awfully mysterious unless he helped you bury the body."

Of course, I'd wondered that myself. "No, Skillet didn't help. I can't be sure how he found out, but my guess is he passed by the grave and was curious about why the earth was turned. He might have dug down to see for himself. He wouldn't have told anyone about finding the body. There being bad blood between the two of them, he might have been arrested for Ben's murder. I suppose by the time he met the Massies, he figured Ben had been dug up."

Rita thought that over and said it made sense.

I turned to go, but Rita stopped me. "There's one other question."

I'd been afraid of that.

Rita lowered her voice. "Was it Mrs. Judd? Was she the one who killed Mr. Crook?"

I thought over that question for a long time. The members of the Persian Pickle Club never talked about which one of us had been responsible for Ben's murder, because we didn't care. Anybody arriving first at the Crook place that day would have

194

picked up the oak ax handle lying on the woodpile and smashed in Ben's skull to keep him from beating Ella. As we saw it, we shared equally in the guilt—and in the credit for saving Ella's life, too. It was important to remember not that a bad man was dead but that a good woman still lived. It wouldn't surprise me if one or two of the members couldn't even recall which Pickle had wielded the ax handle, and among those who did, not a single one would have told, even in a court of law. We were all in it together. The one who actually struck the blow knew that, and it kept her from dwelling on the fact that a man died because of her.

Thinking of that loyalty made a lump come to my throat, and I looked out over the Judds' rusty old steam thresher to the field of winter wheat that Prosper had planted. I wanted to ask Rita if she thought he would get enough moisture to make a crop of it, but how would she know? She wasn't a farmer. Besides, I knew Rita wouldn't let me change the subject.

"We're not supposed to talk about it, even to one another. We agreed," I said at last, not meeting her eyes. I turned a little to stare at the sawhorse where Mrs. Judd killed her chickens. The wood was bloodstained, and feathers were stuck in the ax marks. A puff of wind sent one of them up into the air, where it hung for a minute before floating away. A little yellow head lay on the ground. Mrs. Judd must have killed a chicken that morning, and the dogs hadn't come around yet. "I guess you'd have to say we're all responsible."

"I know that, Queenie, but I'm not going to tell anybody, not even Tom," Rita said. "I'll keep the secret, too. You're the only one I can ask. I wouldn't believe what the others told me."

That was true enough. Still, I shook my head. "I don't want to say."

"Please, Queenie, I promise I'll never talk about it again. Ever. Even with you. After all, I am a Persian Pickle now. I share the responsibility for the secret. I think I have a right to know."

Rita put her hand on my arm to keep me from getting into

the car, but I opened the door anyway and put one foot up on the running board. We'd stayed too late at quilting. Grover would be wanting his supper.

Still, I didn't climb in, because Rita's question hung in the air between us like one of those chicken feathers, and I admitted she was right. She was a Pickle, and now she shared not just the secret of Ben Crook's murder but the guilt. She deserved an answer. I put my other foot on the running board and glanced away at the members of the club, who were getting into their cars. Agnes T. Ritter fluttered her fingers at me, and I waved back.

"Queenie?" Rita said, and I turned toward her again. "Who?"

Mrs. Judd's screen door slammed, and someone called my name, but I didn't look up. Instead, I took a deep breath and looked Rita straight in the eye. Then I leaned over the top of the Studebaker door and said in a clear voice, "I did it."

THE TORTOISE SHELL

Fanny Frewen

Mulberry Cottage is the perfect country retreat, the village quintessentially English. But with a cosmopolitan London background and a lucrative career of her own, Henny Brack is not at all sure she's ready to settle down.

But the village is also home to ninety-five-year-old Cecilia Boxendale. Scratchy, dauntless and devoted to those she loves, she saves her caustic tongue for the ghastly Mrs Phillips (hell-bent on steering her safely into The Elms retirement home) and gradually becomes Henny's greatest friend. As crises loom, Cecilia remains steadfast. Ultimately, though, it is she who will face the greatest ordeal.

Quirky, original and full of life, *The Tortoise Shell* is both unashamedly touching and utterly realistic. It is a welcome first novel from an exciting new talent.

KEEPING SECRETS

Sue Gee

Before Hilda met Stephen, her life was ordered, tidy, self-contained. She had a demanding career, lived alone and had for years kept emotion safely at a distance. Before Hilda met Stephen, her sister Alice, whose childhood she had overshadowed, was flourishing as a wife and contented mother of two children. And Stephen's wife Miriam, removed and isolated in Norfolk, could preserve the illusion of a happy marriage – until Stephen met Hilda.

For a while no one notices that things have changed. Their affair is private, their own. But now the foundations of all these lives have shifted, and the discovery of private happiness brings anguish. Gradually, everyone's secrets are revealed, until, at the end of a long hot summer, their lives are changed irrevocably.

Poignant and absorbing, infused with the emotions of jealousy, passion and betrayal, *Keeping Secrets* unforgettably explores the complexity and dilemmas of contemporary marriage.

'A compelling read' TODAY

Other B format titles available in Arrow

PRICES AND OTHER DETAILS ARE LIABLE TO CHANGE

ALL ARROW BOOKS ARE AVAILABLE THROUGH MAIL ORDER OR FROM YOUR LOCAL BOOKSHOP AND NEWSAGENT.

PLEASE SEND CHEQUE/EUROCHEQUE/POSTAL ORDER (STERLING ONLY) ACCESS, VISA OR MASTERCARD

☐☐☐☐☐☐☐☐☐☐☐☐☐☐☐☐

EXPIRY DATE .... SIGNATURE ....

PLEASE ALLOW 75 PENCE PER BOOK FOR POST AND PACKING U.K.

OVERSEAS CUSTOMERS PLEASE ALLOW £1.00 PER COPY FOR POST AND PACKING.

ALL ORDERS TO:

ARROW BOOKS, BOOK SERVICE BY POST, P.O. BOX 29, DOUGLAS, ISLE OF MAN, IM99 1BQ. TEL: 01624 675137 FAX: 01624 670923

NAME ....

ADDRESS ....

....

Please allow 28 days for delivery. Please tick box if you do not wish to receive any additional information ☐

Prices and availability subject to change without notice.